P9-CSG-625

MISTER
MAX

NEWBERY MEDALIST

CYNTHIA VOIGT

MISTER MAX

The BOOK of KINGS

Illustrated by IACOPO BRUNO

A YEARLING BOOK

 Published in the United States by Yearling, an imprint of Random House Children's Books, a division of Penguin Random House LLC, New York. Originally published in hardcover in the United States by Alfred A. Knopf, an imprint of Random House Children's Books, New York, in 2015.

Visit us on the Web! randomhousekids.com
Educators and librarians, for a variety of teaching tools, visit us at
RHTeachersLibrarians.com

The Library of Congress has cataloged the hardcover edition of this work as follows:
Voigt, Cynthia.
Mister Max : the book of kings / Cynthia Voigt ; illustrated by Iacopo Bruno. — First edition.
p. cm.
Sequel to: Mister Max: the book of secrets.
Summary: Solutioneer Max Starling travels to a fictional South American country to rescue his parents, who have become embroiled in a political power grab.
ISBN 978-0-307-97687-1 (trade) — ISBN 978-0-375-97125-9 (lib. bdg.) —
ISBN 978-0-307-97689-5 (ebook)
[1. Problem solving—Fiction. 2. Self-reliance—Fiction. 3. Missing persons—Fiction. 4. Adventures and adventurers—Fiction. 5. Parents—Fiction.] I. Bruno, Iacopo, illustrator. II. Title. III. Title: Book of kings.
PZ7.V874Mis 2015
[Fic]—dc23
2014017699

ISBN 978-0-307-97688-8 (pbk.)

Printed in the United States of America

10 9 8 7 6 5 4 3 2 1

First Yearling Edition 2016

for Pete & Emily,
the enlightened monarch & his true queen

CONTENTS

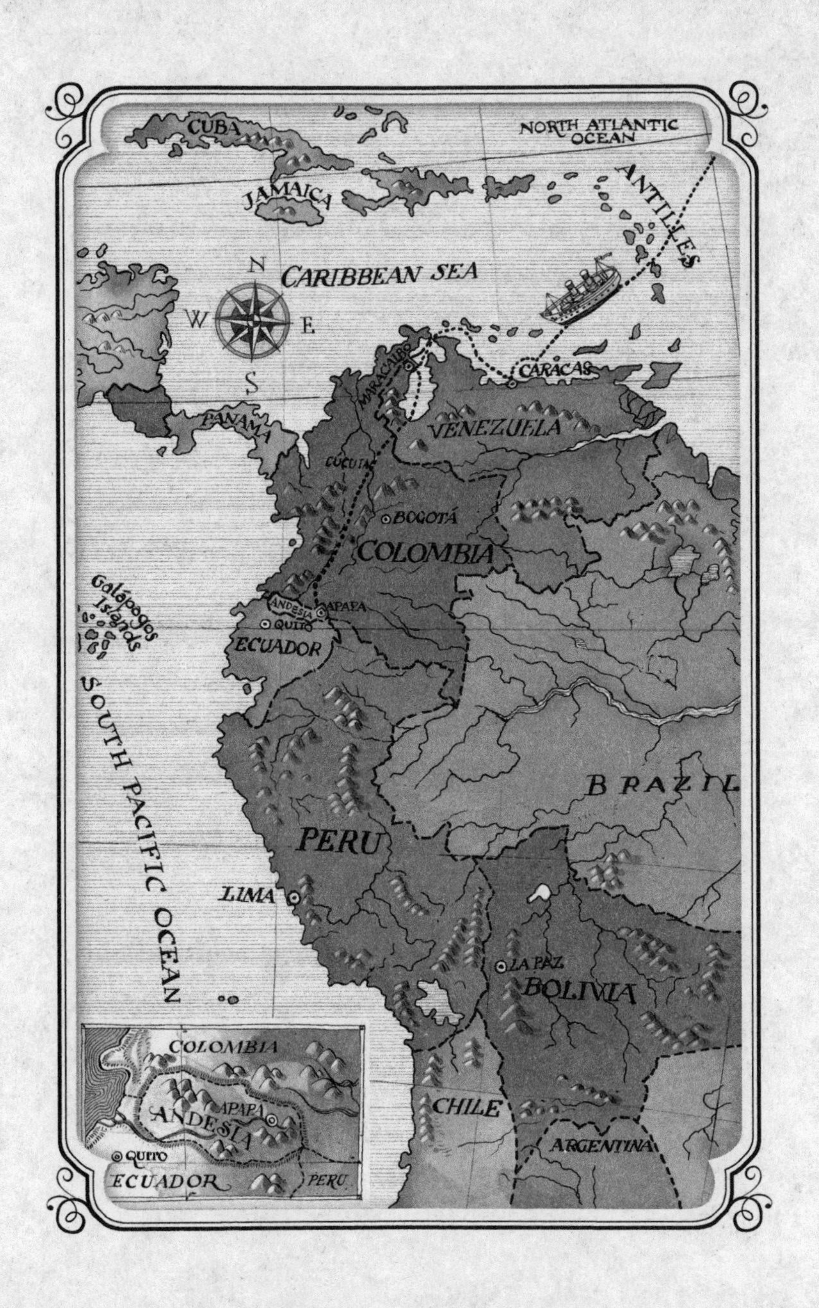
CUBA
NORTH ATLANTIC OCEAN
JAMAICA
ANTILLES
N
W
E
S
CARIBBEAN SEA
MARACAIBO
CARACAS
PANAMA
VENEZUELA
CÚCUTA
BOGOTÁ
COLOMBIA
Galápagos Islands
ANDESIA
APAPA
QUITO
ECUADOR
SOUTH PACIFIC OCEAN
BRAZIL
PERU
LIMA
LA PAZ
BOLIVIA
CHILE
ARGENTINA
COLOMBIA
APAPA
ANDESIA
QUITO
ECUADOR
PERU

"The play's the thing."

—William Shakespeare, *Hamlet*

PROLOGUE

Early on a Wednesday morning in late July, a woman walked alone down a quiet street in the old city. It was usually a woman sent to do jobs like this. Everyone understood that a woman was not dangerous, not threatening, and probably not very intelligent. As long as she wasn't beautiful and didn't carry some other visible peculiarity, a woman would not be noticed. Especially if, like the woman who went along Thieves Alley, she was ripe in years and plump of body, and dressed in a blue-and-white-checked cotton dress and serviceable black boots like a rich man's housekeeper on her half-day holiday. Even her narrow-brimmed felt hat was entirely unremarkable, with a plain blue grosgrain ribbon around its crown as the only decorative touch.

In one gloved hand, the woman carried an envelope, in the other a furled umbrella. She approached number 5 and stopped, distracted by the wooden sign hung on the fence: MISTER MAX, SOLUTIONEER. She considered the writing on the front of the envelope, looked at the sign again, looked at the small house waiting quietly on its well-tended lawn, its gardens weeded and flowering, and made up her mind.

She had her instructions.

The woman pulled once, quickly, on the bell hanging beside the gate and let herself in.

She had not even had time to knock before the door opened and she was faced with a rather tall, entirely ordinary young man. Or he might have been a boy. She couldn't tell and what did it matter?

"May I help you?" he asked, as correct as any butler blocking the entry to a great house.

She was startled enough to look directly at him, even though she knew the dangers of that, and was startled all over again by the odd color of his eyes—like moldy hay rotting in the corners of the stalls she'd cleaned in her girlhood, before she had been recruited away from the farm to her present employment. She held out the envelope, using the words she had been given to speak: "This is Five Thieves Alley?"

"It is," he answered, and he waited for her to say more.

"For you, then," she said, and turned abruptly away. If he had called after her, she would have neither halted nor responded.

1

In which Max is irritated, frustrated, and thwarted

Max didn't have to open the envelope to know what it contained. His fingers recognized the button shape, and a wave of bad feelings—mostly sadness and shame—washed over him.

Max pocketed the button. He didn't need any reminder. Since the April morning when his parents had disappeared—on a ship that didn't exist—Max, along with his grandmother, had worried. At first they worried about what had happened to them, and then, when his parents reappeared in the unlikely roles of King and Queen of Andesia, a tiny South American country, they spent hours worrying about what they should do, and what they *could* do. Max didn't know why his father kept sending these buttons, with the familiar three-peaked symbol stamped on them.

They were as confusing as the few letters that had arrived from Andesia. Max had eventually decoded notes that cried *Help* and *Trapped,* but nothing telling him how to proceed. Even when he'd finally figured out the clues leading to a hidden fortune in gold coins, that had only raised more questions. Where had they come from? How had his father, who earned a good living but was by no means wealthy, gotten them? Why were they hidden away, like some guilty secret?

No surprise, then, that Max could only guess at what the buttons were supposed to mean. Probably *Where are you?* Or maybe *Where the devil are you?* Whatever the precise message, what they hinted at was Max's failure, and he was already sorry enough, every day, that he hadn't yet been able to rescue his parents.

It wasn't as if he'd been sitting under a tree sipping lemonade and munching on cookies while he read adventure books. He'd been busy, figuring out how to earn a living and earning it. He'd become Mister Max, Solutioneer, solving problems for the Mayor, even. For William Starling's information, that was what his son had been doing. Being independent. As ordered.

On his way back through the kitchen, Max ripped up the envelope and dropped it into the trash. He didn't plan to tell his grandmother about this one, just as he hadn't told her about the previous two. He poured himself a glass of water and had a surprising and disturbing thought: the envelope had been delivered by hand. This raised more questions. If his father had an ally in the city, why wouldn't that person come directly to Max? Were these buttons a trap being set by General Balcor to lure Max to Andesia, and if so, what did the General plan to do once he had Max *and* his parents together? Who, besides Max and Grammie and their small circle of co-conspirators, knew about William and Mary Starling's perilous position?

Everything his former-schoolteacher, former-librarian grandmother had been able to find out about Andesia made them even more uneasy: The narrow country that lay along the high foothills of the Andes had been, since the discovery of veins of silver and copper in its mountains, conquered and reconquered by strong men, robber chieftains who styled themselves Kings of Andesia and were soon assassinated by the next conquering invader. Recently, not seven months back, when the downtrodden natives had rebelled against their masters, foreign armies had come to the aid of the King. The royal family had been spirited away to safety in a mountain fortress and order had been re-established, the rebellion put down, its leaders hanged in the public square, and a general left in charge. But despite General Balcor's efforts (or perhaps because of them?), the royal family was discovered and murdered.

Grammie could find out nothing about this General Balcor, other than the simplest facts—Andesian mother, Peruvian father, educated abroad in a suspicious number of different schools. They guessed that his was the shadowy figure in the newspaper photograph Grammie had sighted of the coronation of the new King and Queen of Andesia: William and Mary Starling. The royal couple was smiling down on a crowd gathered to greet them on the steps of the cathedral of Caracas, their hands clasped in a signal Max and Grammie recognized from seeing it as the Starlings took their bows at the end of a bad performance. *Trouble,* those clasped hands meant. Max and Grammie suspected that the trouble had to do with the barely discernible figure lurking close behind them, a high military shako on its head.

The coronation photograph had appeared in June, more than a month after the disappearance, and it was now late July. Max had counted off the slow days and the long weeks, and he knew just how long a time it had been. He was doing the best he could, as fast as he could. There was no need for anyone, most likely William Starling, fake King of Andesia, to be firing buttons at him. He put his glass down on the counter beside the sink and set his feelings down beside it. He could be angry at his parents later, *after* he'd rescued them. Never mind those buttons, he had work to do.

Max finally had a rescue plan, and it was a good one: to arrive in Andesia as a member of a visiting foreign embassy. Ari—Max's tenant, math tutor, and the future Baron Barthold—would be the embassy's head. Max would act as his private secretary. And Grammie would play the housekeeper. He knew that the plan's best chance of success was if it was an *official* diplomatic embassy sent by King Teodor III, but he had no idea how to get into the presence of Teodor to even make the request. One thing in Max's favor was that the royal family had arrived for their annual vacation weeks in the summer palace, so the King was nearby. That was, however, the only thing in his favor.

The summer palace sat on a promontory overlooking the lake, easily visible but thoroughly guarded. During these lakeside holidays, King Teodor and his family could live almost like ordinary people—his children out on bicycles or flying kites, treating themselves to ice cream, going barefoot; he and his Queen out on the lake in a small sailboat, alone together; all of them at the city's best restaurants, just for the pleasure of dining out together as a family. Max needed to think of a way to intrude on the King's well-guarded holiday privacy, and if he could do that, to persuade him to give official standing—nothing more, Max would take care of all the rest—to a rescue party masquerading as a diplomatic embassy. Max had to speak to the King in person, and he hadn't yet figured out how to do that.

He needed to think hard, so he put on his red painter's beret and took his easel out to the front garden, where Grammie would not see him and come pestering around. That morning, luckily, there was a paintable sky. White fluffy clouds floated through air of a color that only happened in July, a pale blue that seemed to include yellow heat. You looked at the sky and you knew it was going to be a hot day. But not—how could the color show this?—a hot and humid day. This was an interesting painting problem, and Max set to work. His hand would paint, his brain would think, and maybe he would have an idea.

He was so deeply immersed in the delicate touches that would re-create the puffiness of the clouds that the bell roused him like an alarm in the night. At the sound, Max spun around. He hadn't known that the little bell could clamor.

A hat was at the gate. The hat was extraordinarily wide and extraordinarily tall and extraordinarily purple. It waved two extraordinarily long and extraordinarily yellow feathers in the air. The feathers were attached to it with the bright green splash of a *Z*.

The hat was wearing a rather small woman.

The woman—who, without being invited in, unlatched the gate and marched onto the path to the front door—was short and round. In a lavender summer dress with a narrow purple belt at the waist, her body was as round as a figure eight. Her face, too, was round and her eyes were round and her little red mouth was almost round. She was not young, not at all young, although she moved up the path and across the grass to where Max stood with the speed and energy of youth. "I expect that you are this Solutioneer person," she said.

Max nodded and bit at the insides of his cheeks, to keep from laughing.

"You know who I am," she told him.

He thought that he might, although it was Pia Bendiff, his

assistant, who had handled the correspondence. The woman must be R Zilla, the city's most well-known milliner. He didn't know which was more alarming, her hat or her presence.

"You are not without skill," the woman remarked, staring at his painting as closely as if he had asked for her opinion. "It's hard to tell from this. Although"—eyes as round and streaky blue as marbles moved to the beret he wore—"you have no sense of style."

Max still couldn't speak, for fear of laughing. There was so much *hat* to her . . .

"Who is your teacher? To set you such an exercise, he must have a plan. It must be a man, I think. Who is it?"

"Joachim," Max answered in a choked voice. He had to gather himself together, he knew. He had to become the Solutioneer, the successful investigator, a professional. He hoped she wouldn't ask him anything solutioneery until he had had a chance to become who she thought he was.

"Joachim works in oils," she told him, as if he did not already know. "I once purchased a painting of a branch in winter," she announced, and turned her attention back to Max's skyscape.

He took a deep breath. While she studied his painting, she made little puffing sounds that emerged like timid kittens from under the purple brim of the hat. He took a second deep breath, and a third. He became Mister Max. He asked, "What is it you want of me?"

"I see nothing of Joachim in this," she announced. "A pity. Does he have a studio?"

"Of course."

"Where would that be? I might be in the market for another of his pictures," she informed him.

Max was happy to give her the address. He was sending Joachim a buyer, just what the painter needed.

"Ah, he's in the New Town." She nodded. "A better location than yours, here in the old city."

"He's actually working in two styles now. There's the old way—"

"Fine details. Rich tones. Painted from life," she told him.

"—and a new one, quite different."

"I will prefer the old," she declared.

"He usually works in his garden," Max said.

He had no idea where this conversation was going. They stood side by side in front of his easel. Anyone in the lane would have thought they were discussing the painting on the easel in front of them.

"I expect it's his way of staying away from his family, who would interrupt his concentration," R Zilla said.

"He doesn't have a family."

"I expect he is too young."

"No," Max said.

"Well," she said then, and turned to look up into his face. "It's about my niece, Tess Tardo," she announced. "The girl has no gratitude. I taught her everything she knows, but she is a quarrelsome and stubborn girl. My youngest sister's youngest child. I took her in. I could do no less, since she has a certain talent. She has acquired necessary skills in my workroom. I trained her," R Zilla told him proudly, then announced, "The girl has gone off on her own."

Max did not need to be told that this displeased R Zilla. Her sharp, quick words did that, but what they didn't tell him was what it all had to do with the Solutioneer.

"Thankless child." R Zilla glared up at him. Her expression changed. "You have very odd eyes," she told him. "I'm not sure you can be trusted, with those eyes. They are almost the color of garden snakes," she said. "Much too close to the color of garden snakes, if you ask me."

Max couldn't help himself. He laughed.

R Zilla did not like being laughed at. Her mouth pursed up into a wrinkled red prune.

At least, Max thought, she wouldn't bother him any more about some job.

But he was to be disappointed in that hope. "When will you start on the job?" she demanded crossly.

"What job?"

"Finding her. Well, I know where she is to be found. I'm not a total dolt, whatever *some* people might think." Her glance made it clear to Max just whom she was referring to. "I want you to find *out* about her. I need to know how to get her back. Tess was very good with the girls in the workroom. Which I am not," R Zilla told him, as if this would come as a surprise.

"You've been told that I'm not taking any new work," Max reminded her.

"*You* never told me. It was some assistant telling me that, some secretary."

"And she was correct," Max said.

"There's no time to waste. Who knows what the girl will do? What if she marries? And has to raise children when she should be . . ." But here, words failed the old woman and she waved her hands in the air, as if gathering in some unseen flock of possibilities. "Tess could be one of the great milliners, like me. But no, the girl has her own ideas. She wants to make hats anyone can afford, even servants and secretaries, even schoolteachers. Well, she'll have learned her lesson by now," R Zilla concluded, with satisfaction. "However, she is, as I said, stubborn. I need to know what it will take to persuade her to return to me. Surely you can accomplish that without much effort?"

"I'm not accepting any work."

"I'll expect to hear from you. You can reach me at the shop, on Barthold Boulevard."

Max had exhausted both his patience and his faith in a mannerly approach to this woman. "Go away," he said to her. Then he couldn't help but add, "Please."

"Not until you agree," she said.

He had no choice. He adjusted the red beret, causing her to sniff her disapproval, and turned his back to her. He picked up his paintbrush, dipped it into water, then color, and applied it to the paper. For several minutes, he simply ignored her.

At last he heard a rustle of skirts and her voice. "I'll be back."

At that moment, Max didn't care if she did return. At that moment, all he cared about was that she stop telling him he had to do something he'd said over and over he wasn't going to do.

Once she had gone off down Thieves Alley, the quiet of the day rose up to wrap itself around him until he was floating along in solitary silence, as if he were himself a cloud. Max put down his brush. He sat on his front steps, elbows resting on the step behind him and legs stretched out in front of him. He turned his face to the light and closed his eyes.

The Solutioneer was thinking. What could he say to persuade the King? How might some nobody make his way into the presence of Teodor? He pictured a theatrical scene in which he stood before the King, and tried to hear the lines the King would speak, and think of how he might answer them. In the quiet morning, wondering, almost dreaming, Max was about to have an idea. He knew it. He could feel himself almost having an idea. He could almost see the idea approaching, like a ghost materializing in a mirror . . .

"Max?"

A screen door slammed and Grammie came clattering out of his house, onto the porch behind him.

"There you are. I'm glad I found you. I didn't know where you were."

She plumped herself down on the step beside him. The idea dematerialized and disappeared, an offended ghost.

Max gathered in his legs and held his tongue.

"I've got tickets," she told him. Seeing confusion on his face, she explained, "Two staterooms on the *Estrella,* one for us, one for Ari. We sail August seventeenth for Caracas. We'll have to find some kind of ship to carry us to Maracaibo, and from there we go overland into Andesia. We'll need mules and porters and guides for the last part of the trip, but we should reach Apapa by mid-September. Barring accidents," Grammie added. "Winter will be over, so we won't have that to contend with. You'll need to buckle down to your study of Spanish," she warned him.

Max didn't speak.

"And I need one of those bags of gold coins," she concluded.

He hadn't asked her to find a boat, or to buy tickets. In fact, he had asked her to let *him* figure out the rescue mission, and Ari had agreed that it was Max's business and responsibility, and now she had gone ahead on her own, without even telling him she was thinking of it. Without asking him.

"We can't just sit around doing nothing," Grammie told him.

"I'm *not.*"

"Maybe. But nothing is happening," Grammie pointed out.

Max, who until just a minute ago had been confidently awaiting the arrival of an idea, jumped to his feet to keep himself quiet. He reminded himself of how worried Grammie must be about her daughter, and her daughter's husband, too. He reminded himself that now that she wasn't going to work every day, she didn't have anything to distract her from her worries.

"You know enough Spanish now so that when we're alone that's all we should speak, and don't give me that face, Max. This is serious," she told him, as if he were in any danger of forgetting that. "So how about getting me those coins," she said.

Max would do as she wanted. "Will Ari be home for supper?" he asked hopefully. His tutor-tenant-false-Ambassador-to-be wasn't bossy, or female, and that made him the very person in whose company Max wanted to be.

"It isn't even lunchtime yet," Grammie answered, "and the garden needs attention if you don't have anything better to do."

Gardening was an activity that encouraged thinking, and problem solving, and plan making, so Max went out back, to pull the weeds growing up under the tall tomato plants. His fingers loosened the soil around the weeds and his mind grew loose as the soil, as he thought about the King and pictured Teodor in his summer palace, up on the promontory, with only the one drive leading up into the grounds and a guarded gatehouse at the start of the drive, and he wondered how a schoolboy—or dogcatcher or university student—how anyone might make his way—

That was when Pia, who although younger was just as female and just as bossy as Grammie and R Zilla, arrived bringing the morning mail delivery out to the garden.

"Word must be spreading that you aren't taking new

cases," Pia complained. "There are only two letters, which isn't at all fair to me, if you think about it, if I'm your assistant. Part-time assistant," she corrected as soon as she saw the look on his face. "You know, Max, if you had a phone you could read your own mail and then telephone to tell me you don't need me and spare me the trouble of riding my bike into the city to hear you say to my face you don't need me, even if a case comes along that I could perfectly well solve. Or probably. So get a telephone."

Max had an urge to rip a tomato plant or two out of the soil and just throw them onto the ground.

Pia had an opinion about the situation to once again share with him. "It's not fair that just because you're going off I can't do anything but answer letters. And do you know what? If people stop talking about the Solutioneer for a while, and it won't take very many weeks, they'll forget about you and there won't even be *letters* for me to answer. That's just basic business sense. And if you're out of business, what will I do? It's not as if I want to learn how to draw or play the pianoforte—a word she pronounced through pursed-up lips—"or dance a waltz or . . . do needlework," which was, from the sound of her voice, no different from being drawn and quartered. "Although I wouldn't mind learning how to drive a motorcar. They can go really fast, over twenty miles an hour, did you know that? Don't you want to learn to drive one? I bet it's easier than driving a carriage. Don't you think?"

Rather than destroy perfectly healthy plants, not to mention the tomatoes ripening on them, Max thought he'd like to pull Pia up, out of his garden, the way he'd uprooted R Zilla earlier. He pictured himself doing just that, and grinned.

And there it was. An idea. A great idea. A two-birds-with-one-stone idea.

"I want to talk to you about the R Zilla job," Max said.

"Don't bother. I don't know anything about hats and I don't want to," Pia announced. Then, "What does it have to do with me?" she asked, with both hope and suspicion, reminding him, "I already turned it down for you. Twice."

"I thought you might work on it," Max said, and thoroughly enjoyed the moment of stunned silence from Pia.

Of course she spoiled it. "You're taking my advice!" she crowed. "You're listening to me!"

Max shrugged. Maybe it hadn't been bad advice, but what had really decided him was the chance to get rid of R Zilla and Pia together, bird one and bird two. There was, however, no reason for Pia to know that.

"I'll notify her that you will be coming by to talk with her," he said. "She can explain her problem to you, and you can figure out a way to solve it."

"And you won't interfere?" Pia asked.

"Not unless you ask."

"I won't ask," she promised, and leaped to her feet. "I'm going now. I need to think about . . . ," she mumbled, and took a quick glance back at Max from the doorway. "Don't worry, you can just go ahead with your expedition to South America and I'll take care of R Zilla before—"

Pia stopped speaking as abruptly as if someone had put a

plug into her mouth. She turned hastily to leave, then turned back to demand, with a wouldn't-you-like-to-know, sly-cat smile on her face, "You don't think she'll make me wear one of her hats, do you?" Then she went off at a run, leaving Max to wonder what she was up to. Because Pia was up to something, he was sure of it, and not because he was the Solutioneer and so clever, but because Pia was terrible at being subtle.

But he didn't have time to think about Pia, not right then. What he should do was get away from where everybody could come and interrupt him. After a quick lunch of bread and cheese, an apple, and a glass of milk, he got on his bike. He would have liked to give himself the treat of lemon raspberry cake, or maybe a lemon tart, but Gabrielle Glompf, the girl Ari wanted to marry, had left her job in the ice cream shop and gone to be pastry chef at Pia's father's new restaurant, B's, so instead of stopping in the busy center of the New Town, Max rode out to the quieter university area. He would sit in Joachim's garden and think. His teacher was not female, and neither was he bossy, and neither was he a talker. Joachim was a painter, an artist, and, except for the skyscapes, had no interest in what Max did. At the alley behind Joachim's house, he dismounted and leaned his bicycle against the fence, then let himself into the garden.

"I'm working," Joachim, who stood at an easel, greeted his student.

"Hello, Sunny," Max called to the golden dog, curled up in front of the open door into the house. Her tail wagged. "I just want to sit," he told his teacher.

Joachim ignored him.

That afternoon, Joachim wasn't painting a flower from his own garden. Instead, he had a long-stemmed bloom of Queen Anne's lace set in a jar on a tall table. This was such a surprise that Max had to ask, "A wildflower?" He tried to decide if it looked more like a burst of firecracker against the night sky or a dusting of snow on the wide branch of a spruce. Mostly, he decided, it looked exactly like itself and nothing else: That was what was wonderful about it. "When did you start painting wildflowers?"

"Quiet, *please,*" Joachim grumped. He stepped back to study the picture, in which each tiny blossom of the lacy white head was painted in perfect detail. Each threadlike stem was there, too, and a section of the rough central stem as well, although in the painting the flower seemed to float against a silky background the dark green color of ivy.

Max sat cross-legged on the ground, and Sunny came over to settle herself down beside him, her head on his thigh. Obediently, he started to stroke her silky skull and pull gently at her floppy ears. Her feathery tail thumped against the ground.

"Although there isn't anyone who'll want to buy this," Joachim announced, breaking the silence.

Max hadn't settled into thinking, so he was happy to try to cheer Joachim up. "It's summer," he said. "There will be all kinds of tourists around, for weeks and weeks, as well as everybody in the court who travels with the King. You'll sell some paintings."

"Worrying all the time about earning enough is hard on

a person, Max," Joachim said, as if Max didn't already know that himself.

Max understood what his teacher meant. Most painters don't earn a lot of money for their work. In fact, most painters don't earn a living by painting. They have to paint for the joy of it, and the challenge of it, and to share with anyone who cares to look—even if only a few people care to *really* look—their vision of the world, of its shapes and colors and creatures. It's not easy to be an artist.

"Did you ever think about finding a patron?" Max asked.

Joachim snorted, disgusted at Max's thickheadedness. "A patron's the last thing I want. Think about it, Max. I'd be terrible at having a patron and having to get along with him. Or her. It's a buyer I want." Joachim turned his gloomy gray glance from the painting to Max. "But I might as well be making hats, for all anyone cares about what I paint. I don't know why I bother." He shifted his position and raised his brush. "Why don't you go away?" Joachim asked, without looking at Max. "Why don't you take Sunny and go away? Don't come in when you bring her back. Just open the front door and let her through. I need to work on this."

Max understood that need to work on something, and maybe taking the dog for a walk in the park would get his brain going along a useful track, so he went off happily enough to get her leash.

On a hot summer afternoon, the city park was almost deserted—although Sunny, as usual, made new friends, a pair of nursemaids taking their charges out for some air. The two women cooed over Sunny, who always welcomed attention, and Max stood back, watching, thinking.

His earlier ideas for approaching the King had come to nothing: Mr. Bendiff had flatly refused to let Max be a temporary waiter the night the royal family came to dine at B's. Pia had returned from the Mayor's office with the depressing news that a letter would take at least five months to make its way through all the city and national checkpoints that surrounded the King. None of the city's three elected Assembly representatives could hope to make a personal request of any of the courtiers before October. And there were no jobs in the town of Summer where a boy might hope to meet his King strolling down a street, no jobs in kitchens or gardens or taverns and especially not on the grounds of the summer palace, no matter how willing a worker that boy was.

Max watched Sunny trying to tempt a nursemaid into a game of throw-the-stick and tried to think of something, anything at all, that might work. He might well fail again, but he wasn't giving up yet. All he needed was an idea.

It was late afternoon when he got home again. If he kept being interrupted out front, painting, and out back, weeding, then he would stay inside, pacing. Sometimes pacing could give a person ideas, even if his house was so small that going from the front parlor through the dining room to the kitchen and back again might make him dizzy. Sometimes, if he glanced at the framed posters advertising the Starling Theatrical Company's performances that hung on the dining room walls, Max might find an idea in one play or another, or one character or another, or one plot twist or another. He drank another glass of water and set about pacing. Thinking. Picturing.

A sharp rapping at his front door was followed by the opening of the door and the arrival of another alarming hat. This hat was peacock blue and so wide it almost filled the doorway. Its *Z* was a black satin streak holding a bouquet of raven feathers to its crown. R Zilla didn't greet him. She didn't look around the entry hall and she didn't hesitate. "The man needs someone to look after him. He shouldn't be encouraged to work a minute longer in that wishy-washy style. It's not what he's known for, and why he has a dog . . . I ask you, what does a painter need with a dog? The man should have a wife, but not some needy, admiring little creature. A man like Joachim needs someone independent. With a life of her own. And a business, and a large house, especially if he *must* have a dog. Why haven't you begun the job?" she demanded. "Do I have to tell you again I'm not taking no for an answer?"

She glared up at him.

"I'm not giving no for an answer," Max said, rushing to have his say before she decided she knew what he was going to say and could argue with it before he'd said it. "My assistant—"

"A snippy person," R Zilla told him. "You didn't read the letter I was sent."

"I will not be taking the job myself," Max said firmly, in the manner of the young patriot Lorenzo Apiedi announcing his resolution to name no names to the judge, to die alone.

"My assistant will be able to present your case to Tess Tardo. It's the assistant or no one," he declared.

R Zilla stood absolutely still for a full half minute. Then she nodded, a swooping event of peacock-blue hat. "We'll see," she decided. "If this assistant isn't up to the task, you'll have to take care of it yourself. But you can tell that painter this: He should think about marrying me."

She left abruptly, and when the little house was quiet again, Max allowed himself a long, theatrical groan. The voice from upstairs surprised him. "Max? Are you all right? Who *was* that?" Ari ran lightly down the stairs, his red hair freshly combed, his face alight with happiness, as it always was these days, tucking a fresh white shirt into dark trousers. "What do you say? It's time, shall we go see what your grandmother is feeding us tonight?"

And all Max could do was laugh. Maybe when he went to bed there would be a chance, in the long, dark silence before he fell asleep, for an idea to make its way forward, and come close enough for him to get a good look at it, and get a good grasp on it.

2

In which Sunny proves useful

The next morning, Max sat at the kitchen table with a plate of cookies to help him work his way through a list of Spanish words for household objects, such as frying pans and linens, including four kinds of spoons (soup, tea, serving, mixing) and two kinds of sinks (kitchen, bathroom). He planned to finish the vocabulary list and then disappear on his bicycle. If he could only have a couple of solitary and undisturbed hours, he was sure he could figure out a way to talk to King Teodor. After that, he could wonder *what* to say. He worked with full concentration, and fast, and was at the bottom of the list (towels, soap) when the bell rang.

His caller was Joachim, Sunny at his side. Max invited

them in and led them back to the kitchen. Something must be wrong, he thought. Joachim had never come to his house before.

Joachim dropped down onto a chair. "It's all your fault," he said. "She's all your fault, and the woman won't leave me alone."

"R Zilla," Max guessed, and Joachim nodded. "Didn't she buy a painting?" Max asked.

"Two, but—" Joachim shrugged that unimportant fact away. He slumped in his chair, like a farmer whose crops have been destroyed by drought, or a teacher whose students have all failed an exam. "I don't *want* any fancy-dancy beret with a *Z* on it. I don't *want* a bigger house with a bigger garden and bigger studio, and a wife to go with it." He sat up straight and glared at Max. "I only want to paint. I'm a painter!" he cried.

That said, and off his mind, Joachim took a couple of the snickerdoodles and rose to look out at the garden, where tomatoes hung down from their leafy vines. Absent-mindedly, the way he talked when he was thinking about a painting, he said, "Good cookies. Did your mother make them?"

"My grandmother," Max told him.

In the same distracted voice, Joachim asked, "Are your parents back? Are they ever coming back? You don't know, do you?" But this didn't interest him, not really. What really interested him was "That tomato there, see how its color *shines*?" He turned around briskly. "How about you take Sunny for a walk? Take her down along the river, beyond the city limits, where she can run free. I can wait here. You have a sketchbook, don't you? And a pencil? Get them for me and I'll be fine. Take as long as you like."

He reached down for another cookie.

Actually, Max thought, a walk by the river, with nothing to distract him, might be even more effective than a bicycle ride. As he went through the front door, the large dog pulling him out toward the street, Max called a warning to Joachim: "R Zilla knows where I live."

It was another fine day, especially fine for a riverside ramble, with a good breeze to keep the air from becoming uncomfortably hot. Sunny at his side, Max went first down Thieves Alley into the heart of the old city, where they stopped in the little square in front of the Starling Theater, so Max could satisfy himself that the building was undisturbed, dark and empty of life, the locks and chains on its doors all secure. That done, he and Sunny wound along through the narrow streets, toward the River Way.

As they came to the end of Eel Lane, two girls rushed up to Sunny. They were about Pia's age, he guessed, ten or eleven, in summer pinafores and sandals, their long hair in braids. The dog, of course, wagged her tail and nuzzled them and welcomed their caresses and cooings. The girls were enchanted. "What's her name?" and "Where did you get her?" they wanted to know. "How old is she? If she has puppies, can I have one?" they asked. "May I hold the leash? Please?" Sunny seemed to bring out the friendliness in people, and

Max could have been a lamppost for all the attention they paid to him: the perfect thinking situation.

When Max and Sunny came to the road that led south out of the city, following the river's path, their progress slowed. They ambled along by the blacksmith's forge, past the warehouses and chandleries, with Sunny tracking down every new smell, to find out what it was and if it was good to eat, while Max looked into shop windows and let his mind drift. Opposite B's, the gates to its courtyard closed at this hour of the day, Sunny pulled Max across the road and onto the grass. He let her off the leash and she ran down to the water's edge to drink, ran on ahead, biting happily at the air, ran back to check up on him, then ran ahead again, ears flopping with every bound. Max followed. He was in no hurry. He was drifting through the morning like some cloud afloat in a clear sky. He watched the river water flow by, murmuring to itself as it went. Little fishing boats, a day's work already behind them, rested at their moorings, booms lowered and sails furled. A tugboat chugged its way upriver to the Queensbridge docks, perhaps having taken an oceangoing vessel safely down to the sea. In only three weeks, Max would be boarding just such a vessel, he thought, and unless he could talk to the King, and talk him into helping out, it would be just the three of them—himself, Grammie, and Ari—doing their best not to look like the pretenders they were.

He wondered if he could become an embassy himself, a one-person embassy, sent to King Teodor III from an exotic, previously unknown foreign land. He could wear the potentate's robes from the Starling Theatrical Company production of *The Caliph's Doctor,* and he could say that his visit concerned the Cellini Spoon. He happened to know something about the Cellini Spoon, didn't he? The scene played out in his imagination: Caliph's Ambassador Max, a gold turban on his head and gold chains draped around his neck, being presented to King Teodor, saying . . . saying what? What lines might he speak that would persuade Teodor to hear a private appeal? he wondered, dreaming at the edge of the river while Sunny ran back and forth, nose to the ground, tail high and happy. She barked, for the joy of it.

A little ways down the bank, two men seated on an overturned rowboat mending fishing nets looked up, then called out to the dog. She loped up to satisfy her curiosity about these new smells and the people attached to them, and Max thought dreamily that if he ever wanted to guarantee himself a welcome, he should have Sunny with him. Sunny was the real diplomat here, he thought, and the idea surged up under his feet like some monster rising out of deep water, and Max was riding on its broad back, swept forward through foaming ocean waves.

He raced home to find Joachim seated on the back steps, pencil in hand, sketch pad on his lap. Before Joachim could say anything, even grumble a greeting about being interrupted at work, Max asked him, "Can you teach me to draw landscapes? Not paint them, just make pencil sketches."

"Probably," Joachim said, folding the sketch pad closed,

"but why? You've never done anything but skyscapes before. Why the sudden change? Is it one of your jobs?"

"No," Max said.

"Well, sort of," he allowed.

"*Will* you teach me?" he insisted. "Can you?"

"Of course I can, but not here. I teach in my garden. You can explain there, tomorrow. Today, I'm going to try painting this tomato."

By the next morning, Max had his explanation ready. Without going into any details about the exact kind of trouble his parents were in, or the messages he had finally deciphered, he could keep it simple. "You remember that my parents disappeared?"

"Why would I forget that?" Joachim asked.

"We've found out that they're trapped in South America. To help them get out, Grammie and I have the idea of pretending to be an embassy from King Teodor, with Ari—who can look the part, because he's a Barthold, the next Baron in fact—with Ari as the Ambassador. Grammie has already booked passage on the *Estrella,* which leaves me only three weeks to figure out a way to persuade the King—"

"Your grandmother is going, too?"

"It's her daughter, plus I'm her grandson. We're all the family she has. If I can't persuade the King to send Ari officially—"

"He probably won't. The royal family refuses to have

anything to do with the Bartholds. Even *I* know about that, and nobody blames them."

"Grammie says we'll go anyway, make do with fake credentials. Or maybe just the two of us will go, and she'll be an eccentric old botanist or geologist and I'll be her assistant or her secretary. But if it's a genuine diplomatic mission, we'd have the best chance."

"She's intrepid, isn't she? Your grandmother."

Max had never thought about it in those terms. "She does what needs doing, if that's what you mean."

"But what does all that have to do with landscapes?"

When Joachim put it that way, Max was no longer so confident that he had a good answer. But since it was the only answer he had—the only plan he'd been able to come up with—it was the answer he gave. "If I'm an artist sketching the gates that guard the drive up to the promontory, maybe I'll be able to get onto the grounds. If I can get onto the grounds, maybe I can find a way into the summer palace, and if I can get in, I might be able to talk to the King. Maybe, if I can talk to King Teodor myself," Max concluded, "I might be able to persuade him. To make us an official embassy."

Max couldn't help but hear how many *might*s and *maybe*s there were. "It would give us our best chance," he explained.

"Sounds pretty wild-eyed to me," Joachim commented.

"*And* I need to borrow Sunny, because everyone likes her," Max explained.

"But your grandmother has a sensible head on her shoulders," Joachim commented.

"To be a distraction," Max explained.

"What are we waiting for?" Joachim asked, adding, "I hope you brought good pencils. A real artist always has good pencils."

3

The R Zilla Job

• ACTS I, II, AND III •

It was a girl that R Zilla expected, in part because of the secretarial position an assistant occupied and in part because the snippiness of the notes that had turned down her job sounded female to her. So when she saw the boy loitering outside her window that Monday morning, she was suspicious. There might have been assurances from the Mayor's office that the vandalism that broke out in the spring had been taken care of, but R Zilla made a habit of not believing everything she was told, especially when it was a man telling it to her. And she had been proved right, time and again, the most recent example of which was that she was still waiting for this Solutioneer's Assistant to make her appearance.

Reminded, she looked again at the boy outside the

window, who appeared to be studying the hat on display. He was too young to have a sweetheart he might give such a gift to—a schoolboy, really. Unless he might be shopping for a gift for his mother? He was certainly well-dressed, despite the informality of a tennis sweater. She could see that, although ill-fitted, the linen trousers were stylish, and made of good fabric. The disorganized strands of tow-colored hair emerging from under the red-and-blue-checked cap were just what she would expect from a boy.

Of course the Solutioneer would hire only boys. Now that she thought of it, she was not surprised. She stood behind the long sales table in her showroom and waited for the boy to enter. Impatiently, she considered his face, the dark straight eyebrows drawn together in concentration and resolution; then—had the boy seen her watching?—he reached out to open the door. The shop bell rang and R Zilla waited until he stood silent in front of her, his dark blue eyes staring.

R Zilla was not about to permit unmannerly behavior in her own shop, even if this was a person sent to solve her difficulty. She said, "Don't you know enough to remove your hat when you come inside?" and was pleased at the hasty and, she hoped, embarrassed grab he made for it, and the nervous way he held on to it. His cheeks were flushed and he couldn't seem to think of what to say—not a bit like that cheeky Solutioneer—but she didn't feel sorry for him. She might just fire him on the spot. He wasn't even looking at her hats.

Pia almost turned around and walked out, and if she had she would have made sure to slam the door behind her. R Zilla was even less likeable in person than she was in writing. Pia squeezed the cap she now held in her hands. And why hadn't she just refused to take it off? She exhaled abruptly and thrust her right hand at the woman. "Lorenzo Apiedi," she said, and reminded herself to have a boy's firm grip.

The old bat had a pretty firm grip of her own.

"Can you do it?" R Zilla asked. She gave Pia's face a quick, birdlike glance, then announced, "He didn't tell you anything, did he. He just sent you over. Did he tell you to get me out of his hair?"

Pia badly wanted to say yes, and say it with the kind of smirky grin her brother Elgar had on his face when he'd grabbed the last piece of bacon off her plate and swallowed it before she could do anything to stop him. But she was the Solutioneer's Part-Time Assistant, on her first case, so she took a small notebook from her rear right pocket—Elgar's right rear pocket, if he only knew—removed a small pencil from the left, and asked, "Just what is the problem?"

R Zilla had more to say. "Your barber should be drummed out of business. That haircut is slipshod work."

Pia shrugged. She had chopped off her braids that morning. Standing in front of her mirror, she held each braid stiff with one hand while the other wielded the scissors, after which she'd trimmed her hair all around to even it up. Her mother had been too shocked to say anything, and her father had looked at her for such a long time that Pia became a little anxious. But it had always been part of her plan to chop off her hair. The R Zilla case had just made it happen sooner, and she was pretty sure that if her father had guessed what she was planning, he'd have put his foot down, immediately and hard—which he hadn't done, so she was safe enough for now. She wasn't really worried.

"I'm not here about my hair," she pointed out, and stared back at R Zilla as intently as the woman was staring at her, as if they were equals in age and importance and anything else that mattered. She knew how to win a staring contest.

"You might do," R Zilla concluded. "We'll see."

"Tell me what you expect of me," Pia said.

"I expect you to return my niece to me. I want her back, here, working for me. A contract was signed and I would be within my rights to take the law to her. She could drive me to that. She should know that about me, and about the contract, and about the law especially. I promised her mother I'd teach her the milliner's craft," R Zilla said. "The girl knows that's what her mother wished for her."

Pia was beginning to feel sorry for this niece, with her mother and this aunt ganging up on her. "What is her name?" she asked, pencil poised above the notebook page.

"Tess Tardo. She's a young woman who can't stand not to get her own way, that's the all of it. You'll have to manage her."

"You employed her?" Pia asked, hoping her face didn't give away the furious activity of the mind hiding behind it. In fact, she had met Tess Tardo and had rather liked the young woman, who had a small millinery shop in the old city.

"She's my apprentice, didn't I just tell you? I am teaching her the trade because talent isn't enough, not by itself. However talented you might be." R Zilla spoke solemnly; this was the heart of things. "You might not know anything about my art—you're a man, or will be—but any man can understand that it's not just talent that makes the kind of success I enjoy. Or earns the kind of fame I have. I expect the Queen will bring Princess Melis by, any day now."

Pia wrote down *Tess Tardo* and announced, as if it were a logical guess and not something she already knew, "She will have founded a rival business—"

"Can you believe that? After only three years! With two years still left on the contract, let me add, the contract she signed herself. She said she understood things I didn't." R Zilla snorted, and slammed an angry hand down flat on the table. "She said my hats were fit only for fat old rich ladies. I don't deny that many of my clients are neither young nor slender, but there *are* others."

Pia quoted her father: "It is the business of a business to make a profit."

The milliner stared into her face for a long, uncomfortable moment. "Is there more to you than meets the eye after all?" she asked.

"Of course." *How could there not be?* Pia almost asked, but stopped herself and merely glared at the milliner. She asked, "This niece, this Tess Tardo, is she copying your designs?"

"She's too proud to do that. No, Tess believes that *every* woman should be able to buy herself a pretty hat, *and* she thinks stylish hats can be as easily made out of cheap straw and felt as out of silks and satins, *and* she says she prefers the look of flowers to feathers. She says this to annoy me." R Zilla puffed and huffed and was, clearly, annoyed.

Pia couldn't help but wonder, "Why do you want her to return?"

"She's my niece, didn't you hear me? I promised her mother. Do I have to repeat everything? Her contract has two more years to run. It's the law."

Pia waited. She had seen the Solutioneer in action and knew a couple of his tricks.

"As well, she is not without a certain ability," R Zilla admitted.

Ha! Pia thought.

"And I still have much to teach her, whatever she may think."

Now Pia understood. This was a matter of somebody wanting her own way, trying to work things out to her own advantage. Pia was on Tess Tardo's side in this quarrel, even if it was R Zilla who was paying the Solutioneer's bill.

"What work did your niece do here?" she asked, pencil poised above paper.

"She wasn't with me in the salesroom, I can assure you of that. Her manner was entirely too familiar for the ladies who come to buy my hats. No, I kept Tess in the workroom."

Pia gestured toward one of the closed doors, as if it were a question.

R Zilla nodded. "When she came to me, she knew nothing.

Nothing. And now, after only three years? Now she's decided she's good enough to produce her own hats."

"You don't agree." This was not a question.

R Zilla folded her arms across her chest, as if everything had been explained and no further words were needed. She asked, "Well, young man? Can you do it? Can you get her back and spare me the expense of a lawyer?"

"Would you really take her to the law?" Pia asked.

"I would certainly be within my rights in doing so," R Zilla said, which was no answer, really. She looked at Pia, suspicious. "You think I'm a greedy, vain old woman, and, moreover, you probably don't care for my hats. Well, you needn't think that surprises me. How can a mere boy appreciate my great achievements? In my designs, in my success, in my life."

For some reason, this claim Pia did believe. R Zilla spoke with such energy and authority that Pia could now see her not as a foolish woman taking advantage of the even greater foolishness of other women, but as someone like her own father: someone who had ideas and did all the work necessary to turn those ideas into reality, someone who believed that the work he did was important. Pia turned to look at the hat in the shop window with new eyes. It was still outrageous, but it wasn't unintelligent.

She announced, "I'm ready to see the workroom." The place where Tess Tardo had spent her days might tell Pia something, although Pia didn't wonder why the niece no longer wanted to work for the aunt.

When the door opened, six human heads swiveled up from

where they were bent over six wooden ones. The wooden ones were eyeless and earless and had no mouths; the human ones wore cloth caps over their hair and darted quick, curious looks at Pia as they rose to stand beside their work stools and waited to hear whatever the milliner had to say.

"Keep on," she ordered, and all six women sat down again, twelve hands and one hundred and twenty fingers immediately busy, like a classroom of students anxious to show a feared teacher that they were working diligently on the assignment, that they were being good.

R Zilla stood at the front of the room, considering each table, one after the other. Then she wheeled around abruptly and returned to the shop.

Pia remained where she was for a brief moment, hands in her trouser pockets in a pose her brothers often struck, but none of the women even looked up at her, so she followed R Zilla.

Back in the sunny salesroom, the milliner positioned herself behind the long table and indicated that Pia should stand facing her. "About your payment," she said, and waited.

Pia folded the notebook back into her pocket. "The usual rates, fifty now and fifty more if I succeed." She pocketed the coins R Zilla gave her from a money box and announced, "I'll report back to you when I've learned something."

"You haven't asked where you can find the girl," R Zilla pointed out.

"I don't need to," Pia pointed out right back, and the shop bell rang before either one of them could say more.

A woman wearing a broad, sunflower-yellow hat, peacock plumes waving, followed her daughter into the shop. Pia recognized them both. The mother was someone her own mother kept trying to make a friend of, and the girl was Clarissa, from the Hilliard School, someone for whom Pia had little affection (the feeling was mutual), someone in whom she had little interest (also mutual), and someone of whom she expected the worst and was never disappointed. She looked around, but the open room offered no hiding place.

Clarissa entered talking, assuring her mother, "I *am* old enough. It wouldn't be a hat like that one—" She waved a hand at the black hat in the window. "I know better than that. My hat would be designed especially for me, Mamà, and I'd be the only girl in my school to have an R Zilla hat and everyone would know that you were the best, most generous mother in the world. All the other mothers would wish they'd thought of it. Don't you see? Won't Papà be proud of us?" She was smiling up at her mother and shaking her head so that her curls bounced while keeping one eye on the milliner.

R Zilla had an eye on the girl, too, but it was the mother to whom she spoke. "I see you wear the hat I made for you last April. It's quite elegant, if I say so myself. And this is your daughter? I'm very pleased to meet you, Miss. You will wear hats well, I can see . . ."

By then, Pia had slipped through the door and onto Barthold Boulevard, where she moved quickly out of view. Not until she was alone did she allow the grin to spread itself all over her face. Clarissa hadn't had a clue. She'd thought Pia was a boy, just as R Zilla had, just because she was wearing clothing she'd taken piece by piece from her brothers' closets. Max wasn't the only Solutioneer in town.

Her hair back under the checked cap, Pia stood in the narrow street, looking into the window of Tess Tardo's shop in the old city. Displayed there were wide-brimmed summer hats woven of straw and decorated with plain ribbons or delicate cloth flowers, as well as bonnets and boaters and sun hats and even a child's hat, made to fit a tiny head. A bell over the door rang as she entered the shop.

At the sound, the milliner turned from her worktable, smiling. Tess Tardo was a tall woman, no longer a girl but still young, wearing a simple white blouse and a plain blue skirt. Her brown hair was piled messily on her head, and her brown eyes welcomed a customer.

"Good afternoon, ma'am," Pia said, the way she thought a boy looking for work would talk to a possible employer. She'd worked it all out in her head. Removing her cap, she said, "You should hire me as your assistant."

Tess Tardo said nothing.

"You make the hats, the assistant sells them," Pia explained.

Still Tess Tardo didn't speak. She stared intently at Pia, like someone working hard to understand a foreign language.

"I could be that assistant," Pia concluded. Really, she'd thought Tess Tardo was quicker than this.

Tess Tardo merely raised her eyebrows.

"Or apprentice," Pia said. She'd just had the idea. "I can pay."

"If I cared about coins, wouldn't I have stayed on with R Zilla?" the milliner asked.

Tess Tardo's voice was *not* friendly. Pia had a lot of experience with unfriendly voices, so she knew. But what did the milliner have to be hostile to her about?

Pretending ignorance, Pia asked, "*Were* you with R Zilla? Why did you leave?"

"Take yourself off now," the milliner answered, and turned her back. "I have inventory to produce."

Pia was cross. How could she complete her case if Tess Tardo acted like this? She opened her mouth to say . . . say something, she didn't know what might come out, something to make this stubborn woman change her mind.

The bell jingled and a red-cheeked girl entered, asking excitedly, "That boater I tried on yesterday? In the window? Can I try it on again, please?" She set a small cloth reticule on the counter.

This would be a sale, Pia knew. Tess Tardo now ignored Pia, who stood with her hands jammed into her pockets, thinking hard.

When the girl had left, boater perched on her dark curls, Pia spoke quickly, before Tess Tardo could object. "I know about business. I can keep books. I could make advertisements to put in shop windows."

Tess Tardo folded her arms over her chest. She had large, long-fingered hands that looked strong enough to wring a chicken's neck. When she sighed, as she did now, it was not a sound of weakness, nor of sadness or resignation, but of boredom—or perhaps exasperation. Pia couldn't tell which. The milliner spoke slowly. "I don't know who you think you're fooling. You've been in here before and you've cut off your beautiful hair. There are too many untruths circling all around you, like flies. I don't know what you're up to, young woman, but I don't want to have anything to do with it."

Taken by surprise, Pia admitted it. "Your aunt thinks I'm a boy."

"She never sees past her own nose," Tess Tardo declared.

Pia was getting panicky. Max never panicked, she was sure of it, but she couldn't stop herself. "I *could* help you. I could sweep. I could buy ribbons, I could—"

"No," Tess Tardo said, so firmly that she didn't even have to shake her head for emphasis.

"How can I do my job if you won't even talk to me?" Pia demanded. Even while the words were tumbling out of her mouth, she told herself, *No wonder Max doesn't want you for a partner.* She couldn't really blame him, which was a discouraging realization.

It was also infuriating. Wasn't she even going to have a chance? She glared at Tess Tardo. "If you won't talk to me and you won't let me find out what your business is like and why you like it—because you do like it, don't you? Otherwise, why would you stay here when your aunt wants you back? Although I don't blame you, even if you do have to work alone and your shop isn't at all as fancy, or comfortable, those women in the workroom didn't look happy to be there, working for *her.* She isn't . . ." Pia waited impatiently for the right word to come to her.

"Isn't a nice person?" Tess Tardo suggested. "Cares only about her own success? But what do you mean your *job*? I thought you wanted to work for me."

"Well, I'm working for your aunt," Pia told the woman. "That's my real assignment. Your aunt hired me . . . Actually she wanted to hire my . . . I'm the assistant," Pia said. "To Mister Max, the Solutioneer, you probably haven't heard of him, but he—he has cases he's hired to work on, but he's busy with something else"—that was one way of putting it, Pia thought, even if what he was busy with was going out of business—"so your aunt had to take me instead. She's not too happy about that. She wants me to find out what it will take to get you back working for her, and she does have the law on her side. Do you know that? Because the apprenticeship contract you signed has two more years on it. That's my job, to find that out for her, and how can I do it if you won't even talk to me?"

After a long minute, Tess Tardo had a question. "Why would I tell you?"

This, Pia had no doubts about. "Because then I can go back and say nothing will change your mind. She said you were pretty stubborn and I don't blame you. If you ask me, I'd much rather work for myself than her. I like your hats better, too, if you want to know."

Now the milliner seemed thoughtful. "*I* like my hats better, too, but she's right. I did sign a contract, didn't I? Also . . . I need to think about this. Come back later," she told Pia. "Come back in an hour, but in a skirt and, please, without that cap. My aunt might not mind lies and pretenses, but I do."

Pia didn't waste words. "One hour. I'll be here," she said, and left before Tess Tardo could change her mind.

When Pia returned, wearing a sundress and sandals, Tess Tardo announced her decision without being asked. "You can tell my aunt that I'll come back if she makes me an equal partner, allows me to show my own designs and ask my own prices for them, *and* gives me sole management of the workroom. Just management, tell her that, nothing more, I don't need to be involved in hiring or firing—as long as the wages are fair."

Pia didn't need her notebook to remember three things. "Why the workroom, too? Won't that make your job a lot more complicated?"

"Maybe, but it pays off. If Aunt were a better employer, she'd get better work out of her people and also they wouldn't run off as soon as they could, to work for someone kinder, or who pays more, or to get married. One girl went back to working on her father's pig farm just to get away from Aunt.

They're proud to be good enough to be hired by her, but they don't stay long. But they do like me and I like them. We work well together. Tell all that to my aunt, and we'll see what she says. You know, even with what you've done to your beautiful hair, a boater would suit you."

It might have been easy to find out what Tess Tardo wanted, but it was not easy to make R Zilla even listen to her niece's terms. As soon as Pia, back in her boy's clothing, spoke the word *partnership,* R Zilla began to stomp around her showroom. It wasn't enough to sputter angry protests—"Upstart minx" and "Too sure of herself by half"—or to slap her hand down flat on the tabletop in anger at just the suggestion of equality. R Zilla also changed the hat displayed in the window, then put it back again, then tried a third choice, all the time muttering, "Impossible. Unthinkable. Arrogance of youth. Ruin me in a year, she would."

Pia realized that she had made a tactical error. She'd been so busy rushing to change out of the dress and back into trousers and cap that she hadn't made a plan. She should have pretended that it was her own idea, and added some other, entirely impossible conditions for R Zilla to be outraged by. Then she could have dropped the impossible ones and pretended to settle for the ones Tess Tardo had demanded. Max would have done better. R Zilla was stomping around the showroom and ranting on without a glance at her detective, and Pia knew she was going to have to accept failure. She said, "That's that, then," and turned to leave.

"Where are you going?" R Zilla demanded. "Are you quitting?"

"You just said you didn't want to—"

"I didn't say I *wouldn't.* Did I? You don't expect me to relish the thought of giving up half of my business, do you? Of having an equal"—spitting out the word as if she couldn't stand to have it in her mouth, and spitting out the next as if it tasted just as bitter—"partner. And if I know my niece, that's not all she'll want."

Pia didn't bother trying to understand.

"She won't compromise, that girl," R Zilla went on. "Stubborn as a mule. What else did she say?"

"She wants you to show *her* designs—"

"Hats any nobody can afford," R Zilla grumbled, but she stood planted right in front of Pia, and fixed Pia with a beady glare. "And ask her own prices for them, too, I expect."

She *did* know her niece, Pia had to admit that. So maybe this partnership was a good idea, if the two women really did understand each other. "Also, she wants to have charge of the workroom. *Sole management* is what she said."

"I guessed as much," R Zilla muttered. "Did she tell you why she walked out?" The milliner shook her head in disbelief. "When Tess quit, it was because she didn't like the way I talked to my girls. I told her it was the same way I talked to her, but she just said she didn't like that, either, and she'd had enough. When I saw some shopgirl wearing one of the little bonnets Tess liked to draw, I knew. She can't fool me," R Zilla announced.

“What do you want me to tell her?” Pia asked, plain and direct. She was no good at being subtle and tricky and she guessed she never would be. Not like Max. But maybe she didn’t have to be. Maybe the plain truth was the best way for her. She tucked that insight away, to be brought out and used when the right time came. For example, the time when she was pulled out from under an overturned lifeboat and some furious sailor demanded to know what this well-dressed boy was doing there and dragged her along to see the captain of the *Estrella,* who wouldn’t be at all pleased.

The plain truth it would be, so Pia asked, “Do you accept her terms? Or not?”

“You can tell her I’m willing to meet with her, and talk.”

“I don’t think she wants to talk about it,” Pia pointed out. “I think she wants a yes-or-no answer.”

“I didn’t ask you what you thought,” the old lady snapped.

“I’m telling you anyway,” Pia snapped back.

R Zilla continued snapping. “All right, then. Yes. I do.”

And Pia had solved her first case. She’d done it, and by herself, and successfully. She couldn’t wait to tell Max. She turned to leave.

“On one condition,” R Zilla said.

Pia didn’t groan, but she wanted to. She turned around. “What condition?”

“She has to come back and live in my house.”

These two women were ruining her day. “Why would she want to do that?” Pia demanded.

"Because if she doesn't, there'll be no partnership. Also," the aunt announced, with a smile that was very pleased with itself, "I've made her a separate apartment. You might advise her as well that I'm thinking of making other changes in my life, and a dog might be involved."

4

Pawn to King

Because it was now August, the fine, steady rain felt to Max almost like a warm mist as he went to Joachim's for another lesson in landscape drawing. Joachim greeted him gloomily. "Rain before seven, clear by eleven, so I'll be out painting in the garden later. When I'm in the garden, she can see me. She brings treats for Sunny and says she has to talk to me about hanging pictures in her shop. It's a hat shop," he pointed out, as if Max didn't already know that.

"Her clients are society ladies," Max pointed out right back at him. "If they see your pictures in her shop, they'll start buying them for their own houses. Won't that be a good thing for you?"

"I wish I didn't have to earn a living," Joachim answered.

"She's trying to get me to like her by winning Sunny's affections. What kind of a person takes advantage of how simple a dog's heart is?"

Since he, too, hoped to take advantage of the dog in the same way, Max didn't answer the question. Instead, "Sunny's coming with me this afternoon."

"Good idea," Joachim said. "That way she can't use the dog as an excuse to come in."

"She might not come today," Max suggested hopefully.

That possibility made Joachim almost cheerful. "Or tomorrow, either," he said.

"Or tomorrow, either," Max echoed, with a tone to his voice that made the painter look sharply at him. The boy had no expression on his face, but there was something dancing in his eyes, those eyes that always reminded the artist of his palette, which had drunk in so many colors over the years that it possessed a color of its own, a color without a name and impossible to reproduce. Could the boy be laughing at him?

After lunch, the sun did come out to dry the roads and fields, so Max and Sunny boarded *The Water Rat* at the city docks. At Summer, the two left the ferry, along with other holidaymakers who were taking advantage of a hot afternoon to stroll along the lakefront and have ice creams and sodas in the cafés, to visit the many small shops, and maybe, even, to catch a glimpse of some member of the royal family out for the same lazy stroll. Slowed only a little by Sunny's friendliness,

Max left the town and headed for the deep meadow on the lakeside, tantalizingly close to the high gates that were the entrance to the summer palace.

The guards noticed him right away. That was their job and they took a long, careful look. However, it didn't do to rush at everyone who came within a hundred yards of the gates to accuse them of being up to no good, so the four guards only kept close watch on the young man and his galumphing dog, who wandered together into the meadow.

Was this someone dangerous? they wondered. Not everyone who wore a beret was an artist. Some of them were only French. Although this was not merely a beret—it was a bright crimson red, and the young man was carrying what could be a drawing pad.

"Artist," Marc announced confidently.

"Looks like," Timmy agreed.

"He's letting that dog off its lead," Warlon remarked, and Kent commented, "That's a golden retriever, gentlest dogs you'll ever meet. Not easy to train," he continued, being the one of the four of them who knew something about dogs, "because they're not too smart. But they're fun. Much more fun than a hound, and better-natured than any terrier."

While the dog ran around the field in wide, excited circles, the young man folded his pad open and sat down in grass grown so tall that all you could see was his red beret.

"Artist," Marc repeated, this time with the satisfaction of being proved right.

Warlon, the most cautious of the four on their watch, worried. "You can't be sure, at a distance. He could be . . ."

"Could be what?" Timmy laughed. At nineteen, he was the youngest of the guards. "Our King has no enemies, not in our own land and not abroad, either. It's our elected officials who gather enemies to themselves, not our King. Probably because they're the ones who hold the power now."

"Not all of it," Marc argued. "It's the King who deals with foreign countries, and he has to approve the appointment of any new judge."

"A king is also a symbol," Warlon pointed out. "So to harm him would be to harm the country."

"It's not as if we're the only ones guarding him," Timmy said. "We only watch the gate."

Warlon insisted, "His children, too. They could be taken and held for ransom, or they could be used as pawns by some . . ." He couldn't think of the word, so he blustered, ". . . enemy."

"With all those nannies and nurses and tutors and governesses and maidservants and menservants always around, to watch over them?" was Kent's question.

Marc, who was the most sensible of them as well as the oldest, said, "If you're worried, Warlon—and I'm not the man to say there's no reason to worry—for how can I know?—you should go and talk to the fellow. Ask his name, ask where he lives, ask him his business."

"And leave my post?" Warlon demanded. "I know my duty."

"Then I'll go," Marc said. "Besides, my grandfather painted decorations on chests and wardrobes to beautify the homes in our village, so I'll know if the fellow is really an artist or no. If no," he told them, "if he is some . . . someone passing himself off as an artist for reasons of his own? You will see me raise my hat. He will think that I doff it in farewell, but you will know to join me and take him into custody. In that event, leave Warlon to guard the gates," he ordered.

"What about the dog?" Kent asked. "If he's taken into custody, what will become of the dog?"

"A dog can make its own way in the world," Marc answered.

"I'll see to the dog, then," said Kent, who preferred animals to people.

"You two, keep your eyes on me," Marc ordered. "Warlon, you watch the road."

In the event, no hat was raised, nobody had to dash down through the long grass, pistols out and shouting *Halt!* In fact, the dog followed Marc back to the sentry post, circling happily around his legs so that he had hard work not to stumble over her. Kent crouched down to pet her and learn her name, but nobody fed her. It was clear that she was not a well-trained, disciplined dog. If you gave a dog like this a treat, she might never leave you alone, so Kent only petted her, wished her well, and watched her bound off in pursuit of a stick he'd thrown, then get diverted by something moving in the grass—a mouse? a moth?—and chase after it.

The artist, identified as such by Marc, looked across the road to the lake, paying no attention to either the dog or the guards.

"Name's Tancred, lives in the old city, he's good enough that he must have studied some. I've never seen eyes like that," Marc told his fellow soldiers, looking back thoughtfully at the figure bent over its sketch pad. "Almost the color of the inside of a gun barrel. Not that he's dangerous. The opposite," he laughed. "The fellow wouldn't even swat an ant that crawled up on his paper. He took a leaf, coaxed it onto the leaf, and then set it down on the grass. An ant!" he laughed again, and they all laughed with him, at the way some people would literally not hurt a fly.

Max and Sunny returned to the meadow the next afternoon, to sketch (Max) and run about after butterflies, greet new friends, sniff along a stone wall, and nap (Sunny). By the end of the day, each of the guards, even Warlon, had taken a turn throwing sticks for the big, friendly dog, and Marc had paid Max a compliment on "the three-point perspective" of his drawing, which Max made a mental note to ask Joachim about, since he wasn't sure what it meant about his picture of the gates and guardhouse and curving drive, with a thick bank of trees behind.

At mid-afternoon, he had a bit of luck. The light sound of hoofbeats preceded the sight of a pony cart emerging from the band of woods to approach the gates. The driver was a boy of about eleven, and in the cart were two girls of about eight or nine, plus a middle-aged woman in a gray uniform. She wore a straw hat but the others were bareheaded. The children spoke in high, excited voices. The woman clutched at the wooden side of the cart as it jounced along while the two girls reached over the sides to grab at tall stalks of Queen Anne's lace.

"Look!" one of them shrieked as they came up to the gates and the guards. "A dog!"

"Slow down, Your Highness!" the woman was yelling. "Slow this thing down! Immediately! I'm warning you," she said sternly. Then she added, because he was a prince, "Please."

Max had already recognized Carlino, the Second Prince, and the royal twins, Marielle and Marguerite. He removed his beret and bowed his head, in case they noticed him. In fact, he hoped that they would notice him.

But it was only Sunny they had eyes for. "Does the dog need a home?" he heard as he kept his eyes fixed on the long grass around his shoes. "Slowly, slowly on the turn, Your Highness," one of the guards advised while the others greeted the children and their companion. "Afternoon, Your Highnesses, Mrs. Nanny. It's a nice one, isn't it?"

Max raised his head to watch the Second Prince maneuver the pony cart in a wide circle just inside the gates. Sunny bounded through the meadow, barking, and Max heard himself identified for the woman as "an artist, the dog's very friendly."

"She's beautiful!" one of the Princesses cried. "Why can't I have a dog like that?"

Max risked a smile and a humble bow in the direction of the cart. The little girls waved while the Second Prince sat up straighter, prouder, on his wooden seat. He snapped the reins smartly, the cart pulled away, and Sunny did not follow it.

Max would have liked Sunny to follow it so he could run after her. But she didn't, so he couldn't, and so as the hoofbeats faded away, he returned to his sketching of the curve of drive and the height of gates, and the line of leafy trees beyond.

He found Ari and Grammie together in her kitchen, reading aloud to one another from a Spanish newspaper, correcting one another's pronunciation and discussing the meaning of what they'd read. "You should be working with us," Grammie told Max.

"First things first," he answered, and she shook her head to let him know she thought he was making a big mistake. But Max couldn't worry about that.

"Any luck?" Ari asked.

"I'm making progress," Max reported. "Maybe."

"I'm not at all sure that I want you to succeed," Ari admitted. "I have about as little desire to meet King Teodor as he does to meet me. What could I say to him? Other than apologize for how my family has behaved for the last hundred years, and more, about which I can change nothing. How could I make up for the kind of people I come from?"

Max couldn't worry about that, either. His job was to

make contact with the King. He had less than three weeks before the *Estrella* sailed. If the painter-with-dog plan didn't work, this masquerade of theirs became a lot more dangerous for everybody, including not only the three of them but also the two people it was supposed to rescue.

Max needed to succeed as painter-with-dog.

It was as if Nature herself were on Max's side. The next day dawned windy, and bright with the kind of light that makes anybody want to pick up a paintbrush, or colored pencil, or pastel stick, or ordinary crayon, and put down on paper what they can see in that light. On the journey up the lake to Summer, the waves tossed the little ferry about and spray drenched the decks, so Sunny and Max were at the center of a crowd in the passenger cabin. Nobody paid any attention to Max, although Sunny came in for her usual caresses and compliments. That morning, there happened to be two small, yappy chows and a lively Jack Russell also riding in the cabin, so Sunny was praised for her calm and friendly nature and nobody minded the sweep of her tail.

By this third day, a couple of the café waiters nodded at Max, recognizing the painter—or at least his dog—as he crossed the square. He made his way along the road to his usual spot on the meadow, gave a quick wave to the guards, then turned to his business. That morning he wanted to sketch the view back across the lake to the hills beyond, with the distant western mountains little more than a backdrop to the scene. By then, Max and Sunny had become such familiar figures that the four soldiers on guard only waved carelessly back.

The wind pulled at the pages of Max's sketch pad and ruffled the feathers on Sunny's tail. It washed across the top of the tall grass, a wind strong enough to carry the sound of waves splashing against the shore. Max sketched, and wondered if he was changing, being changed by necessity, by what had happened to him and what he was doing about it, changed into something other than what he had always been before. He was accustomed to thinking of himself as a skyscapist who had no interest in scenery, artistically speaking. But he was enjoying this sketching of landscapes, and was already wondering which of his watercolor skills would be useful to him if he were to paint the scene. So that for long minutes at a time, his real purpose here slipped from his mind. So that he almost failed to see his opportunity when it happened. So that he almost missed the sight of Sunny leaping over the stone wall to chase something into the woods, barking happily.

But Max didn't miss it. He grabbed his sketch pad, jammed his pencil into a jacket pocket, and tore off in pursuit.

He heard voices, which he knew belonged to the guards. His feet wanted to just run, and get there, but his brain was wiser. He stopped, turned, and waved at them, where they watched after him. By then, he was halfway across the field, and farther from them, so he didn't have to pretend not to be able to hear their words, in the wind, at the distance. He lowered his arm to indicate the space where, if she had been at his side, Sunny's head would have been. Then he pointed to the trees and spread his hands out, helplessly. *What else can I do?*

They waved him off and he thought they were smiling, at the dog's mischief and the artist's embarrassment. That suited Max just fine.

Once he had scrambled over the stone fence and was out of sight among the trees, Max had to move fast. The soldiers would give him what struck them as a reasonable amount of time to catch his dog and bring her back out, but after that time had passed they would come after him. He had no idea how much time would strike them as reasonable, and—he now realized—he had no plan for what he would do once he had broken through the barrier of trees that kept the promontory and its inhabitants private. But his feet didn't need a plan. He raced through the trees, not even trying to call Sunny. He wanted to get to whatever lay beyond.

Stumbling over roots and dodging around bushes, ducking under low branches or broken limbs hanging down from the thick canopy of leaves above him, Max ran. Not knowing how far it was made it feel like a good distance, and not knowing how much time he had made it feel like it took too long; but in fact it wasn't all that far or all that long before he burst out of the woods onto a wide, sloping lawn, the grass mown short and glowing green. Sunny was dashing across it, toward three figures that were circling around under three kites that swept across the sky, dragging long, bright tails. Max heard the voices of children floating through the air.

In the distance, the summer palace shone white and the sky shone blue behind it. Even with the little he now knew about landscapes, Max could see a painting: children flying brightly colored kites in the open sky and a dog romping up to them, while from the background the palace kept watch over the scene. He slowed to a brisk walk, panting for breath, his sketch pad clutched against his chest.

Sunny lolloped up to the children and the kites swooped to the ground. It was then that Max noticed two men in green livery who stood close enough to oversee the children but not so close as to interfere in their play. He noticed the men because one of them raced forward to pick up the spindle the smallest child had dropped onto the ground in the excitement of Sunny's approach. The other man moved forward to collect the other two spindles and rewind the long kite strings, while the same gray-uniformed woman from the day before rushed to head off the little boy, who ran toward the dog with his arms outstretched. The woman said something that the wind blew away and the little boy ignored her, but one of the girls caught him by one arm and bent down to say something into his ear.

Max was close enough by then to recognize the Princesses, Marielle and Marguerite, twins but not identical, and so he knew that the littler boy must be Horatio, the youngest of King Teodor's children. These three did not look like two princesses and a prince. The girls wore green cotton dresses under white pinafores, and Horatio had short green trousers with a white short-sleeved shirt. All of them had the bare feet and wild hair of any child on a summer morning.

Max had no plan for what to say. He heard two pairs of booted feet slow to a marching pace as they came up behind him.

He had hoped to find the King taking a morning stroll. That would have been a gigantic piece of luck, he knew, but it was what he had hoped for. Instead, he found himself surrounded by children and their guardians. Luck had failed him.

Max walked even more slowly, ignoring the various adult voices that first demanded, "Just who are you?" and then called loudly, "*There* you are, Kent. Are you all asleep at your post?" and shouted at him to "Get back! These are the royal children." One of the girls, the one with honey-colored braids, asked him, "Is she your dog? Does she bite?"

This, Max responded to. "I've never known her to bite, Miss, Your Highness," he said. He hadn't even asked Grammie how you addressed royalty, that's how unprepared he was. Luckily, Sunny had the sense not to jump up, and as usual she wagged her tail with enthusiasm at everybody and was especially interested in the creatures who were her size, and one even shorter.

"Are you an artist?" the twin with nut-brown braids asked.

Max had never played an artist on the stage. He hadn't even ever *seen* a play that had an artist in it. He was only

Max Starling, a boy with missing parents and a plan to rescue them. He hadn't prepared the script for a scene in which royal children and their guards met up with an artist.

"You're wearing a beret," the brown-braided girl explained, "and I think that's a sketch pad you're carrying."

"He's an artist, Your Highness," Kent said. "Name's Tancred. We know him."

"The dog's gentle, no need to worry about her, Mrs. Nanny," Warlon told the woman. "She's a sweetheart."

"Sweetheart," Honey-Colored Braids crooned, and she wrapped her arms around Sunny's neck. She laughed happily when the dog's wet tongue swept down her cheek.

"Marguerite!" exclaimed Mrs. Nanny.

"Lick me, too! I want a lick!" cried Horatio, and he thrust his cheek up against Sunny's muzzle.

The dog obliged. The little boy dropped to the ground in a fit of giggles.

"Do you offer lessons?" Marielle inquired, as if she were years older than her twin and her brother, as if she were a princess grown.

"Your parents choose your instructors, Your Highness," one of the liveried men said, but in a kind voice.

"Of course!" she cried, and held out a hand to Max. "Come on, we'll ask Mother if you can give me drawing lessons, because I don't have an art teacher for the holidays."

"I don't know . . . ," Max mumbled, looking from Kent and Warlon to Mrs. Nanny, and then to the men in livery, trying to show them by his voice and facial expression, by his humble lowering of the head, that he had no idea how to behave in this unexpected and overwhelming situation.

Mrs. Nanny reminded the Princess, "Your mother has gone into Queensbridge this morning."

"For a big, big hat!" cried Horatio, who jumped to his feet so he could show Max how wide the brim on his mother's hat would be. "With feathers, isn't that right, Marielle? That's what she said, and Melis, too. Melis wants one, too." Then he heard his own words and laughed, repeating them to himself, "One, too, she wants one two three."

Max was trying to think about who the artist Tancred might be, what kind of person, and if he could—could he?—seem enough like a drawing teacher to be allowed into the summer palace. Max was trying to think and little quarrels were swirling around him and at the same time Marielle had him by the sleeve and was pulling him up the grassy slope.

"Wait! Wait!" wailed Horatio, and then, "Carry me!"

Marguerite hurried along beside Max and her sister. She held Sunny by the collar. "Poor dog, doesn't she have a leash? I could buy her one, can I, Nanny Rose?"

Max gave her Sunny's green leash and decided he'd have a French last name, *Dumas.* Yes, Tancred Dumas, that was good. With a name, Max felt better, as if he knew who he was and what he was doing. With a name, he felt like the Solutioneer at work.

5

King takes Pawn

They trooped along together, the two footmen, the nanny, the three royal children, and Max. Sunny romped, sometimes at the rear, sometimes at the fore. Sometimes Marguerite held her leash, sometimes it was Max. At first, as they went up the long rise at the pace dictated by Horatio's short legs, Max paid attention to learning as much as he could—the woman was Nanny Rose, the two footmen Will and Pierre, and all three had traveled with the family from the Capital to the promontory. After that he was free to worry about what to do once he was inside the palace. He wasn't at all sure how to play the role of the artist he'd taken for his disguise. He thought of Joachim, who was a real artist;

but he didn't think grumpy and obsessed would set the right tone here.

As they came closer to the palace, Max saw that it was a long stone building, painted white, and not the shining marble temple it resembled when viewed from the lake below. Flagstone terraces surrounded it, many French doors and tall windows interrupted the flow of its walls, and the whole long building seemed to curve around a wide garden crisscrossed with grassy pathways, bursting with flowery color and all of it just a little untidy, a place where children could go barefoot and take long, looping rides on the swings that hung from the branches of the sturdy old trees, where a scattering of balls and sticks and wooden train sets looked at home on the grass. The party followed Nanny Rose through wide-open French doors into the nursery.

This was a large, welcoming room, with warm wooden floors and crowded bookshelves, with a fireplace for cool August nights and a long table, low enough for small children to sit at but not so low that a full-grown person couldn't fit her knees under it. There were maps on the walls, among pictures illustrating some of the old familiar stories—Long John Silver with a parrot on his shoulder, Cinderella running toward her coach, a fox leaping up to secure the grapes that hung just out of reach, and the infant Hercules strangling snakes—the same stories Max had been told or read for himself. Could it be that under their crowns, inside their palaces—as if crowns and palaces were the costumes and settings for a dramatic production—the royal family was made up of real, normal people? A special kind of real, normal people, granted, but all the same, at heart, not so very different from everybody else. It looked that way, at least in this nursery, so maybe it *was* that way. Max hoped this idea would help him know what to say to the King. He had a letter explaining his request clipped to his sketch pad, and he knew he wouldn't have time to say much more than *Please, read this* or *Lives depend on this* before—as was bound to happen—he was seized by the scruff of the neck and jerked back, before he was identified as a fake and a possible danger and dragged away to prison by armed guards.

What would happen to Sunny when he was taken into custody? He hadn't thought of that, either!

Max needed to make a plan, but his attention skipped around like a small child, distracted and delighted by details of the rooms they paraded through, the murals of gardens in which gods and goddesses picnicked, or played lutes, or simply draped themselves with flowers. In other rooms, painted animals lived in harmony together, the lion and the lamb asleep under the same tree, the fox and the rabbit peeping out from under the same rosebush at an infant asleep in its cradle. Cool marble floors flowed under his feet and huge mirrors in wide golden frames reflected the light pouring in through tall windows. After a while, they arrived at what one of the liveried servants, Pierre or Will, he didn't know which, called the anteroom, which was small, wood-paneled, chairless, and empty. There, they waited.

It took Sunny no time at all to smell out everything in

that little room and settle herself at Max's feet. Marguerite sat cross-legged on the floor beside the dog, to whisper into her ear and scratch under her chin. Nanny Rose pulled a little wooden horse on wheels from her apron pocket and gave it to Horatio, while preparing Marielle for disappointment. "You mustn't set your heart on lessons. It's only a few weeks until you return to *Monsieur.* Your mother would want you to be patient."

Marielle looked sideways at Max and gripped her hands together behind her back.

Max couldn't help her out, although he sympathized with her. He, too, had had to argue his case in order to be allowed art lessons. Why was it, he wondered, that parents—even actors, even Kings, neither of whom *had* to be conventional about things—didn't want their children to learn the things the children chose, but only the things the parents preferred? He tried to put an expression of artistic dreaminess mixed with trustworthiness on his face.

They waited and waited, the young members of the royal family more well-behaved than any other children Max had ever seen as they waited and waited. Even when Horatio tired of his toy horse, he was contented with the stories Nanny Rose told him in a low voice.

Max shifted from one foot to the other and tried to find something to look at. The room had two doors. There were only two windows, tall and narrow and uncurtained. There were no murals, only mirrors, and he did not want to look into any mirrors. He shifted his weight again and half listened to Nanny Rose: "And then, the three billy goats gruff all ate their fill of the sweet grass on the other side of the bridge." Horatio yawned and Max thought it must be past noon, past lunchtime, although the way time was dragging it might be only eleven o'clock; and he himself yawned.

Finally, a door opened. Four men in shirtsleeves and linen trousers, not suits, came out, talking among themselves and turning back to consult with younger men, who *were* wearing dark suits and starched collars, who carried notebooks and piles of papers and had pens in their hands or, in one case, behind his ear. Max had no time to think about who they might be, because the two servants in livery were hurrying *his* group into the presence of the King, and Max had Sunny to keep hold of because in this new, long, wide, carpeted, and window-lined room there were places to run to and sniff out, and the tempting oiled leather of the boots worn by the four soldiers who stood on guard. Sunny tugged at her leash, but Max held her close to his side.

The three children ran up to their father but halted a foot away from him and stood silent until he bent down to give each one a kiss on the top of his or her shining head. In the company of his children, Teodor gave them his complete attention, and this gave Max a chance to consider the King, close up.

The King was a slight man, and not tall. His dark hair was graying and his face, as he addressed his children, was amused, the dark eyes alight, a smile dancing on his mouth. His close-shaven chin was a firm one, his nose was long and thin, and he looked at that moment like any other fond father in the company of his family. "What is it that's so urgent with you three?" he asked the two Princesses and Horatio, bending a little to be closer to them.

"I have my horsie!" Horatio answered, thrusting the toy at his father, who chuckled while also listening to Marguerite and Marielle saying at the same time, "I want to play with the dog" and "I could have drawing lessons. He's an artist, he could teach me."

"One at a time," said the King. He didn't even look up at the people who had accompanied his children into the room, the usual two servants and the nanny, and a fourth, non-childish shape. He didn't look at the dog, either. His attention was captured and held by his children.

"*And* the billy goats gruff all ran safely across the bridge," Horatio offered.

"That was lucky," the King said. "You do know, don't you, Horatio? That there are no trolls under any bridge in *my* land. So you can cross bridges just as slowly as you like."

Marielle grabbed her father's sleeve and pulled gently. The King bent to listen. "I really want to take lessons from him. Nanny Rose says I have to wait, but he's here and Kent-at-the-gate says he's an artist and if I have to go for four more whole weeks without even one lesson I'll forget *how,*" she pleaded.

"I don't like to contradict Nanny Rose," the King said. "She has good reasons for whatever she says."

"He has a dog," urged Marguerite from his other sleeve.

"Oh, well," the King laughed. "A dog changes everything, doesn't it?" he teased, and then he did glance up.

He glanced up and saw a stranger, a red beret, and a large dog that wagged her tail in a friendly fashion, a golden retriever, probably safe for his children. Max unclipped his envelope, to have his appeal ready in his hand, and the King's attention was caught by the movement.

Then Teodor looked right at Max, and he straightened to his full height. He looked at Max and his expression became . . . became what? Not angry. Became kingly, rather stern, thoughtful. The King looked the way Lorenzo Apiedi, the hero of *A Patriot's Story,* might have looked, had his uprising succeeded in ousting the tyrant, had he not been hanged young. There was a hardness in the King's face now which reminded Max of the portraits of all the past Barons Barthold, men of wealth who exercised great power. Just because this King was wise enough to listen to his advisers and forward-looking enough to give over many of his royal powers to the elected representatives of his people, that didn't mean he wasn't also the King, wealthier and more powerful than any baron, much more formidable.

"Sire," Max began, and wondered if he should fall onto one knee.

"Nanny? Take the children," the King ordered. "Leave me now, children. No discussion. Will, Pierre, you'll accompany them. Let the Queen know I may come a few minutes late to luncheon and she should sit down without me," he said. Then he held out a hand to halt the four soldiers, who had stepped closer, ready to defend him, and he gave the order. "Withdraw to the anteroom. No need to fear. I don't think he has a weapon." He looked into Max's eyes to demand, "Do you?"

Max could barely speak. He shook his head and mumbled, "No, sir. Your Majesty."

This was worse than stage fright, when you know that if you open your mouth, nothing will come out of it. Or if something does, it will be only a little high squeak, nothing that makes sense. Max had almost forgotten what it felt like to be a twelve-year-old boy, in trouble with someone in authority.

As the soldiers left the room, Max thrust the envelope at the King. King Teodor took it, but he did not look at it. Instead, he studied Max's face.

Sunny sat quietly at Max's side.

Max took a breath. "That letter explains—" he began, but King Teodor waved his hand impatiently.

"Where are your parents?" he demanded.

"What?" Max asked. "What?"

"It is customary to remove your hat in the presence of your King," Teodor instructed sternly.

Max took off the beret and clutched it in his hand. He didn't know what to think. He could think of nothing to say. He had no idea—

"I hope it's my buttons in this envelope, now you've finally— You took your own sweet time answering the signal. What the devil are your parents playing at?"

"What?" Max asked again, stupidly. "What signal?" He

was dumbfounded, dumbstruck, and almost afraid. He didn't understand anything—and then, to make everything worse, at the look on Max's face the King burst out laughing.

It was a fine laugh King Teodor had, rich and royal. Max felt a goopy smile begin on his own face at the sound of that laugh.

"All right, boy, come here. I don't mean to bully you. It's just that I've been waiting ever since I arrived . . . and I've been very worried. Let's have a glass of lemonade—" And the King led Max, Sunny still close at his side, to a long table where he pulled out a chair for Max to sit in and pulled out another for himself.

Sunny, reassured by something in the King's voice, moved over with great sweeps of her tail to sniff at the hand that was held out, inviting her attention. Max, also reassured, took the tall glass the King offered him. He drank.

The King drank. He watched Max.

Max had the feeling that a subject should always wait for the King to speak, so he waited.

The King smiled, perfectly pleasantly, an ordinary nice smile on the face of an ordinary nice man, and said, "You've got the look of your mother about you. You're the boy, the son. Max. They never told me much about you. How old are you?"

"Almost thirteen, but why would my parents be talking to *you*?"

"They're my agents. You didn't know? They've been my agents since before you—"

Max interrupted. "You mean *spies*?"

The King shrugged.

Max insisted, "You mean, people who sneak into other countries and steal their secrets?"

"If you think about it," King Teodor answered with a teasing, teacherly expression, "not all of the secrets a nation keeps have to do with weapons or planning attacks. If you think about it, sometimes knowing what is really going on in a nation—or in a city, or in a countryside—can allow you to offer the right kind of help at the right time. Nations are proud, at least as proud as people and maybe even more so—and national pride can be just as dangerous as personal pride. Or it can be a strength, of course; that, too."

Max thought of the Baroness Barthold and how her own pride and her ancient family pride made her life a prison. He thought of Lorenzo Apiedi, even if he was only a character in a play, and how pride had helped him make, and keep to, the noble choices. He thought about history and the things that had happened because one nation or another, or one tribe or another, had felt shamed, or insulted, or even just—and this was often the case—so proud of its own strength or the rightness of its position that it made foolish and self-destructive decisions.

After he had thought for a long minute, Max asked, "Exactly what did they do? When they were your agents."

"Three years ago—for one example? You will remember that the Company toured in the northern countries."

Max nodded. He remembered that time and how his

parents had refused to let him go with them, despite all his arguments. Their reasons were good enough, and genuine, as he had known even at the time. But he had also seen that they were sorry to miss the chance to introduce him to a new landscape and new peoples, for which reason they would have liked to say yes. He remembered thinking at the time that if he could just think of one or two more arguments that would tip them over the line, they would notify his school and he would pack his bag and they would be off together. But that hadn't happened. Maybe now he knew why.

"While touring there, especially in the smaller cities, they heard rumors about a failed wheat crop—too much spring rain, then a long summer drought, if I remember. Knowing that, I could see to it that our grain and beer, our cheeses, were made available at a consistently low price, and I could build up a store of woolens and medicines to offer, should the winter prove harsh and sickness spread, especially among the poor. Not all information gathered in secret is intended to be used to the disadvantage of another, Max," the King said. He took a long, slow drink and admitted, "It happens that I am proud to think of myself as a king who is also a good citizen of the world."

"That was the kind of information my parents brought you?"

"Mostly. Perhaps four times over the fifteen years they brought back word of armies being increased along one of our borders, or someone spreading rumors among his people to make them fear us. Or they smuggled someone across a border to safety a few times over the years, because— You must know that your father's an adventurer, and such men enjoy danger. You do know that?"

"Yes, and my mother . . . is not unwilling."

"Your mother is not any kind of a coward, I agree. So now you know, and I'm glad they told you about the buttons."

"But they didn't," Max said. "Do you want them back? Because I have them at home."

"Your father didn't tell you about the signal code?"

Max shook his head.

"About being my spies?"

Max shook his head again.

"Hmm," Teodor said. Then, because a good king has a broad streak of practicality, "Yes, I would like the buttons returned. But in that case, why have you come here? Unless—is it an accident that you're here?"

Max shook his head for the third time.

Now it was Teodor taking time to think. After a while, he asked, "Where *are* your parents? Your father fobbed me off with some story about India, but that's too far-fetched to be believable. I know they've left the city, but they didn't tell me their true destination, and, frankly? I think I've put too much gold into their hands for your father to try to gull me."

Suddenly it was very important to Max that the King should know that his parents had been telling him the truth. "They believed they were going to India. There were first-class tickets on a boat called the *Flower of Kashmir,* which didn't exist. We all thought we were going. Really, sir. Sire. Your Majesty."

"*Sir* will do. You mean the invitation was a fraud?"

"Yes! It wasn't until after they'd gone that we realized . . ." Max let that sentence drift off, distracted by a sudden realization: "That's where all those gold coins come from, isn't it? You paid them in gold coins."

King Teodor looked confused.

Max waved his hands, to wave this unimportant fact away, and told the King, "They really did believe the invitation was genuine. There was a ticket for me, too, when they asked for it. Or at least they were told it would be on the ship, waiting for me." Now he wondered, "Do you think it was? But I had an art lesson that morning, a final lesson, with Joachim."

Now it was the King who waved away an unimportant fact, so that Max would get on with the story.

"When I got to the docks, I was on time, but it turned out there was no vessel with that name there. And," he added quickly, "none of the manifests of any of the ships that sailed from Queensbridge that morning had any passengers on them that sounded like they could have been my parents."

"If they were in disguise?" the King suggested.

"Except, I was given a message by the Harbormaster, a note from my father. It was just a few lines which made no sense at the time, so we had to conclude that they really had sailed on one of the boats. My grandmother and me."

"What do you mean, made no sense at the time?"

Max took a large swallow of his sharply flavored drink

and told the King the story, as it had come to him and as they had figured it out, including the long first weeks of waiting, until Grammie had seen the photograph in the newspaper, then the odd response he'd received in answer to his schoolgirl's letter to Andesia, and finally how he'd decoded his father's messages. The King listened carefully, not once interrupting.

"They need help," Max concluded.

"I see that," the King answered. "Yes," he said, in the inattentive way someone speaks whose mind is busily at work. "You know I can't send in an army," he said, apologizing. "Getting an army across an ocean is bad enough, and it's not as if Andesia has attacked one of our towns, or even one of our merchant ships. It wouldn't be legal, or right. I don't see how to do it."

"I have an idea," Max said.

"Somehow, I'm not surprised," the King remarked as he poured them each more lemonade. "When I sent someone to have a quiet look at your parents' house, there was a sign, I was told. Quite a professional sign, I heard . . . So," he concluded, with a smile, "I have a suspicion about you. Just a hunch"—he raised his hand to silence Max, who was about to deny everything, deny it all—"which I'd never voice to anyone."

Max subsided. He looked with interest at this King.

"What's your idea?" King Teodor asked, with equal interest.

Max explained the plan to send a diplomatic embassy to Andesia, which would include himself as secretary to the

Envoy and Grammie as housekeeper. He admitted that he had no idea how to actually manage a rescue but argued that he would be able to think of something, once he was on the spot and knew what the actual situation was. He told the King about the uprising in Andesia, almost a year ago now, and the invasion of armies from neighboring countries, which was probably motivated by the silver and copper mines. He talked about how General Balcor had been given control and had stayed on in Andesia, how the deposed former royal family—"who were cruel, greedy, tyrannical, yes, but still . . ."—had been slaughtered by robbers in what was supposed to be a safe fortress. He described what he and Grammie had read about the poverty of the people of Andesia—excepting, of course, those who owned the mines. He explained why he had settled on this particular rescue plan.

King Teodor nodded and nodded and said, "I see," and "Yes," until the question of who the Envoy would be was raised, by the King, and answered, by Max. When he heard Ari's name, the King pushed himself up from his chair and his face turned to stone. He was angry. "I have no dealings with that family," he announced.

Max admitted, "That's what he said, that's exactly what he said you'd say."

"Who?"

"Ari. Yes, he's the next Baron, the Baroness's heir, but he's also my math tutor, and tenant, and friend, and he said you wouldn't have anything to do with him and he didn't blame you. Because how could you know he isn't the same kind of

Barthold as the rest of them. After all, the Baroness is like that, too, even if she has a couple of good points."

"I didn't know the Baroness had an heir. I thought that family was finally going to die out, poisoned off by its own evil character." The King, however, was now listening again.

"Actually, Ari would prefer not to be the Baron Barthold, but you can't help the family you were born into. And he'll be a good one, *I* know—but how would *you* know that?"

"In fact, I know the opposite. They're lawless, they always have been. They're pirates and thieves. Bad masters and worse subjects."

"The Cellini Spoon," Max said, to show that he understood the King's point of view.

"What do you know about the Cellini Spoon?" King Teodor asked, adding, "Mysteriously stolen from that old woman. Or so I was told," he concluded in a tone of voice that said he was pretty sure he hadn't been told the truth.

"It's been found," Max said. He did his best to damp down the pride in his own voice, but his eyes must have shone with it, because the King sat again.

"Found? Was it really lost?"

Max nodded.

"And I think you might have found it."

Max hoped he was keeping his face expressionless as he nodded again.

"You *are* your parents' child, through and through," the King murmured, talking to himself more than to Max. "So now it's back in the hands of that terrible old woman—"

"That's what Ari says about her, too," Max said.

The King looked at him thoughtfully.

"You could meet with him, if you were willing to. Just meet him, nobody has to know," Max said. "Ari could surprise you. It might be time for things to change."

The King stared a minute more and then said, "I'm willing to wager that you have an idea about how such a meeting might be contrived, in absolute secrecy."

Max nodded yet again, remembering the front deck of *The Water Rat,* available for just such occasions under the discreet eye of Captain Francis, but he didn't explain. He sat silent and let the King come to the decision in his own way, in his own time.

Finally, King Teodor picked up his glass, and took a long drink. "If a king can make a peace within his own country, or at least consider that possibility, it has to be a good thing. For everyone concerned. All right, then, Max Starling, you can have it your way. I'll talk to your Barthold. But I think you *had* better agree to give the Princess Marielle those drawing lessons she longs for, so that I can keep you informed about this . . . this rescue plot."

"But I don't—I don't know how to—"

"I expect you'll think of something. Shall we say at ten in the morning? The day after tomorrow? This business is in *my* hands now," King Teodor announced as he stood up again. "Don't forget your beret," he told Max, with a smile. "Or your dog," and he left the room.

6

In which the King acts, while Max adjusts, accommodates, and adapts

Then began a strange period in Max's life. He was the spider at the center of the web, but he wasn't the weaver. His long arms spun out the threads, but those threads were being arranged as if they had nothing to do with him. He was powerful and helpless, both at the same time; he knew what he was doing and he had no idea what was going on, both at the same time. He was the Solutioneer and at the same time he was just one part of the solution.

What mostly kept Max occupied during those long days was the matter of teaching drawing to the Princess Marielle. When Max asked for his help in giving drawing lessons, "You're neither an artist nor a teacher!" Joachim exclaimed. "What are you thinking?"

Sunny went to examine something under a bush at the farthest end of the garden.

"Even the dog knows better!" Joachim expostulated, waving his arm in the air so violently that paint spattered on the grass. "I don't know what's happened to you, Max. First you drag that woman into my life and now you want to set yourself up as a drawing teacher. Who is it that needs *you* for a drawing teacher?"

"Princess Marielle," Max admitted.

"Shouldn't a princess have a *real* drawing teacher?" Joachim argued.

"The King told me to do it," Max explained, adding, "I'm supposed to bring Sunny, too, for Marguerite to play with. She doesn't have a dog of her own."

This seemed to satisfy Joachim, who remarked, "So you found your way to the King. And you already have tickets, thanks to your grandmother."

"She's getting worked up now about how to get from Caracas to Apapa, which is the capital of Andesia. It's way up in the mountains, isolated."

"An enterprising woman, your grandmother," Joachim observed.

Max certainly agreed. Grammie was enterprising, and more. She got things done, and done right. He couldn't resist the temptation to boast. "She has us all learning Spanish."

"You wouldn't think it, to see her," Joachim remarked. "Are three people enough to rescue your parents?"

"How would we know? We don't even know what kind of

plans we can make. We don't know *what* we'll find when we get there," Max admitted.

Something had decided Joachim. He announced, "You should start with perspective. Perspective's easy to explain and I know a couple of exercises even a little girl can do."

It was a good thing Pia wasn't around to hear that, Max thought, but didn't say. In fact, in general, it was a good thing Pia wasn't around at all these days. He decided that it had been brilliant of him to give her the R Zilla job, to keep her out of his hair.

After about fifteen minutes of being an art teacher, Max understood how much easier it is to do something yourself than to try to show somebody else how to do it and put your hand in your pocket while her hand did it wrong, then explain yet again, then watch again to see if you had explained it in a useful way. He said, "Good. Now try again, and hold the ruler steady." He'd only said *Good* because Joachim never did, and especially when he had first started lessons it was a word he would have liked to hear. Another fifteen minutes went by, slowly. Through the open French doors, Max watched Marguerite and Sunny playing throw-the-stick out on the lawn. Excited barkings mingled with excited laughter. Marielle concentrated on the assignment he'd given her, which was to draw a room using one-point perspective. In fact, he now saw that she had successfully created the back wall. "Good," he said, and this time he meant it. "Now can you put in a near corner?" He forced his hand to stay in his pocket and not point out the very spot on her paper where she should put the ruler to begin the next straight line.

At the end of the lesson, Pierre told Max that the King wanted a word with him and that Will would take him to the King, and then wait to bring him back so he could collect his dog. What the King wanted to see Max about was the name of the ship Grammie had booked them on, and the date on which she was due to depart. *"Estrella,"* Max answered, and "the seventeenth of August."

The King nodded. "Thank you. On your advice, I'm taking a sunset ride around the lake on the ferry," he said.

Max nodded. He'd already heard about this from Ari.

Teodor, wearing no uniform more than the light linen suit and panama hat of a wealthy gentleman, stood at the prow of *The Water Rat* and enjoyed the solitude, and the way the moist early-evening air on the lake brushed his face. He watched the houses of Graffon Landing come closer and determined that on the next fine afternoon, he would take his three youngest children on this journey. It was time those three had their father's full attention for an entire afternoon—*and* time their father got to spend an entire afternoon with just those three. The little Princesses and Horatio would love the ferry ride, and the waterfall, and the attention from whoever happened to find themselves unexpectedly sharing the ferry with the royal family. Teodor smiled to himself in anticipation.

How this evening's meeting might turn out depended on whether the Starlings' boy was a sound judge of character.

Historically, the Barons Barthold had been grasping men, with little respect for the law and no concern for the well-being of their women, servants, soldiers, and serfs. Teodor had little hope for this Baron-to-be, but he would meet him, and listen to his appeal.

It was a young man who approached the King under the watchful eye of Captain Francis, a slender, handsome young man, with the Barthold red hair. He, too, wore a light linen suit for the occasion. Teodor waited.

The young man had either the wits or the arrogance *not* to bow, which kept the King's identity concealed from the other passengers, but he knew how to greet his monarch appropriately—"Your Majesty"—and this show of diplomatic good sense did not go unnoticed. Then the young man looked directly at the King and said, without preamble or apology, "The Cellini Spoon belongs, by rights, to you. Whatever comes of this meeting, I promise you I will put it back into your hands. Exactly when this will happen, however, depends on the present Baroness, to whom it is a comfort and a source of much pride."

Having announced this, he fell silent, and waited for the King's response.

If he had promised to deliver the spoon within a week, or on condition that the King agree to name him Envoy to Andesia, Teodor would have ended the interview right then. But he had not, had instead made the promise with the only condition a concern for an unlovable old woman, and with a full acknowledgment of the royal rights in the matter. This might be a new breed of Barthold indeed, and Teodor did not hesitate. "I thank you. Now, tell me about this proposed embassy of yours."

The young man smiled. "It's Max's embassy. Not that I'm unwilling. On the contrary, I owe Max a . . . a great debt. Which it's a pleasure to be in the position to repay, if you decide I am worthy of your trust."

Teodor had already decided. This only confirmed his opinion.

Max had thought that he would teach Marielle one-point perspective the first day, two-point the second, and maybe on the third day three-point. But it turned out that she needed at least another day, and maybe even another after that, to master one-point perspective. It turned out that when you were teaching, you had to be patient not only for the length of the lesson but also day after day, while your student progressed from learning to knowing. Max amused himself trying—and failing—to sketch Sunny. Sunny seemed entirely happy with her new best friend, and Marguerite was obviously delighted. It made Max wonder why the girl didn't have a dog of her own. Was there a law that the royal family couldn't have pets?

If there was, it would have been just something else to wonder about. Max was wondering if the King would give official status to the embassy, wondering if he was teaching Marielle anything useful, wondering if he was finished being the Solutioneer, wondering why Pia didn't come to his house to pester for help or boast about success. This wondering but not doing was uncomfortable for Max. Also, it struck him as he received a second summons to the King, there was the wondering what Teodor was up to, wondering if the King's interference would actually help his parents.

Their second meeting was brief. "I should be paying you for these lessons," the King said, and passed him a small cloth purse with coins in it. "I will make only one major change in your plan," he announced. "The others are minor."

Max wanted to know what these changes were, but before he could work up the courage to ask, the King said, "You may leave me now," and Will stepped forward to show him the way back to the terrace, and Sunny, and the road to Summer. It wasn't until the ferry was making its approach to Graffon Landing that Max realized what he had been told:

Teodor had agreed to send a royal embassy to Andesia.

As arranged, King Teodor arrived almost half an hour early, and alone, for the royal family's dinner reservation at B's, Queensbridge's newest fashionable restaurant, yet another success for Hamish Bendiff. Teodor ignored the bowing, overawed maître d' and strode into the dining room, leaving his guards at the street entrance. As if in royal displeasure or royal fussiness, "I'd like to see the room you've given us," the King said to the man who stepped forward to welcome him, Bendiff himself.

With the gesture of an arm—respectful, but not subservient; the gesture of a man with a vote, who also knew better than to introduce himself to the King—a doorway was indicated. Through it Teodor saw a round table, as private as he could wish, set with bright white linen, gleaming silver, and small bowls filled with flowers. The windows were open to the fresh evening air, which carried into the room the soft music of the rushing river.

Teodor walked around the table, nodding so that anyone could see his satisfaction. He crossed to the window, where whatever he said would not be overheard but also where, because he could be seen to be only talking quietly—about seating arrangements? the menu? the wine?—nobody would be concerned for his safety. "You're Bendiff's Jams and Jellies," he told his host. "Bendiff's Cheese and Crackers. Bendiff's Beers and Ales."

"I am," the man said, wasting no words. He wondered what a King might want with him. Not, he was sure, to invite Hamish Bendiff and his wife to dine at the summer palace, for which (he made a mental apology to his wife: "Sorry, Grete") he was grateful.

The King said, "I've heard of you, your successes, your way of doing business. Your employees are contented. Your products give good value." He waited a few seconds here, then added, "I've also heard that you came from nothing."

"Not nothing, Sire. A dairy farm in the hills on the western lakeshore and my parents knew the value of hard work, and careful husbandry. I was lucky enough to have the right wife at my side. I came from a great deal, I'd say."

As if the man hadn't spoken, "And now this," the King said, indicating with a gesture the restaurant behind them.

"We are all hoping that you will enjoy your meal here," the man said. "But I'm thinking that you want something from me? I mean, something particular, to ask for a private conversation."

King Teodor, who was accustomed to the worldly sophistications of courtiers and the politically circumspect conversations of foreign ambassadors, not to mention the irritatingly ornate good manners of an old aristocracy, smiled happily at this frankness.

"I think you are a man who welcomes a challenge," he observed, just as frankly. "And I wonder: Would you be willing to step away from your current businesses?"

Mr. Bendiff considered the question, and its implications. Eventually, he said, "I have an excellent head accountant, although no one ready to maintain my current endeavors." There was a time, he did not tell the King, when his wife had been such a person; but now she seemed to care only for her hats and her social position, even though that pursuit just made her unhappy. "Why would this concern you?"

Teodor smiled again. "I have a use for your skills and gifts. And your time, too, perhaps even months of your time." He went on to explain about the embassy to Andesia under the leadership of the young Barthold, who would be accompanied by a private secretary. "The present King, and his Queen, too, were until recently residing in Queensbridge," he said, to explain *why* Andesia. "There is wealth in the country, mining industries—although the people themselves are poor farmers, uneducated, as you can imagine, and all the wealth is in the hands of the one family that owns the mines. At this point, I believe it is governed by the army of occupation that put down a peasant uprising." There were many things he wasn't saying.

"Residents of Queensbridge, and now a King and Queen in South America?" the businessman asked. His dark blue eyes sparkled with curiosity. "I'd have expected to hear something of that in the newspaper."

"A certain William Starling and his wife," the King said.

This startled the businessman. He thought for another long moment, then asked, "The Starling Theatrical Company?" There were things that Mr. Bendiff, too, wasn't saying.

"I believe so," the King answered. "My thought is that you would be qualified to understand the economics of Andesia, to see where an industry might flourish, and what that industry might be. It may prove a dangerous assignment," he added. "I can't swear that diplomatic credentials will offer safety in that part of the world."

Hamish Bendiff studied the King, thinking his own thoughts. "I'm tempted," he said at last.

"I hoped you might be," the King said.

"May I take a few days to consider your proposal?" the businessman asked.

"Don't take too long," Teodor advised. "The ambassadorial party sails on the *Estrella* August seventeenth."

As if that confirmed something—but what could it confirm?—Bendiff nodded briskly. "In that case, I'll let you know within twenty-four hours," he promised his King. "And now, would you like to see the kitchens? I'm rather proud of those kitchens."

King Teodor, who was seldom shown the working areas of the institutions and businesses he visited, was happy to do just that while he waited for his party to arrive. If he was any judge of character, Bendiff would agree to become a member of the Andesian embassy—and perhaps, someday, the royal Minister of Commerce, although Teodor suspected that the man's independence was more important to him than a position at court. The big man had an adventuring look to him, and he had—in his way—led an adventurous life. The addition of Hamish Bendiff would give the embassy more credibility and increase its chances of bringing his spies safely home. That it might also bear economic fruit for his own country and his own people was another of Teodor's thoughts. A good king is always thinking of his country's well-being, and a wise king knows how seldom armies and wars achieve that goal.

At their next meeting, the King had announcements to make to Max. "I've made an addition to your party" was the first.

By that time, the strangeness of everything had Max so far off balance that he couldn't have stopped himself from objecting if he'd wanted to. But he didn't want to, King or no King. "Why would you do that?" he demanded.

"The embassy needs one more addition as well," the King announced, as if Max's protest had never been made. "You're the best person to choose that one. I speak of someone to act as servant to the Ambassador's party. A King's envoy on a state visit to establish diplomatic and commercial relations with another nation would have a personal servant, as well as a private secretary and a housekeeper and an economic adviser."

"What economic adviser?" Max demanded. "What commercial relations?"

These are my *parents,* he was thinking. *This is* my *plan and it's a good one, what are you doing messing around with my plan, I don't care if you're King, my father's a King, too . . .* but when he reached this point in his thoughts, he almost laughed, and only the seriousness of his parents' situation stopped him.

"A genuine embassy, seeking to establish diplomatic relations, would include someone experienced in economics," the King said. "I have appointed someone. A Queensbridge man."

Max thought he could make a guess about which Queensbridge citizen King Teodor might mean, and even if the idea was entirely new, and not his own, he could see that it was a good one. When profits are possible, everyone becomes friendlier.

"Surely you know someone reliable who would be able to act as the Envoy's servant," Teodor said, no longer surprised at the way he talked with this ordinary boy—although the

King doubted that any ordinary boy could get done what this one had gotten done. There was something about this boy's eyes, something as undefinable as their color, a rough gray like the stones at his waterfront fortress at Porthaven, massive blocks of granite that were covered by every rising tide and then left exposed to the oxidizing air as the waters receded every day. "Some boy who might be useful in a scuffle, someone resourceful, strong, but young enough to be overlooked by a military governor. The kind of person who asks *what can I do,* not *what do I have to do,* and clever enough to learn new things quickly . . . Do you know someone like that? I think you must."

In fact, Max did, and that silenced his protests.

"I'll pay his wages, of course," the King said. "All costs of the embassy will be met by the royal treasury—"

Now Max interrupted. "No," he said. "That will not be necessary," he added, because a one-word refusal sounded rude, and he did not want to be rude to the King. "Sire."

The King studied him.

Max met the royal gaze steadily.

"Max," the King said, as gently as if he were talking to one of his own children. "It's an official embassy. The embassy you asked me to send. Carrying the credentials you asked me to give to it." He watched the boy understand this, and accept it. "Your grandmother will need to cancel her booking. The palace will arrange all passages, yes, still on the *Estrella.* The palace will establish a line of credit for your Baron in Caracas. It's safer for everyone this way," the King advised. "We want

Ari to have all necessary credentials. I'd give you an army if I could, Max. These are two of my people," he explained in response to Max's expression, which was mostly dismay because what would he do with an army? "But war is a burden and an expense, especially when private citizens are willing to undertake what may well be"—and this was what he really wanted to get said to Max, to warn the boy—"a very dangerous mission."

"I know," the boy said.

He knew but he did not understand, the King thought.

Max wanted to be sure Teodor understood him. "I don't want an army," he told his King.

"So we're agreed?"

Max nodded.

"Can you continue to give lessons to Marielle until your ship sails?"

Max nodded.

"And bring the dog for my little Marguerite, who so badly wants one?"

Max nodded.

"Then it's left to me only to await news of your return, and hope that you do return, accompanied by your parents and with your embassy intact."

Max nodded, and bowed, and left the reception room.

This was the last meeting the King requested. After that day, Max the drawing master came and went, Sunny at his side, taught his lessons, and returned home on the midday ferry.

The strangeness, however, did not end. It was strange to be taking out one of the small bags stuffed with gold coins and deciding how to conceal the coins in luggage and clothing, "just in case." Ari would be in charge of whatever funds the embassy was given, but Max didn't know how generous King Teodor would be, or if Ari would refuse to pay a bribe, should one be asked. Grammie agreed. "Better safe than sorry," she said.

It was strange to be offering employment to Tomi Brandt and strange that Tomi didn't seem reluctant to act as Ari's personal servant. Max had watched Tomi across a schoolroom for years, admiring his forthright character, and not been surprised when, recently, Tomi had proved a clever and trustworthy ally, but he wouldn't have predicted that the boy would agree so eagerly to alter his own plans and fit in with Max's. "Firefighting wasn't what I thought it would be," he explained. "I might try the police when we get back. But I never dreamed I'd get a chance to travel, and on a ship, across an ocean. Maybe I should just go to work for *you,* work my way up to a partnership. Just joking," he said then, but added, "Maybe," as if he knew Max well enough to tease him.

It was also strange for Ari to take Max out onto Barthold Boulevard to purchase the kind of clothing a private secretary would wear, the dark suits and narrow ties, the stiff collars, the low boots, and even the fine cotton pajamas, as well as a leather portfolio. Tomi, too, needed outfitting, and Grammie made sure she had a good supply of the kind of pinafore aprons a housekeeper-cook would prefer. It was strange to have a weaponry discussion in which his grandmother took part, all of them deciding together that a nobleman might carry a sword, as might his private secretary, who would have to be ready to protect his employer in the unpredictable dangers of an ambassadorial career in foreign lands. Their servant, also, would be armed, although only with a knife. Pistols, they agreed, were not appropriate for a royal embassy.

Strangely, it was Max—who had often carried a sword at his side onstage—who showed Ari how to walk and sit while bearing arms, although it was Ari who had been trained in sword fighting. They practiced with one another. However, more strange than all the rest was the visit from Mr. Bendiff, Pia's father, to the little house at 5 Thieves Alley.

Pia herself had been keeping away, day after day. When she brought Max R Zilla's final payment, she boasted to him that both milliners were satisfied with her work on the job—only, being Pia, she called it "the case." Max congratulated her and fully expected her to become even more insistent about being given assignments, but he hadn't heard a peep out of her since that time. As more Pia-free days went by, Max grew puzzled. This behavior in his part-time assistant was not at all what he expected, and now here was her father, come to find him at home.

Like his daughter, when Mr. Bendiff burst into the house he started talking right away, giving orders. "You have to do something about Pia. She's stealing her brothers' clothes, she has a hoard of coins, she hacked off her hair. You know what she's going to try, don't you?"

When Mr. Bendiff put it like that, Max was afraid he did know, and he guessed he shouldn't be too surprised. But it was her father's responsibility to deal with Pia. "Can't you—?"

Mr. Bendiff cut him off. "I've got enough other trouble at home right now. You're the one who's involved Pia in all this—and to her benefit, I won't deny it. But as I see it, Pia is your problem. I expect you to solve it, young man. Right away."

The idea came as quickly as if it were a natural thing for him to ask of Pia—which in fact it was, if he planned to continue his new, independent life when he returned to Queensbridge. "Would you object—" he began, expecting to be interrupted. When he wasn't, he asked, "Would you object to Pia running my business for me? Only while I'm away and I don't want a partner, but . . . I think she could do it. I think she'd like to do it," he added.

Mr. Bendiff didn't hesitate. "You'll have a hard time turfing her out, later, after," he said, but that was his only objection. "It's a clever solution," he said thoughtfully, "very clever," and he shook Max's hand. "Thank you, young man," he said, then turned on his heels and left.

7

In which the *Estrella* sails

August seventeenth finally arrived, and Max walked along the docks in the company of his grandmother and Tomi Brandt, the Envoy's household, boarding together. Great steel hulls in various stages of being loaded with supplies, and with luggage, and with passengers, loomed beside him, like unscalable cliff faces. Gangplanks led up into lower decks, and it seemed as if the people ascending them approached a mysterious and quite possibly dangerous and maybe even doomful future. He watched a family (husband, wife, two young children, a babe in arms) come to the top of a gangplank; when they stepped into the ship and disappeared, Max thought of his parents.

On that April morning, his parents had stood just where he

was, their feet on the same thick boards, eager to catch their first glimpse of the upper decks, where first-class passengers would stroll at their ease. He could imagine how they had looked, his father's arm gesturing as he exclaimed about something to the woman at his side, both faces bright with anticipation of the adventure to come. Captain Francis had noticed William Starling that day. Well, William Starling was the kind of person you noticed, and it raised your spirits to see him, his gladness in being alive, in being himself, in being about to do whatever it was that he was about to do. Mary was not so noticeable. Her particular skill was the ability to be anybody: a proud queen, a flirtatious village beauty, a homely middle-aged shopkeeper, an aged crone—each one distinctly herself.

A wave of sorrow washed over Max and might have sucked his feet out from under him, had not a jolt of fear held him upright. They had walked into one of those dark entries, William and Mary Starling, and he did not know what had happened to them then, except that it was not what they had expected, not what had been promised them.

This embassy had to move fast, it might already be too late, and the ocean voyage was going to take too much time, too many long days and . . . Max felt like a dog at the end of a leash, desperate to run ahead and cruelly pulled back.

"Slow down, Eyes." Tomi Brandt spoke quietly from behind him. "We're the Envoy's household, servants and the private secretary, we don't hurry anywhere."

Tomi was right. Max fell back into step just in front of the other two.

"We're doing everything we can." Grammie spoke as quietly as Tomi, but he heard in her voice the same fear that was quickening his steps. "All you can ever do is everything you can."

The side of the *Estrella* loomed above them as they entered. But they were greeted by the uniformed purser and then led by a sailor up to the first-class deck, along a narrow but well-lit and carpeted hallway to their accommodations. Their trunk and valises awaited them, and like the good servants and secretary they intended to be taken for, they set to work.

Grammie withdrew to her small, windowless servant's cabin across the narrow corridor from the Envoy's stateroom. There, she hung up the clothes she would need for the voyage and unpacked the books and notebooks with which she intended to continue her study of Spanish, as well as teach as much as she could in the time they had to Ari, Max, and Tomi. Her housekeeping duties would not begin until they reached Apapa.

Tomi, the Envoy's personal servant, unpacked Ari's clothing into the narrow closet and deep drawers. He set Ari's shaving gear and toiletries out on the shelves built in behind the mirror of the tiny bathroom. Only when his employer's things had been entirely arranged, and the supply of towels and blankets checked, did Tomi withdraw into his own cabin, next to Grammie's but, unlike hers, a double, which he would share with some person who had not yet come on board. Tomi claimed the lower bunk.

Max and Ari were to share the stateroom, with Max in the small second sleeping cabin. Max first unpacked his new shirts and suits, socks and underwear, leisure trousers, sweaters, a modest enough wardrobe for a young gentleman employed as a personal secretary, but an extensive one for an about-to-be-thirteen-year-old, who might or might not eventually return to being a mere schoolboy. That done, he went into their sitting area, where armchairs and a table and even a long desk with bookshelves over it awaited the important man. There, he set out pens and notebooks, stationery, a chessboard, and a two-volume history of South America, with which they could pass the long days and evenings of the voyage.

Once the rooms had been made ready, Max, Grammie, and Tomi went out onto the deck to watch the activity on the docks below while they waited for the rest of their party to arrive. Ari would be the last to board the *Estrella.* His would be a ceremonial entrance, since he was not only the King's Envoy but also the next Baron Barthold.

Max leaned against the metal railing of the first-class promenade deck and looked down, at the crowd of people gathering to watch friends and family off, at the carts and carriages taking supplies and trunks to two liners berthed nearby, at the Harbormaster, hurrying from one man in nautical uniform to another, carrying papers, talking and gesturing importantly. The commotion of departures filled the air: voices and hoofbeats, the dull sounds of great engines muffled by thick layers of steel, the higher-pitched motors of the tugboats that would pull the liners from their docks, one after the other, to lead them under the raised drawbridge and out onto the broad river. The air itself shimmered with the excitement of the journeys about to begin. Even Max, whose journey had a dark and dangerous purpose, not to mention a worrying and fear-filled cause as well—even Max couldn't help but feel eager. He turned to look at Grammie, and saw in her face the same unwilling excitement.

As the hour of departure approached, more people crowded up around the *Estrella*'s gangplank, more faces looked up at the faces looking down, and more travelers made the ascent. Max caught a glimpse of a blue beret in the crowd and thought for a minute that Joachim had come to see him off, but he couldn't find it again, and besides, he hadn't seen Sunny, so it couldn't have been his teacher. At his shoulder, Tomi Brandt asked, "Who's that? Is that Ari?" as he pointed toward a long black motorcar making its slow way through a throng that moved clumsily and reluctantly aside, to let it pass.

Max suspected that he knew who it was, but all he answered was "I think Ari will arrive in one of the royal carriages."

He felt Tomi's sharp glance. "What haven't you told me, Eyes? What are you up to now?"

Max grinned. Tomi Brandt was nothing if not blunt. You couldn't fool him. "It's not me. I'm not up to anything, it's the King." Then a chauffeur opened the rear door of the vehicle and now they could see the ornate golden *B* painted there.

"Pia's father?" Tomi demanded.

The first to emerge was Mrs. Bendiff, wearing a wide-brimmed yellow hat adorned with four green feathers and a silky green *Z.* Pia followed her mother, on her head a simple straw boater, its crown circled by red and blue ribbons that had been braided together. The round brim of her hat emphasized the shining white-blond hair that was cropped so short, she might have been a boy disguised as a girl. Mr. Bendiff was the last to get out. He stood for a long moment, fedora in his hand, looking toward the upper decks in a measuring, assessing way.

"Are the Bendiffs traveling on the *Estrella*?" Tomi wondered, then asked, suspiciously, "They aren't coming with us, are they, Eyes?"

"Just Mr. Bendiff, I think," Max said. "The King felt the embassy needed an economic adviser."

"Oh?" Tomi said, with nothing more than curiosity, but when they saw a fifth figure walk around the front of the motorcar to stand just a little apart from the small family group, they both fell silent.

This was like a play without words, Max thought, like a mime show. When he looked down at the group standing beside the big automobile, he could see their faces and their gestures but he couldn't hear their words, so he had to guess from their faces and their gestures what was being said.

Mr. Bendiff turned to the fifth figure and his mouth moved. The figure, a boy with corn-colored hair, nodded, picked up three suitcases, one in each hand, one beneath an arm, and stepped onto the gangplank. "That's not Colly, is it?" Tomi asked. "Isn't that Colly? What's he doing here?"

Max was too surprised to answer, but Grammie reminded them, "Ari sent him to work for Mr. Bendiff, didn't he? And you," she said to Tomi, "told us how smart he was, and honest, despite what you'd caught him doing. Hamish Bendiff might easily have noticed him, and asked him to come as his personal servant. Like you and Ari."

"We'll find out soon enough," Max said as the motorcar backed slowly through the crowd, away from the docks. The King wouldn't send the entire Bendiff family to Andesia, would he? Max asked himself unhappily, and was relieved to see the motorcar park itself, out of the way until it was needed again. Mr. Bendiff said something, and bent to kiss Pia on the cheek. He took his wife's gloved hand and spoke seriously with her for several minutes, while Pia waited with uncharacteristic patience and also an uncharacteristic lack of interrupting. Then Mr. Bendiff wrapped his arms around his wife, kissed her on the lips, patted the top of Pia's head, and walked alone up into the ship.

Pia and her mother fell into a lively conversation, glancing occasionally at the crowd of people lining the upper decks. As if they were in fact skilled mimes, Max understood that they were discussing Mr. Bendiff's departure and then something else, something more, about which they were in agreement. Some common interest. But what common interest could Pia have discovered with her silly, social-climbing mother?

Pia saw him then and waved, grinning happily. She gave him a double thumbs-up, to say—he knew exactly what she was saying even if he couldn't hear a word—that the Solutioneer's business was in good hands, that he'd done the right and smart thing leaving her in charge. Temporarily in charge, of course, but temporarily in total charge of absolutely everything.

The Private Secretary to the King's special Envoy to Andesia could not grin and wave back, but he bowed slightly, *message received.*

Pia continued grinning and waving, ignoring his dignity, and then her gaze shifted to someone standing just along the railing. Max was not surprised to see that it was her father, who looked down at his daughter and his wife. What did surprise him was to see Mrs. Bendiff give her husband the same smiling thumbs-up signal Pia had just given him, and the understanding of what that meant made him laugh out loud. Mr. Bendiff had found solutions to more than one problem when he came to consult the Solutioneer.

As if laughter was his cue, the Envoy entered the scene. He sat alone in an open carriage with the royal crest on its side. The carriage was drawn by two coal-black horses; its driver and the accompanying footman both wore the green livery of the King's household. Ari's black tricorn was topped with a curving white plume and his red military jacket was hung with medals. He paid no attention to the people around him, who quickly realized he was only some diplomat, and not a member of the royal family and lost interest; in fact, as soon as his feet were on the ground he removed the tricorn from his head, swung a short dark cape around to cover the glitter of his jacket, and, instead of striding up the gangplank, merged back into the crowd.

Grammie guessed, "He'll be making his farewells to Gabrielle."

Max kept his eyes on the head of red hair as Ari slipped through the throng. Grammie was right, of course. Ari stood for several minutes, just looking down into the face of the girl he planned to marry, pastry chef at B's and wrongfully accused thief, a girl from a mountain village who had neither fine wits nor great beauty to recommend her, only a kind heart and a gift for the plain truth of things—which happened to be the very qualities that won Ari's admiration, and devotion. "She's agreed to marry me," Ari had concluded when he reported to Max that the young woman had approved of his going off at the head of the rescue party. "So you'd better get me back safe, Mister Max."

The farewell made, plumed hat back on his head and cloak pulled open so that his medals were on display, Ari strode up the gangplank, as self-assured a figure as any prideful Baron Barthold. He turned at the dark opening and raised his hat to the watching people before disappearing. As if the ship had been waiting only for his arrival, the last visitor's bell sounded and soon the gangplank was being pulled up, the iron entrance clanged shut, and the people on the docks were waving more energetically. The engines rumbled more loudly. Slowly, slowly, the great mass of metal began to move, heavily, almost reluctantly. Guided by two tugboats, the liner backed away from the docks and out into the lake while the drawbridge clanked and groaned as it began its slow ascent.

Max looked at his grandmother. They didn't need to say anything. But there was something about the moment that made them both say, "It won't be long now."

Grammie took a deep breath. "I'm going to get myself a scarf. It'll be windy, once we pass Porthaven. Do you want one?" Max shook his head. He didn't want to leave his post.

Mr. Bendiff went to find his stateroom, but Colly, surprised to find Tomi, and pleased to discover that they were cabinmates, hesitated among his valises. Tomi and Colly went off together, Tomi now carrying one of Colly's burdens. Tomi would explain everything to Colly, Max guessed, and probably Colly would explain how it came about that he'd joined them. Not that Max was really surprised. Max would never be surprised at something unexpected coming from Mr. Bendiff's corner.

What did surprise him was to see Joachim. His teacher was beside the doorway into the first-class accommodations, blue beret firmly in place, in conversation with Grammie. Grammie pointed to where Max stood at the rail, then went on her way.

"I suppose you'll send me back on the pilot boat," Joachim announced when he reached Max's side.

"Where's Sunny?" Max was taken off guard, shocked stupid. What was Joachim doing here? How could he afford a ticket of any kind, not to mention first-class? Why wasn't he at home, in his garden, painting?

ESTRELLA

"The Bellerephon sisters have her while I'm— You remember them, you must, they were the ones who found Sunny for you. If you send me off on the pilot boat, I warn you, Max, that woman will have me married and moved in and painting pictures of her hats. She's relentless! She's heartless! She keeps coming after me and it's all your fault. It's up to you to do something about it."

"But, Joachim—" Max began.

"You'll have to pay for my ticket, because I'm not supposed to be here. I skulked when they blew the whistle for visitors to leave, but I have my materials with me, so . . . Expeditions take artists along with them. Even you might know that, and your grandmother certainly does. To make a record of the local flora, and the landscapes, and animals, too, birds like Audubon or— You *shouldn't* send me back, Max, and you know it."

Max knew no such thing, although he did feel responsible for introducing R Zilla into Joachim's life. He'd done it with the best of intentions, for which Joachim never gave him credit, but he *had* done it. "I'll have to ask Ari," he said.

"Talk to your grandmother, she's got a good head on her shoulders," Joachim advised.

While this was going on, the great ship moved slowly through the raised drawbridge, cast off the lines to the tugboats, and, with a rumbling surge of its engines, followed the small pilot boat downriver, heading for the open ocean.

8

The journey

By mid-afternoon, the *Estrella* had entered the open seas, leaving the stone fortress and tall lighthouse of Porthaven behind, and Max had transformed himself into the Secretary. This was too important a job to risk being under-prepared or under-practiced. Until he exited Andesia in the company of his parents, he was Alexander Ireton, Private Secretary to the King's special Envoy to Andesia. Alexander Ireton dressed in dark suits and stiff white collars; he wore slippers and a robe in the cabin in the mornings; he put on a bowler to take turns around the deck, every morning and every afternoon, around and around the length of the boat, as if the distances he covered on foot could cut down the necessary hours of travel that lay between him and Apapa.

Max did not allow himself to be anything other than the Secretary, not even for an hour. He was no longer a grandson, nor one of three boys adventuring together, nor an amateur skyscapist. He could not even be the Solutioneer. He was always and entirely the Secretary, and never his own self, Max Starling, thirteen-year-old boy, crossing an ocean to rescue his parents.

His thirteenth birthday had been not-celebrated in the *Estrella*'s large first-class dining room. There had been no candles on no cake, no wrapped packages, and no singing of the traditional birthday song. Only Ari and Mr. Bendiff were at the table with Max, since Grammie, Colly, and Tomi, as servants, took their meals in the second-class dining room with Joachim, who was an artist and without social position. Alexander Ireton was having no birthday, and besides, if he were to be having one it would not have been his thirteenth, and Max had no choice in the matter: He had to be always and only Alexander Ireton.

He might wish that, like Colly, he could move freely down the carpeted stairway to the second-class deck, or farther, down the plain wood stairs to third class, meeting strangers and hearing stories of their destinations and their lives, in the kind of long conversations possible when you travel by ship across wide stretches of empty sea. He might wish to clatter down steep iron stairs with Tomi to reach the engine room, and learn about the great machinery that worked away deep within the ship, and be the one to bring back an American card game the sailors liked, called poker and involving bets.

He did wish he could sit out on deck to paint the kind of skies that hang over the ocean, vast blue expanses with white clouds stretched thin as veils across them, or thick, densely gray clouds that lie heavy on a rough-edged gray water, with only the uneasy surge of the metal floor beneath him to remind him he was not, however it seemed, motionless, stuck. Often, Max stood at the bow of the ship under a sky so black and pricked with so many stars that he wished he had a chunk of charcoal in his hand, to draw it.

He had never been so alone.

As the great propellers pushed the *Estrella* across the ocean, Max was as solitary as an island among the hundreds of people on board, motionless as an island, and helpless as an island to do anything other than wait for the journey's end.

Mr. Bendiff could be frankly amazed and excited, the whole adventure of an ocean voyage being new to him, but Max could not, even though Max was, like Mr. Bendiff, someone who enjoyed new jobs, new problems to solve, new ideas bursting up in him. Neither could Max spend each day in the happiness of a love left behind and awaiting his return, the pleasures of memory and anticipation, the way Ari did. Grammie could practice her Spanish on native speakers in the second-class dining room, Joachim could sketch a portrait for anyone who offered to pay him, but Max had always and only to be Alexander Ireton. Alexander Ireton spent most of his time in the Envoy's stateroom, doing whatever secretaries do—in his case, studying Spanish from books and learning history from books, and looking out the porthole at the long stretch of sky over the stretch of restless water. On those occasions when he left the stateroom, Alexander Ireton could do little more than pace the decks, long day at sea after long day at sea, and fret.

Luckily for Max's state of mind, once the constant queasiness of seasickness had passed, and they had all established their identities with the other passengers and the crew, the four members of the party seeking more diversion—the Envoy, his Secretary, and his housekeeper, plus the businessman's valet—decided to meet in the Envoy's stateroom every day after lunch, to read one of Shakespeare's plays together. With four of them, the cabin felt cramped and crowded, and they had to leave the door to Max's small cabin open so the tray holding teapot, cups, saucers, and cookies could be set down on his bunk. Grammie served the tea, setting two cookies side by side on each saucer, adding milk, sugar, or lemon according to preferences.

Grammie would have liked to be the group's teacher, but Max had spent many hours in the theater, both onstage and backstage, and Ari had studied at university, leaving only Colly willing to grant her that position, so she had to step down and become just another student. Colly wanted to read *Hamlet,* one of the great tragedies, but "Comedy is more realistic," Grammie argued, and Ari pointed out that *Julius Caesar* had the least difficult language, as well as the kind of political story that might be useful for them to think about in their mission to Andesia.

"I don't want to do anything just because it's easy," Colly protested.

"It's not easy," Max could promise him. "It's Shakespeare, he's never easy, but he's always interesting. He's . . . *great.*"

Grammie started it. "Act one, scene one, line one," she said, and began reading, in a bossy and important voice, " 'Hence! home, you idle creatures get you home! Is this a holiday?' " At the question, she looked at Max, both worried and hopeful.

All of them, especially Grammie and Alexander Ireton, were waiting their way through the long hours of the long days at sea. And the days did pass, and the ocean was crossed, and the *Estrella* berthed in the harbor of New York City.

To arrive in a great city by sea is like stumbling out of a cave into bright sunlight: The muffled darkness that had become normal is suddenly shown for the non-life it is, and all the shapes and colors and sounds of day are right there before you, to remind you of how vivid and lively the world is. Even though the Envoy's party decided not to go ashore during the ship's twenty-four-hour stopover in New York, they all wanted to spend hours at the railing, watching and listening to the business of unloading and then loading cargo, of resupplying the ship with fuel and food, of disembarking and then embarking passengers. Every one of them would have liked to get off to wander the straight streets, but Grammie reminded them, "We can't afford any kind of mishap, any possible delay." Nobody objected, although "Maybe on the return voyage?" Mr. Bendiff suggested hopefully.

They had been away from Queensbridge almost two weeks when the *Estrella* once again entered open waters, heading south. For the first several days, they steamed along the coast of America, which seemed no more than a low, dark cloud on the western horizon; then the ship followed a route through sun-soaked Caribbean islands, wide white beaches backed by tall palms, rows of pink and yellow beachfront homes roofed with the long fronds of those palms. They passed Cuba, skirted Hispaniola, came close to Aruba, and at last the ship came to rest at the one long dock of La Guaira, the port for the city of Caracas. There, long yellow beaches spread like welcoming arms on both sides of a cluster of unpainted wooden buildings, with many more warehouses than homes. Max had been at sea for three weeks when he could finally put his feet down on the soil of South America.

He might be standing on dry land, but it seemed to Max that the ground under his feet was still rocking. He walked uneasily along the dock to the customs shed, where Ari and Mr. Bendiff were presenting credentials and answering questions about the members of their traveling party. Max's attention was turned inland, eyes looking toward Caracas, although he couldn't possibly see it for the low hills and thick woods. That didn't matter. He knew that Grammie, who stood quietly beside him, was also picturing the map they'd spent so much time looking at, a nearly heart-shaped mass of land that tapered down to a narrow point, and the long spine of mountains running from the north to the south of it, on which a tiny worm of a country perched. In that country, huddled together for warmth and comfort, two minuscule figures, half the size of ants, were waiting. He tried not to urge them all to hurry, hurry, get into the coach waiting to take them into Caracas, stop wasting time.

On arrival in Caracas, the travelers went first to the Hotel Magnifica. They planned to take two days to arrange passage to Andesia and ready themselves for a long journey under harsh conditions, to write letters home and walk down city streets, looking in shop windows, eavesdropping on conversations, stopping to eat local foods.

Those plans changed immediately.

Max, as Alexander Ireton, heard the news first, because he happened to be in the writing room setting out stationery and pens for Ari while the doorman gossiped outside a window that was opened to let in the morning air. Max heard it and his hands stopped moving and he fell out of character entirely, concentrating on the Spanish words. It was the name of Andesia that caught his ear, and not many words later—struggling to understand—he heard *los reyes,* which he knew meant the King and Queen. He heard more words but couldn't string them together: *tiro,* shot, *cocinero,* cook, *anarquista,* which he guessed had to mean anarchist, one of those people who opposed any sort of government at all, any order imposed on a society, whether by tradition, or law, or power, or even the people themselves.

Max stumbled back into character and into the reception area, where the rest of his companions were waiting for the desk clerk to give them their room keys. It was Alexander

Ireton who came quietly up to his employer to say, "I think something has happened, sir. In Andesia. I overheard a conversation which I only partly understood . . ." But he couldn't go on and he glanced desperately at his grandmother.

"Oh, M—" she started to say, before his quick head shake stopped her. "M—my goodness."

Mr. Bendiff took charge. He sent Colly to find a newspaper. "In our own language, if possible." But Colly could bring them only a Spanish edition, which Grammie translated, in the privacy of the suite Ari had been given.

As soon as the door closed behind them, Max asked, "Did the palace cook shoot them?"

"Give me a chance to find the article," she snapped. When she had, on the back page where news from unimportant places is reported, her translation was not smooth, or complete—". . . a word I don't know," she often interrupted herself to say—but the bare facts were clear. There had been an explosion in the palace kitchen in Apapa; a serving woman had been killed and the cook wounded; the scullery maid escaped harm because she had just been sent out to dump a bucket of vegetable peelings into the pigs' trough. "Is *chancho* pig, do you think? Is any other domestic animal fed vegetable scraps? Do they have pigs in Andesia? I don't know *enough*!" The article reported that a large confection had appeared in the kitchen that morning, set out on a silver tray. Nobody knew where it had come from, but it was clearly intended for the royal table. A bomb had been hidden within the many layers of a cake that had been frosted with chocolate and decorated around the edges with wildflowers. The cook had had no reason to question its presence, or so she said. The great houses often sent gifts of food to the King and Queen. This cake was larger and more elaborate than most, the cook allowed, but why should that make her suspicious?

"They must have mis-timed the explosion," Mr. Bendiff said.

"Who are *they*?" Max asked miserably.

"There's something else here," Grammie said.

At the end of the article, the writer mentioned an incident that had taken place a few months earlier, a shot that had been fired as the newly crowned royal couple was coming out of the Caracas cathedral—"That's the photograph we saw," Grammie reminded Max, who didn't need reminding. He went to the window and looked down onto a busy street where ordinary carriages filled with ordinary people wandered up and down, and women carried parasols against the strong sun.

"The police blamed anarchists for the shot. They never caught anybody."

"What would an anarchist be doing trying to kill the King of Andesia when he's in Venezuela and they don't even know what kind of a King he'll be yet?" Max protested.

"Anarchists believe that if they can assassinate one member of a royal family, the political structures of the country will fall, one after the other, like a row of dominoes," Ari explained apologetically. "And they're right about places like the Balkans where there are always small wars going on.

Remember, Colombia has just recently come out of a civil war, and Balcor's army just put down an uprising in Andesia, and Venezuela may look like a single country but it's divided up into areas of influence, and they're like small nations under the rule of military strongmen who are always ready to fight."

"The newspaper says the exploding cake happened almost two weeks ago. The reporter got the story from one of the soldiers in the occupying army. One of Balcor's soldiers," Grammie concluded.

"Is this Balcor one of those military strongmen?" Mr. Bendiff asked.

"Was Balcor behind the bomb?" Colly wondered.

"We don't know anything, do we?" Joachim observed.

It was Tomi who said what they were all thinking. "We'd better get there as fast as we can."

Ari and Mr. Bendiff arranged at the hotel for telegrams to be sent announcing their safe arrival: one to Gabrielle, who would take word to the Baroness, and one to Mrs. Bendiff, who would inform Pia, who would, in turn, arrange for Tomi's parents and Colly's grandparents to be informed. Grammie, with Joachim, went back to the dock to locate a boat to take them along the coast to Maracaibo, the clerk at the hotel having assured them this was the fastest way to get there. From Maracaibo they'd go to Cúcuta, Colombia, and if they could be in Cúcuta Tuesday morning, he told them, they could travel on to Apapa with the regular wagon train. "It will be safest," he told them in his simplest Spanish. "Always, there will be soldiers, for the silver and copper, and also they protect the strongbox holding the gold coins for which the ores are sold. No bandits dare attack Stefano's wagons."

Grammie didn't care about discomfort or danger. "We'll have to leave tomorrow to make the connection. It doesn't look like a storm, does it? We'd better pick out what we're carrying with us, and leave those language books behind."

Ari went to the bank with his letter of credit from King Teodor and procured a supply of the local currency—for travel expenses, for living expenses in Andesia, however long they would be there, and for bribes, if they were needed.

"I don't believe in bribing," Mr. Bendiff announced over dinner.

"Neither do I, but it's what the Andesians believe in and what Balcor believes in that concern us," Ari said, adding, "Teodor had a message waiting for me. He's had a response from Andesia. They're expecting us and have expressed their eagerness for our arrival."

"Whoever *they* are. Whatever *that* means," Joachim remarked gloomily, and nobody corrected him.

9

The arrival

They spent two days and one long, wet night on the open deck of the packet that took them along the coast and into Lake Maracaibo, where small square houses standing on stilts out in the water became the first entry in Joachim's expedition sketchbook. Then came two long days and longer nights jouncing in a coach to Cúcuta, and Joachim could not have made sketches even if he hadn't been too disgruntled by the discomforts to be interested in what he was seeing. After a night in a rough country inn, where the entire party slept on cots set out in one room, they joined the wagon train on its regular biweekly run between Cúcuta and Apapa. There followed four days of walking a well-traveled wagon track from damp dawns until gray evenings, with only a brief midday rest, moving at the pace of mules on rough, ascending roadways. After the first morning, Joachim insisted that he and Grammie ride on the tailgate of the wagon that was carrying their luggage.

A company of soldiers marching at the front and rear accompanied the wagons, but the wagon train boss was a loud, stocky civilian named Stefano, who spent much of the journey cursing at the muleteers and porters when anything went wrong. The soldiers and the Andesians all wore loose trousers, rough shirts, and heavy boots, but the soldiers carried rifles on their backs and their chests were crossed with bands of ammunition, while the Andesians, even Stefano, wore woven ponchos against the rain and wide-brimmed *chupallas* against the sun.

The soldiers didn't mix with the Andesians or the strangers, the Andesians didn't mix with the soldiers or the strangers, so the rescue party learned little during the long trek except more than they cared to know about the insect and animal life of the landscapes through which they moved, the lowland tropical forests and the barren uplands. They all slept with their boots on.

They had not understood how close they were to their destination and nobody had warned them that this was the day of arrival, so when the wagon train rounded a long curve of ridge and the valley opened out before them as abruptly as if they were emerging from a long tunnel, every member of the rescue party inhaled sharply, though whether for the unexpectedness of the scene or its beauty none of them could have said. Suddenly a valley lay before them, surrounded by jagged mountains, their crests still white with snow. The lower slopes of the mountains were bright with white and yellow flowers, and occasional one-room earth-colored houses were scattered on the foothills, where movement could be seen, some of it human, some animal. The strong midday sun washed over the whole narrow valley, at the heart of which a small city had grown up on both sides of a fast-flowing mountain river.

Max stared down at the city where his parents had been held for almost five months. His heart beat fast and he did not dare look at his grandmother.

Ari sent word to Stefano that they needed to make a brief stop. When Tomi and Colly had pulled down the suitcases, they washed up as best they could in buckets of water, all the while looking ahead and around, at the hills that rose up from the valley and the endless range of mountains that surrounded it, and the three mountains that loomed close over its western side. These three had scrub forests at their skirts, marked in three places with blotches of bare ground, like mange on a dog.

Joachim and Grammie stretched stiff muscles and rinsed off dusty faces and hands, but didn't bother to change their clothing. "I'll be wearing men's trousers for the return," Grammie muttered to Joachim. "You can be sure of that."

"Maybe they'll hang us and you won't have to," Joachim suggested.

Grammie laughed.

"You're always laughing at me," Joachim grumbled.

"It's either that or take you seriously, and I have no desire to spend my days being a gloomy Gus," she told him.

He didn't argue. Instead, he pointed out, "Do you know how long it's been since I held even a pencil in my hand?"

"About as long as it's been since I had a hot bath," she told him.

Ari interrupted. "It won't be much longer now. I just wish I could understand more of what they're saying. I didn't realize how *hard* it is to learn a language."

Max buttoned his shirt and studied the city. He put on his jacket and slipped his feet into dress boots without looking. On the side of the river beneath the three peaks, the small houses crowded around an open space so perfectly square it had to be a plaza. There was one long, low, brown-roofed building among the houses, and he couldn't see any real streets, just twisting alleys. A single bridge crossed the river. On the western shore, the buildings were fewer and larger, three with gardens behind high walls, one a big stone building with a short square tower at its side, and, built at a distance from the others, a long, whitewashed one-story building next to a wide dirt rectangle, the edges as clear as if it had been cut out of the grass with a sword's blade.

"Do you think the one with the tower is the royal palace?" Max asked Ari.

"Where's your hat, Alexander?" Ari answered, reminding Max of who he was supposed to be. "This occasion requires hats."

Max dusted off the detested bowler and decided, "The

white building is probably the barracks. How many soldiers are stationed in Andesia?" he asked.

Ari settled a plumed tricorn on his red hair and answered, "We'll find out. Enough to protect us, I'm sure."

Not too many to fight our way out through, Max hoped.

Going slowly, the wagon train followed the road down steep hillsides scattered with low adobe houses, some set among terraces that were plowed and ready for planting, others standing solitary in grassy pastures where wildflowers grew thick. They passed herds of woolly-coated animals that grazed close to some of those houses, but they saw no one. No one came out even as far as a doorway to greet their caravan, with its soldiers marching smartly at its front and rear, or even to stare curiously at the foreigners.

From closer up, the three mangy blotches on the mountainsides could be identified. "Must be the mines," Mr. Bendiff said. "See those railroad tracks leading into the mountains?"

Ari pointed out three narrow dirt roads winding down to meet theirs not far ahead. "They must bring the ore down in carts, to be stored." When he looked, Max could identify a low building surrounded by soldiers at the point where the three tracks intersected with the roadway.

In fact, the caravan stopped there, leaving two of the wagons, their empty beds covered tightly by tarpaulins, and all of the soldiers, who took with them a small locked chest. Stefano's own two covered wagons were the only ones to make the final slow descent, through darkening air, into the city.

Night fell fast and hard in this high valley. By the time

Stefano's goods had been unloaded and the foreigners' suitcases piled into a handcart, his single lantern was the only light left to guide the party along winding dirt alleys lined with small houses to a stone bridge, its railings no higher than a man's knees. The only sounds were their footsteps and the creak of cart wheels and the rush of water. The entire city lay in dark silence.

The members of the embassy were too busy being sure of their footing to find anything to say to one another during these final steps of the journey, and too tired, and especially too eager to, at last, arrive. When they came up to a building, they sensed rather than saw the dense shape. Behind them, the three jagged peaks were silhouettes that blocked most of the star-studded sky.

Stefano unloaded the luggage and walked off without a word of farewell, pushing the cart ahead of him. As his footsteps faded away, the embassy banded closer together, facing a mass that seemed to loom in front of them, and above them. Nobody had anything to say. The surrounding silence grew deeper as the darkness thickened.

Then a door was thrown open and a tall, silhouetted figure stood in the blinding burst of light.

Nobody moved. Nobody spoke.

The light from the doorway also showed them two armed soldiers stationed in the shadows at each side of the entry. The silhouette called, "Come! Come forward! Envoy of the King Teodor, welcome!"

They looked quickly at one another, like actors about to

step onto the stage and begin the play, and Ari moved into the light, resplendent in a red military jacket, a short line of medals at his breast, gold epaulettes on his shoulders, gold trim at the sleeves and hem of the jacket as well as gold stripes down the sides of his black trousers. He carried his plumed hat under his arm. A sword hung at his side and he did not smile or extend his hand. Instead, he clicked the heels of his shining boots smartly together. "Andrew Robert Von Bauer Cozart, heir of the Barons Barthold," he announced stiffly, and bowed. "To whom do I present myself?"

The man was taller than Ari and attired with equal formality in a black suit that fitted him close around the chest, with silver buttons down the front of the short jacket and silver trim at the military collar, the sleeves, and the flared hem of the trousers. His sword's scabbard gleamed silver. He was a long-nosed man, with no spare flesh on him and a restless cleverness on his face. "I am Juan Carlos Carrera y Carrera," he announced. His dark hair shone and his thick, dark mustache glistened. "I am your welcome here, into the royal guesthouse. You must enter. It will be warm, there is food." He stood back and swept an arm, to usher Ari in.

Max had a sudden melodramatic impulse to shout at Ari, *Don't do it!*

Ari stepped into the house but stopped just inside the entry to wave Mr. Bendiff forward and introduce him. "A man adept in the field of business, whom King Teodor has named to this embassy."

Mr. Bendiff, his homburg in his left hand and a wide smile

on his face, reached out his right hand to shake the Andesian's. "*Señor,* it is a pleasure."

"Señor," echoed Juan Carlos Carrera y Carrera, with a smile and a bow, "delighted, welcome, enter, enter."

Oily. Max could almost hear his father's voice pronouncing the words, *An oily feller, that'un.*

"My Secretary," Ari announced.

A properly suited Alexander Ireton received a brief nod of the head and a slight gesture of the hand from the Andesian as he stepped eagerly into the light, to see . . .

He didn't *expect* to see his parents waiting. Not really. He did know better. But still, he looked all around, down to the staircase at the back of the entryway and into the two rooms he could see, one to his right, one to his left. Behind him, Ari called in Joachim, Grammie, then Colly as Mr. Bendiff's valet, and finally Tomi Brandt, who was the party's general dogsbody. *"Dogsbody?"* the Andesian asked. "This is a word I haven't heard."

Max paid no attention. He was looking into the house.

The two rooms he could see from the entry were lit by oil lamps and chandeliers, and both were empty of people. One was a long sitting room, furnished with a sofa and chairs, desk and bookcase, where nobody waited. The other seemed to be a small dining room, where a round table offered loaves of bread and thick wedges of cheese, as well as a roast of some kind, ready to be sliced. Tall silver goblets and long-necked silver ewers were also set out, and no royal couple stood at the table, ready to laugh at the surprised look on their son's face.

Grammie had her own part to play, so "I'd like to see the kitchen," she announced, not exactly speaking to the Andesian but clearly not addressing her remark to Ari.

Juan Carlos Carrera y Carrera clapped his hands, once, twice, three times. Immediately, as if he had summoned them like genies from a bottle, two short, olive-skinned women stepped into the shadows at the back of the hallway. Their long cotton skirts were made from red and brown strips of some woven material and their dark hair was braided into thick plaits. They did not look at the strangers, but only at the Andesian, who spoke to them in quick Spanish, of which Max understood the words *Señora Cocinera,* Mrs. Cook, and also he thought he had recognized the word *vigilar.* The two women turned to Grammie, and curtseyed, and nodded, then waited to be given their next order.

"Devera and Suela," Juan Carlos named them, without saying which was who. "They will not know your language," he told Grammie, as if he was happy to disappoint her. "And how should they? The Carrera y Carreras had governesses, but these people cannot even read their own native tongue. And what use would it be to them if they could? They do their work, they are docile. You will find them good servants, *Señora.*" He smiled.

Grammie huffed as if to say she would be the judge of that and followed the two women down the hallway. She was apparently having the same *oily* reaction to their host.

The Andesian turned to give an order to the soldiers, who proceeded to carry in the valises. He announced to

Ari that his servants could take them up to the bedrooms. "While I offer refreshments to the honorable Baron and his welcome compatriot. But"—and he turned to Joachim, who had claimed his one small suitcase and his large satchel of art supplies, whose shirt was not fresh, whose boots were caked with mud, and who wore a blue beret on his gray head, to ask—"who is this man?"

Joachim let Ari answer the question. "An artist."

Their host seemed almost alarmed. "What purpose does the King Teodor have, sending an artist to . . . to do what? Did he not say you are a diplomatic embassy?"

"The King is a man who always wishes to learn," Ari answered. "He has asked for pictures of your country and your people, your animals, your homes, your gardens and fields, and particularly your mountains. Is it not common for an artist to accompany such expeditions into unknown lands? You must remember that it was as an artist that Darwin joined the men traveling on the *Beagle*."

"Of course I know of Darwin from my studies in Lima," Juan Carlos said, then, "You will take the room on the third floor," he told Joachim, and turned back to the important guests. "Come, Baron. Come, *Señor* Bendiff. You," he instructed Max, "follow the artist."

"No," said Ari.

No was a word the Andesian did not welcome.

"The man is my Private Secretary," Ari announced. "A position of distinction," and he walked through the door to the dining room. Without looking at Juan Carlos, Max followed

Ari. The Andesian entered behind Mr. Bendiff, still protesting, "You did not introduce him to me by name." He closed the door behind them. "How am I to know, if you did not introduce him by name?"

Ari gave the man a quick, scornful glance, as if to say, *A real gentleman would have recognized the signs.* He did not have to say it out loud. The man looked daggers at Max, even while his smile did not fade. Juan Carlos did not ask to be introduced, as if to tell this Baron, *He may be your Private Secretary, but he is still a servant. I have no need to know his name.*

"Eat," Ari was told. "Drink," and Juan Carlos poured wine first for Ari, then for Mr. Bendiff, then a goblet for himself. Max stood back, controlling his impatience. Juan Carlos raised his goblet, in a toast: "Welcome to my country. May your stay in our city be pleasurable, may your visit be of benefit to both of our nations." He drank and announced, "The wine is French. As are all the best wines, do you agree?"

"Of course," Ari answered. He tasted its flavors, nodded, swallowed, and said no more.

Juan Carlos had an itinerary for this embassy, and he smiled his oily smile, announcing it to them. "Baron? *Señor* Bendiff? And Secretary, too. Tomorrow my cousin and I will offer a tour of Apapa and at four you will be guests at dinner with my family, and the families of my cousins, and you will see that we know not only wine but also what it is to dine well."

"Tomorrow, I will see the King," Ari announced.

"That is not to be." The Andesian tried to sound sorry

about this, but didn't entirely succeed. He explained to Ari, "Until the General has returned, this cannot be. Nobody can visit the King unless the General also is present. This is necessary for the King's safety," Juan Carlos concluded solemnly.

Ari's displeasure was evident. "The General had notice that I would be arriving."

The Andesian shrugged, held out helpless hands, shook his head. "The General comes and he goes at his own will. He does not explain himself. He is the General," Juan Carlos said, and Max did not know if there was more fear or defeat or resentment in the man's voice. He looked questioningly at Ari, asking him to ask when the General was due back, but it was Mr. Bendiff who spoke.

"I take it he didn't say how long he'd be away." The businessman—who understood how such an undefined absence might expose the soft underbelly of the city—was as displeased as the Envoy at this news.

Juan Carlos shrugged, raised his eyebrows, grimaced slightly, and sighed, a man forced to apologize for the errors of others.

"I find it very strange," Ari remarked, and turned to Max. "Have something to eat, Alexander. You'll be as hungry as I am." He poured some wine into a goblet he passed to Max.

Max took the wine, although he would have preferred cold milk, or even water. For a while, nobody said anything. Everybody was playing a waiting game.

"Your ways are not our ways," the Andesian said, at last. "It is as with your language, which I warn you is not well known here. The Carrera y Carreras have studied it, as you can plainly see. The General speaks well, and understands, for he is a widely traveled man, sent for schooling in Madrid. It was General Balcor—only a captain at the time—who was selected out of all the army as companion to the son of the President of Peru when the boy was entered into the University in Madrid, and later he went with the young man on his grand tour. The natives, as you have seen, know nothing, and the soldiers . . . Who knows what soldiers know? It is asked of them only to follow their orders, and for the rest . . . I leave the soldiers to their Captain," he said, and that sounded like a warning. "They are quick to shoot. It is they who have kept order after the recent uprising."

"Uprising?" Ari asked, as if this came as a surprise to him. "Was this to do with the bomb of which I have learned?" he wondered.

Max waited with anxious interest for the Andesian's response.

But Juan Carlos ignored Ari's second inquiry. "The uprising need not worry you, Baron. It was merely a few malcontents hoping to seize our mines. They brought hardship down on everyone, until our friends sent the General with his army to protect us. Sadly, in the end, the General failed to protect the late King, and his family," Juan Carlos concluded, in the kind of voice designed to spread suspicion without actually accusing anybody of anything.

"I understand your meaning," Ari said.

"So I hope you will be comfortable here," Juan Carlos

went on, satisfied. "We in Andesia are not experienced in the needs of guests, but the guesthouse has water closets, both upstairs and down. The house will serve you well, we hope. You may send Suela or Devera to me if anything has been neglected."

Ari glanced at Max before he asked, "The King is well?"

The question surprised Juan Carlos. "Yes, of course."

"And the Queen?"—carelessly.

"The Queen is suffering from a lingering indisposition, but you need not concern yourselves with that. We have good hope that she will soon be out of discomfort."

"Her healing is much to be hoped for," Ari answered. Then, "I thank you for your welcome, and the food and drink. We will take up no more of your time." He opened the dining room door and held it wide, for Juan Carlos to go through, dismissed.

But Juan Carlos claimed the last word. "You will find soldiers always guarding your door. We wish you to be safe here, during your visit," he said, and smiled.

When the heavy front door had closed behind him, Grammie, Joachim, Colly, and Tomi all came into the dining room. "Close the kitchen door," Mr. Bendiff told Colly, but Grammie answered, "I've sent the servants out to the back. It seems they have their quarters there."

"They know you speak the language?"

"They know I speak a little and do not care how much," she assured him. "What did he say, that man? When can we see the Queen?"

"We can't see anyone unless General Balcor is present, and he's off somewhere," Max told her. "That's sort of curious when there's been a bomb, don't you think, Ari?"

"I think the whole setup is curious," Ari answered. "Hamish? What do you make of it?"

"We're dealing with a military occupation," Mr. Bendiff answered thoughtfully. "Those soldiers sound . . . a little dangerous. Was Juan Carlos threatening us, do you think? Or warning us, when he said there will always be soldiers at the door."

"Those two women didn't dare say a word," Grammie agreed.

"Well, I, for one, am going to have something to eat," Joachim announced. "After which, I'm going to bed. Since for the first time in too long a time I have a proper bed to go to," he grumbled. "And I know it's all my own doing, so nobody needs to remind me."

As if they were waiting for permission, Colly and Tomi followed his example, filling plates with chunks of bread and cheese.

"I don't want you boys drinking that wine," Grammie told them. "There's a jug of water in the kitchen—if you can call that a kitchen. Tomi, could you bring it in, please?"

"Sure," he said. "But do you mind if I just taste the wine?"

Grammie laughed.

"We should all eat and then get to bed," Ari suggested. "We'll make plans in the morning. Hamish, Max, and I are summoned to a city tour, followed by some kind of formal dinner, but the rest of you will be free to wander, and find out what you can."

"Maybe I shouldn't be a secretary," Max said now. His parents were so close and he still couldn't see them. How could there be no way of calling out to them? "Maybe I should be a servant and free to wander, too."

"Not if you want any chance of being present when we're taken before the King," Ari answered.

"That's *if. If* you're taken to meet him," Joachim said. "And I'm pretty sure no artist will be invited along for that. Cooks, either, I'm afraid," he said to Grammie.

"We'll see about *that,*" she huffed.

They finished their meal and carried their plates down a short hall into a kitchen that had a wood-burning stove and no icebox, open shelves, and a faucet that offered only cold water. A square table stood in the center of the room, with benches on each side. It was large enough to accommodate all of them, but Grammie said, "You three can't eat in here, and we shouldn't be eating in the dining room with you. Those servants will notice everything. My room is down here," she told them, pointing to a doorway. "There's a WC attached, things could be worse," she concluded, with a stern look at the painter, as if to say, *We don't need to hear any more from you.* "We'll learn more tomorrow," she promised Max, bidding them all a good night.

The rooms assigned to Ari and Mr. Bendiff took up the entire second floor. Each had a large bedroom, its own water closet, and a separate sitting room with an alcove off it, offering a second bed. The attic Joachim occupied had four beds in it, but Tomi said he wanted to take one mattress down to the hall outside Grammie's bedroom door, so that she would not be so alone, which seemed to them all like a good idea.

Upstairs, unpacked, seated on the edge of his hard mattress in the sleeping alcove, Max listened to Ari settling in, the sounds muffled by a thick wall and a heavy wooden door. After a while, there was the silence of deep sleep. Max was as tired as Ari, but he couldn't relax. A window was set into the wall of this sitting room and he would have liked to look out, but he didn't know if he was allowed to open the shutters. Because he couldn't look out the window, Max crept barefoot down the staircase and into the kitchen. The whole house slept. Only Max was awake. The kitchen door opened onto darkness, but his eyes had adjusted and he stepped out, into the cool air, into the night, into what might have been a small garden within high walls, into a darkness beyond which only one of the black peaks was visible. A dark mass blocked his view of the other two.

Was this the palace, where his father and mother were . . . were what? living? trapped? imprisoned? There had to be windows in the stone wall, shuttered now, but in daytime they might open. His jacket buttoned close against the night air, Max stared into that flat darkness where a window had to be. All during the voyage he had imagined his arrival in Andesia, and how his mother would put both her hands on his shoulders and look into his face, and smile, glad beyond words at his presence. His father was never beyond words. Sometimes Max imagined William Starling crying out, with a laugh, *You took your time getting here!* and sometimes, also with a laugh, *The prodigal son returns!* But always, the next thing his father said to Max was, *Now get us out of here.*

Silence, Max had not imagined. He had not imagined there would be even more waiting. He had not, really, imagined this feeling of not-knowing. He barely knew anything of the language, he didn't know what the situation really was, he had no idea what to expect. Knowing so little, how could he hope to come up with a plan?

But his parents were in danger. That he did know, so he *had* to come up with a plan.

A shape moved in the doorway and he knew who it was. "You're exhausted," his grandmother said, softly. "Go to bed. We're here. We'll learn more tomorrow, and I strongly suspect that we're going to need all our wits about us."

10

Andesia

Before dawn had swept deep night away from the valley, Devera and Suela were in the guesthouse, opening shutters, lighting fires, starting up the woodstove. The rescue party was awakened, but because the servants were present the embassy had no chance to form common plans. Nevertheless, they all determined, each in his own way, to learn as much as they could about the situation in Andesia, and about the King.

Max came downstairs first and splashed his face with cold water in the kitchen sink before hurrying down the hall to the front door. He wanted to see the palace with his own eyes. He didn't know where it was or if he could gain entry, he knew nothing, but he wanted to at least *see* the doorways and windows behind which, somewhere, his mother and father were to be found. He slid back the bolt and pulled the front door open.

Two soldiers blocked his way. They held their rifles across their chests, ready. They didn't speak, only stared.

"I am taking a morning walk," Max said in an ordinary, friendly voice, however angry and afraid he felt, which was quite angry and very afraid. Not for nothing had he spent his childhood appearing on a stage in one role or another. Now he was Alexander Ireton, in service to an important man. He took a step forward, saying at the same time, "Thank you."

They continued to stare at him. Of course they hadn't understood.

He gestured with walking fingers. "May I pass?"

"No," they said in Spanish. A quick, knife-sharp word, a word that did not allow any argument.

The soldiers wore dark blue uniforms and stood straight. One had tied his long dark hair back, at the nape of his neck; the other had a scar that ran from his ear to the corner of his mouth.

Max became imperious. "Let me pass," he ordered.

"No," and now the two rifles were crossed in front of *his* chest.

Gently, the soldiers forced him backward, into the house. He glared from the doorway, then closed the door behind him, sliding the bolt back into place. He strode back to the kitchen. There, he didn't hesitate. He opened the door and stepped outside. "It's not—" Grammie said, but he paid her no attention.

He had stepped into a small dirt courtyard with a lean-to at one end, built against a stone wall so high that he couldn't see over it, even when he stood on the wooden bench set out there. Two ropes for drying clothes were strung across the courtyard. On the third side loomed the square stone tower. Max studied it. It was only three stories, not at all high, but it had crenellations at its top, and for windows there were only narrow slits through which arrows or bullets could be fired.

That had to be the palace. If his parents were living in the tower, and if they ever looked out through the slits to the guesthouse courtyard, and if he happened to be standing outside at the time, looking up, then they would see him and he might—somehow, by the waving of a handkerchief or the dropping of a brooch, maybe—learn that they knew he had arrived.

The tower rose into the clouded sky, silent and motionless as the stony peak behind it. Fear ran lightly up along the long bones of Max's legs. He retreated to the kitchen, where the two servants were heating water in large pots. He wandered into the dining room, where Grammie was setting bread and a jelly of some kind and a pot of tea down before Ari and Mr. Bendiff, who were still in their dressing gowns.

"The soldiers wouldn't let me leave," Max announced, adding, "The courtyard has no gate. How did the servants get in this morning, with the door bolted and the courtyard walled?" Maybe there was another entrance into the guest-house. Through a cellar? Another entrance would be another exit, maybe not blocked by soldiers.

"They sleep in the courtyard," Grammie told him. "So that they'll always be available to us."

But the only shelter in the courtyard was that little roofed lean-to, where spades and a sickle were kept, barely a man's width. You might keep an animal there, but not two women, Max thought. However, all he said was, "I see."

What he saw was that there was no way out.

"Your baths will be ready after breakfast," Grammie said from the doorway.

Max would be glad to wash away the dirt and sweat of travel even if, until then, he hadn't noticed it. He sat down. "We have to get going," he told the two men.

"Breakfast first," Ari answered with a shake of his head and a glance at the doorway. Mr. Bendiff poured him a cup of tea and offered him the bread, without a word.

From the kitchen they heard Grammie telling the two women in her simple Spanish that *sí,* yes, she would bathe, and *sí-í-í,* yes, the boys, too, and the painter, and *no,* there was nothing strange about that. "Not where I live," she said, even though they couldn't understand. Switching back to their language, she asked if they, also, would wish to wash.

Max heard the laughter of the two women, a normal, happy sound, at even the idea of being offered hot water to bathe in. *"Oh, Señora,"* they laughed. *"Oh no."*

Four soldiers accompanied Juan Carlos Carrera y Carrera as he led the foreigners around the city. The first part of the tour took them past the high palace gates, where guards stood at attention, to the high walls surrounding the Carrera y Carrera compound, equally well-guarded. "We will not enter, I will leave it until tonight to show you my home," Juan Carlos announced, then introduced the man who had been waiting for them, standing far off from the soldiers, "My cousin, Juan Luc Carrera y Carrera." The man bowed slightly and greeted the two men, "*Señor* Baron, *Señor* Bendiff," gave Max a quick glance and a nod, and then turned to his cousin, awaiting instructions, or leadership. Juan Luc wore the same brown corduroy jacket and close-fitted trousers as Juan Carlos, and the same high boots. He was a shorter, stouter version of his cousin and his English was more hesitant, a little clumsy. He fell in beside Max and Mr. Bendiff as they followed Juan Carlos back to the palace gates, where they observed the changing of the guard, an event not without its pageantry.

Juan Carlos Carrera y Carrera, gentleman, mine owner, and father of a beautiful daughter, knew himself to be a man of destiny. That morning, he had two reasons for requiring his cousin Juan Luc to accompany the embassy on its tour. First, he wanted somebody to keep the businessman occupied while he found out whatever the Envoy could tell him of Balcor's purposes in welcoming these foreigners. Second, Juan Carlos was aware that, although Juan Luc had the long Carrera y Carrera nose and the velvety Carrera y Carrera eyes, when the two cousins stood together, the difference between them was as clear as the difference between shining veins of silver and dull green copper deposits.

In fact, he'd have preferred that all three of the Carrera y Carrera cousins might be present that morning so that the strangers could see his own superiority, but the mines could never be left without an owner on watch, so Juan Antonio was not available. The soldiers kept the workers in line and also beat off occasional attacks by those men who had fled to the mountains after their uprising failed, but unsupervised soldiers can run amok. A second uprising was no part of the plans Juan Carlos had for Andesia.

He could tell from their uneasy glances at the military guard marching ahead and behind them that his guests were unused to such an escort, so without being asked Juan Carlos told them, "My country is not so old as yours. There is no police in Andesia. We have soldiers to keep order."

The businessman was quick to wonder, "Who keeps the soldiers in order?"

This fellow was too bold for Juan Carlos's taste, as if he were the equal of a Carrera y Carrera or a Baron. "The General and Captain Malpenso," he snapped, and demanded, "Who keeps in order your police?"

There was a brief hesitation, a glance exchanged between Envoy and businessman, before the young Baron answered this. "The law," he said. "We have the law to govern and to protect us. I wonder that your new King has not told you about my country and will ask him about that, when we meet.

For he must be eager to greet us, just as we are eager to present him with the compliments of King Teodor."

"The General will know that better than I," Juan Carlos answered smoothly, and promised, "He will soon be back among us, I have heard." As if struck by a sudden thought, he added, "If it pleases you, perhaps one morning you would like to ride up into the hills? General Balcor keeps a fine stable. Do you ride?"

"Of course," the Envoy answered, a little disdainfully, while *Señor* Bendiff shook his head and remarked that he used to drive workhorses in front of a wagon but now he went about in a motorcar.

"And the Secretary?" Juan Carlos asked, barely glancing at the fellow. "But of course he must. He is, as you say, a gentleman, with a gentleman's accomplishments. We can find worthy mounts for you both."

"I look forward to it all," the Envoy responded.

"You will not, of course, be able to repay our hospitality," Juan Carlos told him, in proud forgiveness of the Envoy's unavoidable failure to keep up his end of the social bargain.

"Unhappily," the Envoy agreed, untroubled. "Unless your King were to send an embassy to our country, or perhaps even come himself, to revisit our cities, to discuss forms of government and taxation with our King and elected representatives."

Juan Carlos was leading his group past the bridge to show them the parade ground, with the long barracks just beyond.

He dismissed the Envoy's suggestion. "I don't think the King of Andesia will want to travel."

"How could he not?" *Señor* Bendiff seemed surprised to hear this. But how could a businessman understand a King's behavior? *Señor* Bendiff insisted, "Surely he has the funds to do so, and in style, I would think, for do the mines not pay a part of their profits to him? And all the people of the land, too. Am I to believe there are no taxes in Andesia?"

Juan Luc laughed and, not understanding as his cousin did what might be learned from this information, foolishly assured their visitor that half of the revenues of the mines were paid into the royal coffers. "Of course a mine will eventually, inevitably, give out, but for now there is no hardship for us to pay a tax," he said. "As you can see," he added, indicating the large carved silver buckles he and his cousin wore at their waists.

Juan Carlos changed the subject again. "The soldiers parade at midday. They are very proud of their drills, which they work hard to make perfect. I don't know if you've ever seen a company of soldiers on parade?" he asked the Secretary, graciously including him. "You will not be disappointed, I think."

The little Secretary acknowledged the Andesian's words and his graciousness with a slight nod, and this irritated Juan Carlos. Who did the young man think he was? He had no reason for pride, as far as Juan Carlos could see. He served a master, following him about like a dog, and he was not by any means a distinguished figure in his own right, a slight fellow with ordinary features—Juan Carlos looked coldly into that face. Ordinary except for the eyes, he corrected himself. The Secretary's eyes were, really, an unpleasant color, a color Juan Carlos had last seen during the uprising, on the blades of spades and hoes raised into the smoking air, their metal still stained with the dirt of their normal uses. Or perhaps it was blood that stained them—he had not lingered to find that out. But this Secretary was an annoyance, no more, a gnat, a cog, and Juan Carlos was sorry he could not fob him off on Juan Luc so that he himself could continue making an impression on the Baron. The man would be a good match for Elizaveta, and she in turn would make a fine Baroness. A father need never consider his child's fate sealed until the wedding vows have been exchanged.

Juan Carlos could see now in how many ways this embassy might suit his own plans.

The party crossed the river, Juan Carlos pointing out the solidity of the bridge ("Erected by the Carrera y Carreras more than fifty years ago"), and entered into the wide plaza, with its sculpted fountain in one corner ("Designed by my great-uncle, who studied in Rome with the most modern sculptors of the time"), around which a few women were gathered, filling jugs and buckets. On benches around the sides of the open space, old men sat in the spring sunlight, watching the small children who chased one another around, shrieking with the excitement of the game. More women sat cross-legged on woven blankets with whatever they had to bring to market spread out before them. Soldiers lounging in shady doorways snapped to attention when the party entered but did not speak to the escort, and neither were they spoken to. When they saw the strangers, the children fell quiet and stared, but everyone else studiously ignored them as they crossed the plaza. The alley they were going down now was dirt, and the houses along it low, without gardens, almost windowless. The Baron, Juan Carlos noted, looked back over his shoulder, as if memorizing the tranquil and picturesque scene, or perhaps admiring the great fountain.

Juan Carlos directed the young man's attention ahead and upward. "From here are seen the mines, on the mountain. You see how the workers move about?" and then he pointed toward their right. It was time to include the three others in the conversation. "Our *mercado,*" he announced, and they all turned to the low, flat-roofed building, with its single door of solid wood. Its few windows were set high on the walls, and barred.

"This is Stefano's store, where your housekeeper can find anything she desires," Juan Carlos said, and then told the businessman, "Our Stefano is a clever man. He has used the profits from his wagon trains to purchase farmlands, and there he grows vegetables to supply the tables of those who know the pleasure of good food. He is a man you will understand, I think. He is often invited to dine with us, with his two pretty daughters, whom he is educating as best he can."

"Ah. So there is a middle class in Andesia," *Señor* Bendiff remarked.

"Oh no," Juan Carlos assured him. "There is only Stefano and our doctor, Doctor Hawkins, who brought his wife up from the coast for the healing mountain air many years ago, and when she died he stayed on to care for our families. They do not form a class, not at all."

Señor Bendiff humphed, as if he knew better than Juan Carlos, who was born and raised in Apapa. He asked, "Why are the store windows barred? They're too high for any thief to enter. Why are there six soldiers here? On guard? Must the store be guarded? Is there such unease about its security?"

Juan Carlos did not care for this businessman, who had no idea that there were topics gentlemen didn't discuss.

"The soldiers keep careful watch because of our recent troubles," Juan Luc explained. "There was an uprising."

"Do you expect another rebellion?" the businessman asked. "Was that bomb a part of a plot?"

Two more unacceptable topics, and Juan Carlos spoke quickly, before his cousin could make things worse. "The uprising was nothing, only some of the farmers from the countryside making things difficult. But our neighbors sent Balcor and his soldiers to help us, and Balcor named Captain Malpenso, who was a member of the late King's special guard, as his second-in-command. We have a good prison in the cellars of the palace," he promised the visitors, lest they worry. "And we are not afraid to fill it."

Grammie had asked Joachim to go out into the countryside and discover whatever there was to be learned beyond the city confines. During the long days on the *Estrella,* separated from his garden, Joachim produced drawings of ships, of sea and sky, of deck games and orchestras. He completed two portraits and a still life of the buffet set out every afternoon for the first-class passengers. He had learned to enjoy new subjects. However, he was not entirely pleased about this change and he suspected that it was all—somehow—the fault of that woman. Hadn't she virtually chased him onto the boat?

Now he protested the assignment. "I don't know the language."

"One picture is worth a thousand words," Grammie reminded him unsympathetically.

"Don't you want to help?" Colly wondered.

"Isn't that why you're here?" Tomi's voice was full of enough surprise to embarrass even Joachim, so when Grammie added, a little desperately, "We need all the information we can get," he said, "All *right.* I'll try, but I'm not making promises."

He accepted a slab of flat bread wrapped in a napkin from Suela, and from Devera a canteen of water, tucked them into his rucksack, added a few pencils and a sketch pad, and slung it over his shoulder. The guards stopped him at the door.

One soldier said something to another, in which Joachim might have heard the word *serviente,* which he thought he might have understood, so he nodded, *sí, sí.* The soldiers shrugged and let him pass.

The few people Joachim saw out and about on the narrow city streets were obviously unaccustomed to strangers. Women pulled shawls more closely around their shoulders and kept their eyes fixed on the dusty road. Old men in ponchos pulled their *chupallas* down low. Soldiers watched him from doorways and street corners. Uneasy at all this attention, Joachim walked fast, hurrying toward the hills. It wasn't long before he'd left the little city behind and could walk freely, slowly, looking about him. He stopped whenever he saw a vista or a plant he wanted to sketch, or anything else that caught his eye: the arrangement of three curved terraces, like a schoolchild's contour map, or a solitary building next to a small garden, its doorway empty, or a particular stony peak that had been sharpened like a spear point by wind and weather. Sometimes his attention was caught by a distant horseman moving across the hillsides, the only sign of human life to be seen.

At midday, Joachim sat on a grassy hillside that rose gently up toward the mountains to have his lunch. He was not far from one of the small houses, but nobody seemed to be at home. For company he had one of the herds they had noticed the day before. Between taking bites of the chewy bread and swallows of tepid water, Joachim opened his sketch pad. The animals came in varying shades of brown and gray. With their furry faces, they were appealing creatures who reminded him of Sunny, although they didn't have her smooth coat or soft, floppy ears. In fact, their coats were thicker even than the heavy spring wool on a sheep, but their sympathetic dark eyes and fearlessness about a stranger reminded him of his dog. Quickly, he sketched a creature, and next to it drew the form of a man, to show its size.

As he sat there, the ground solid beneath him and a sharp pencil in his hand, he pictured himself, as seen from above, a lone man on an isolated hillside, beret on his head, working at the sketch pad on his knees—and he realized with a jolt that halted the movement of his pencil that this landscape drawing was a change, and there had already been several others in the last weeks. He'd thought he could work peacefully only in his own garden, but that woman with her hats had taken that peace away from him—thanks to Max, Joachim thought, with a comfortable grumbly feeling. Still picturing himself from a bird's-eye view, a man on a hillside grumbling contentedly about something that had happened hundreds of miles and many weeks before, Joachim almost smiled.

Could he be laughing at himself? And if he was, what was the harm in that?

One of the woolly creatures approached him with the soft clucking noise a large, contented chicken might emit, and Joachim did smile as he began to draw the long-lashed eyes and furry muzzle of the first friendly face he'd seen in this country. The sun flowed over him, gentle as water, and the air shone clear. The ugliness of the mines was at his back, so he saw just a hillside sloping gently down to the river, along the sides of which the city nestled. Joachim felt as if he had been dropped into a new-made, unspoiled world.

Something moved at the edge of his vision and reminded

him of what he was: a foreigner, with a secret purpose for being on this hillside. It was human movement and he lifted his head to look. A woman was walking toward him. She must have come out of the silent house, and when Joachim looked at it now, he glimpsed two children peeking through the open doorway.

The woman was short, square of body and of face, and she marched right at him. She wore a loose shirt and a heavy skirt. Joachim turned his attention to his drawing until she came up close and stared down, at him, at his sketch pad. To show her that he was friendly, he turned the pages back to find the drawing of the herd, which was probably hers. She grunted, then crouched down beside him for a better look. She reached out a finger, which was not clean, and touched one of the animals on its rump. She grunted again, and smiled, and Joachim couldn't help but see the gaps where teeth had once grown.

He risked asking her a question, using the Spanish word and pointing at one of the animals. "Dog?"

Laughter bubbled out of her. She shook her head. "Alpaca," she told him.

"Alpaca," he echoed.

She nodded and took the hem of her skirt in her hand. She held it out to him so that he could feel it while she said again, "Alpaca."

"Soft," he said without thinking, and she stared at him out of dark, serious eyes. Then she surprised him. She sat down cross-legged beside him and ordered him with words and gestures, "Draw me."

Joachim did, the quickest of sketches. He tore the page out and gave it to her.

She rose to her feet and told him, with more gestures and words, to accompany her back to the house. He did as he was told.

Later that day, trying to express everything to Grammie and the two boys—because he was too impatient to report his success to insist on waiting for the others to return from dinner at the Carrera y Carrera compound—he spread out his sketches: of the old woman seated on the one wide, low bed, where apparently everybody slept, weaving on a back-strap loom; of the little boy holding the carded wool while an older sister turned the spindle, twisting it into yarn; of that first woman as she worked on a vertical loom; of the pile of woven fabric on a shelf, waiting to be sewn together into some article of clothing for warmth against the next winter. His last sketch showed the one room of their home, a small fire in one corner, the cooking pot hanging from a tripod over the low flames.

"She gave me some kind of corn bread. She insisted on feeding me," Joachim reported, "and the children couldn't take their eyes off of it. But she wanted me to eat it, so I did, but . . . I drew the two children for her and that's when . . ." Joachim stopped speaking, to arrange his thoughts, which were not thoughts, really, so much as feelings.

His hesitation made Max's grandmother anxious and she demanded, "When *what,* you irritating man?"

"Was it something bad?" Colly wondered.

"Dangerous?" Tomi hoped. "What was it?"

"It was hoofbeats," Joachim told them. "And the next thing I know, the woman and her mother are shoving me into the bed—rucksack, sketch pad, pencil, and all—and burying my beret under the blankets. The old lady stayed there, sitting beside me, rocking back and forth and making little moaning noises. If they hadn't looked so frightened, I'd have asked what was going on. And the children just . . . they disappeared. In a flash. Just—gone. Onto the roof, as it turned out, but all I could figure out was that they wanted me to lie there and be moaned over. So I did," he said, smiling, "and I groaned a little, too, when the hoofbeats stopped right outside the door."

His listeners waited, watching his face.

"A soldier came into the room," Joachim told them, and they nodded as if this was what they'd expected.

"He said something, short, sharp. He took out a notebook and a pencil. The mother shook her head. Two, three times he said it and each time she shook her head, until at the end she said something and waved her hand, as if to say, *See for yourself,* and he wrote something in his notebook. The old woman just watched him and so did I, and I didn't have to pretend to be afraid. He looked—he looked like the kind of man who might do anything, anything he wanted at any moment. And he was just one of the ordinary soldiers," Joachim said.

"Oh my." Max's grandmother put her head into her hands. "Oh my oh my."

"Then what?" Tomi asked.

"Then he went away. Angry, I think, and we stayed where we were, listening to be sure he didn't come back."

"How long?" Colly asked.

Joachim shook his head, he didn't know. "Then they let me get out of the bed. The children came back. I wanted to help, but she couldn't understand what little Spanish I remember, so—so I gave her the sketch pad."

"She can draw?" Grammie asked, wonder in her voice.

"Anyone can draw. Well, enough to show a stick-figure child belly down on what had to be a horse, pinned there by the rider. I asked, using signs, pointing at the picture, pointing at the door, if the rider was that same soldier. She said no, but she might not have understood me because she spread out her arms, as if she was trying to be a bird on the hunt, which makes no sense."

"Taking children? Kidnapping them? Why?" Colly asked.

Tomi's question was more practical. "Taking them where?"

"I think the mines. At least, she pointed in that direction when I asked— Well, I shaded my eyes like a portrait of a mariner peering into the distance and she seemed to understand. Then they shooed me off," Joachim concluded.

"You'd be a danger to them," Grammie said.

"We didn't see any children today except for really little ones," Tomi remembered.

Then Grammie reported to Joachim and Colly on the

scarcity of goods offered in the plaza—a few yams, a few eggs, a bowl of cornmeal—and the contrast of that with the well-stocked shelves at Stefano's store, with its supplies of vegetables and canned goods, French soaps and bolts of silk cloth. "The women who waited on us were all smiles. They didn't speak a word, but their smiles never left their faces."

"They were very friendly," Tomi agreed.

At his tone of voice, Colly, who had not gone with them to the *mercado,* wondered, "But?"

"But maybe too friendly?" Tomi answered. "As if they were afraid not to smile. Afraid of us? Or someone I couldn't see, watching? Afraid of one another?"

"They didn't take our coins, they kept saying *Balcor, Balcor,*" Grammie reported. "Is the General paying our bills?"

"What is going *on* in this country?" Joachim wondered.

Golden-haired Elizaveta Maddalena Antonetta Carrera y Carrera turned wide-set, velvety brown eyes on the Envoy, who her father said was a Baron in his own land and was, besides, a handsome man, if you didn't mind dark red hair. Then she modestly lowered her attention to her soup plate so that he could appreciate her long eyelashes, and reflected that she preferred dark-headed men, next to whom her golden beauty appeared to more advantage. But she knew what her father expected of her and she asked the Baron the kinds of questions an eager girl should ask about his long sea voyage. Shyly, she confided that she hoped someday to take such a voyage as her honeymoon, and let him see how much she enjoyed imagining the pleasures awaiting her. "Did the ladies have new gowns for every evening? Did everyone take part, all the gentlemen and ladies, in the morning promenades? Did the chef present dessert soufflés? Was there not also an orchestra?"

The Baron stubbornly refused to flirt with her. Instead, he told her the plain truth and asked straightforward questions. "Often the ladies sat in deck chairs, to read books from the ship's library. Do you think your Queen would have done that?" or "The orchestra was an array of stringed instruments, plus a piano. I'm sure your King has many more skillful musicians at his command?"

He was always trying to talk about the King, she complained to herself, or the Queen. She told him, "The King does not dance, I have heard. There have been no coronation balls. Not even a feast," and she smiled so that he could admire her perfect teeth.

"Perhaps when summer has arrived and the weather is fair, the King will offer a feast *and* a ball. For I think he must be happy in his good fortune?"

Elizaveta detected in his eyes the hope to be here for that occasion and especially the hope to dance with her. He might be a Baron and he might come from a more civilized country, but was he not a man? She lowered her eyes again, as if to conceal her thoughts from him so that he could hope that she, too, longed for a chance to waltz in his arms.

She might even think of marrying him, if her father wished her to. In any case, new faces at the table were welcome, and this embassy offered not only this Baron but also a businessman of some sort and a secretary for her sisters. Since the army had arrived to save them, it was the Captain her father had seated her beside—a man of crude manners and conversation who either relentlessly praised her beauty or endlessly boasted of his prowess in battle, in duels, in any conflict; a man, also, whose long, spidery fingers made her skin crawl as she watched them wrap around one of the heavy silver forks. Only once had she been placed next to the General, who was the most important man in Andesia and widely traveled, besides. On that occasion, the General had advised her to study hard at her English. "It is good for a young woman to be educated," he said. He had called her a woman and not a girl, and he had seemed confident that she was capable of learning. "Educated in languages, of course," the General said, "but also in history. If you know something of history, you will be better able to understand the things that happen in the world, and the people who make them happen." He had spoken seriously but not sternly, and he had seemed interested in her, Elizaveta, not in her beauty. For this reason, Elizaveta had never been able to fear the General, as the others did.

She had followed his advice, and was proud of having done so even if she had not yet been able to display her achievements to him. But perhaps now, when he returned and there was this visiting party to be entertained, she could hope to talk with him again. Sometimes she did not want to be her father's beautiful daughter—although, to be honest, even less did she want to be one of her mother's ordinary daughters.

Her sisters, that evening, were seated far down the table with the Secretary between them. Elizaveta did not care for the Secretary, who was not handsome or even interesting to look at, and apparently had nothing to say for himself, since she could see how her sisters were chattering away and he only listening. The eyes of this Secretary made her uneasy. They were an odd stone-and-earth shade, the colors of the high mountains that walled her in, she sometimes thought, and kept her safe, as she thought at other times. Elizaveta Carrera y Carrera longed to cross those mountains, and feared that she might not find her way back. And that she might not wish to find her way back. The mountains made her uneasy, so she turned her attention away from the Secretary, and his eyes.

The businessman, on the other hand, was like the jolly father in an English story. Her own father was not at all jolly, even less so in these days than before, and Elizaveta might have been beautiful but that didn't mean she was silly, or blind. She wondered what it was about this embassy from far away that had her father so worried.

At that moment, her father was smiling with satisfaction as the businessman talked earnestly to his quiet little cousin Juan Antonio, presentable enough now that he had changed out of the rough clothing he had worn for his day's overseeing of the mine operations. How could her father not be happy tonight, Elizaveta thought, with his long dining room lit by heavy crystal chandeliers and wide silver candelabras? This was a room where the guests were served elegant foods on white porcelain plates edged in gold, where the silverware

had been forged from the output of their own mine, heavy forks and spoons and knives, each incised with an ornate *C*. The entire Carrera y Carrera family was present: both cousins and all their children, except for the boys of eight and more years, who were off at one school or another, and those children judged too young for the company; all the wives, in richly colored, many-flounced satin, displaying costly jewels; and the three mine owners in bright cummerbunds and silver buttons. Two guitars played softly in an anteroom . . . How could her father be anything but happy?

"Perhaps there will be a ball to honor you," she said to the Baron, looking up at him through thick lashes, flirtatiously, for everyone to see and admire, like the foolish, careless beauty they were all so sure she was.

"I feel sorry for her," Ari said when the evening had at last ended and soldiers had escorted them back to the guesthouse, where they could share news of the evening with the whole party.

"Her father is all pride and does nothing, as far as I can tell," Mr. Bendiff said. "He's lucky he's got those cousins to keep things in order. He doesn't understand anything about running a business."

"They certainly live well," Ari said.

"Expensively," Mr. Bendiff agreed, adding, "None of them will talk about the bomb," before he asked, "What did you boys learn?"

Max reported first. "Soldiers aren't allowed inside the

Carrera y Carrera compound. Malpenso often dines with them, but he's a captain, not a soldier. *El Capitán,* the sisters call him, and I don't think they like him, although, since he's always left to Elizaveta, they don't worry about him. The one time the General came, only Elizaveta was allowed to be there. Her sisters had to dine in the nursery with the little children that night." He took a minute to think. He hadn't learned much, but maybe there was something to add. "They haven't had a governess or word from beyond Andesia—except for monthly letters from the brothers and cousins at boarding schools in Peru—since the army arrived. They've never talked with the new King, or his Queen, and only seen them from a distance. I didn't dare ask them about the bomb."

Colly and Tomi had wandered the city late in the afternoon, to find out whatever they could, which was little enough.

"People stopped talking as soon as they saw us," Colly said. "Soldiers followed us."

"Even when we were buying *chupallas*—we got you one, too, Eyes—they'd barely even look at us."

"They wouldn't take coins," Colly said.

"Coins are useless in a barter economy," Mr. Bendiff pointed out.

"They pushed away our hands," Tomi said, "and all they said was *Balcor, Balcor.*"

"It would seem that the General is paying our bills," Mr. Bendiff said.

"So what have we learned?" Ari asked.

"They're poor," Joachim announced. "Hungry, too. I can't imagine where they got the strength to rebel."

"They're afraid of us," Tomi said, but Colly didn't agree.

"More wary than afraid, I think. It's the soldiers they're afraid of."

"Nobody will talk about the King," Max said, and added unnecessarily, "or the Queen."

Mr. Bendiff was thinking his own thoughts. "Would you buy me a poncho?" he asked Colly. "The next time you're in the plaza. Or two would be better. Where did you find ponchos?"

"We can't *buy* anything," Tomi reminded him.

"In Stefano's store," Colly told him. "There are plenty more there."

"There's a lot of wealth in Andesia," Ari remarked. "It wasn't just that dining room. Did you notice the furnishings in the salon? Uncomfortable, with those spindly legs, but elegant. Very expensive," he added thoughtfully. "It's huge, that home, and there are two others, just as large."

"We were certainly entertained in style," Mr. Bendiff agreed. "I wonder how they display their wealth when there are no strangers to show off to?"

Max could answer that. "They invite Stefano, and the doctor. Stefano has two daughters, the sisters told me, although they assured me that Stefano's daughters were not being nearly as well educated in everything a girl should know as the Carrera y Carreras. Also, they are not so pretty. They thought I would like to meet Stefano's daughters," he added, and smiled, pleased with the success of his performance as the unimportant Alexander Ireton. "But hasn't anybody else noticed?" he asked.

Six puzzled faces looked at him.

"Noticed what?" Grammie asked impatiently.

"Where are the young men? And the boys, has anyone seen any boys over eight? Or men under—I can't tell, I think they must age quickly with the lives they lead, so men under maybe forty?" Max asked his question again: "Where are the men and boys?"

"Can they all have been taken by soldiers?" wondered Joachim.

Which made Ari wonder, "Without men or boys to make things difficult, why are there so many soldiers?"

11

Balcor

Slowly, slowly, the next two days passed. The first morning, it rained, a cleansing spring rain, but that night, as Max stood in the kitchen doorway, the moon shone bright onto the dark tower. The second afternoon, a sun-warmed breeze blew through the valley, smelling of moist earth and new grass. There was no word of Balcor. There was no word from the King.

Grammie marketed and cooked and supervised Devera and Suela in the work of keeping the house clean and the clothes laundered, the wood chopped and stacked beside stove and fireplaces. And she fretted.

Joachim wandered the hills to sketch plants and flowers, the terraced slopes, the herds of alpaca, the steep, enclosing mountains. He saw not a living soul, except for that first woman and her small family when he made a return visit to the little homestead. He was pleased to leave the guesthouse in the morning, to spend a day sketching whatever caught his eye, and to return in the evening to a good meal and good company.

Tomi and Colly, when they weren't needed for one chore (peeling potatoes, stirring corn pudding) or another (taking notes as Mr. Bendiff paced his room, back and forth, having ideas), liked to disappear into the city streets. The book-Spanish they had studied did enable them to understand much of what people said, and since it was assumed that they, not only strangers but also young, would not understand, people spoke freely in front of them. Often people spoke of things the visitors were not supposed to hear about.

Ari and Mr. Bendiff were kept busy meeting one Carrera y Carrera or another, talks that decided nothing and revealed nothing but took hour after tedious hour. Max sat beside Ari, listening and taking notes. And fretting.

Every midday, rain or shine, they were required to be at the parade ground to watch the soldiers drill. Joachim, off in the hills with his sketch pad, avoided the duty, but Juan Carlos had made it clear that the rest of them had no choice. Everyone in Apapa was expected to attend, the only exceptions being those few soldiers left to guard the palace, those protecting the *mercado,* and the one detail charged with rounding up anybody in the streets and in the houses who tried to stay away. During the midday hour, the city emptied onto the parade ground, from the youngest and least important child up to and including the three Carrera y Carrera families and their array of serving women.

When the bells rang out from the palace tower to announce the noon hour, the visitors left the guesthouse, in two groups. Grammie and the boys went first; Max, Ari, and Mr. Bendiff a little later, as befitted their higher status. A raised platform had been erected on one side of the parade ground, with benches on it to seat the Carrera y Carreras and the three important visitors, but everybody else stood, spread out along the perimeter, to admire and applaud, to be the audience.

Balcor's army consisted of four companies of soldiers, which rotated assignments every month. Two companies had their headquarters at the mines, one to stand guard there while the other accompanied the wagons that made the twice-monthly round-trip to Cúcuta, carrying copper and silver down to the coast, bringing back foodstuffs, fabrics, furniture, and whatever else was needed to stock Stefano's store, as well as the rare letter. The other two companies, almost three hundred soldiers, each man armed with rifle and pistols and sword, stood ready to protect the royal couple, the Carrera y Carreras, and the city—as if the native Andesians, armed with hoes, spades, pitchforks, and hunting knives, represented a constant danger. Since the soldiers on duty in the city had so little to occupy them—feared as they were by the Andesians and disdained as they were by the Carrera y Carreras as landless mercenaries, unfit companions for even the servants of their haciendas—the parade drills made a rare source of entertainment for them. Every soldier wore a freshly laundered black shirt. All weapons shone with polish, all caps were stiffly creased. The parades were, as Max could see, well-rehearsed performances, filled with the drama of sharp drumbeats and the thud of feet marching in unison, with orders snapped out and instantly obeyed, the guns fired, one after the other, down entire lines of infantry.

Only the Captain was on horseback, a lean, narrow-eyed, unsmiling man in a dark green uniform, astride a leggy gray stallion that seemed to require both tightly held reins and sharp spurs. The horse was fretful, his hooves dancing, his mouth pushing against the bit, but Captain Malpenso was its master, and he could both control his mount and direct the drill with the same unsmiling authority. The Captain reviewing his troops on parade was like an orchestra conductor, who needed only the slightest gesture of a gloved hand to instruct his instruments. He sat straight in the saddle and his boots gleamed as brightly as the sword he held up, unsheathed. When that sword fell, his men moved in perfect formation, forward or back, left or right.

Max couldn't help himself. Once he'd gotten over the sharp disappointment of seeing—again—the two empty thrones at the center of the dais, he enjoyed the show. This was good theater. His heart beat in time with the drums, his eye savored the ballet-like precision of the marchers. Even the third day of the same performance didn't bore him. He might, he suspected, have been the only person who felt that way. Although each maneuver was answered by loud applause, cries of *"¡Olé! ¡Olé!"* and sometimes gasps, Ari and Mr. Bendiff took advantage of an occasion for private conversation, and Max was not surprised when Grammie, Colly, and Tomi, who had stood among the crowd, reported that this was not only a forced attendance but also a forced enthusiasm, and a forced applause.

The other honored guests on the dais, the large Carrera y Carrera families and their aging doctor, always applauded loudly and called "Bravo!" to the Captain as his gray pranced by, tail high in the air. But they gasped in so much unison that Max knew it was a well-practiced spontaneous cry of delight. And what they said, leaning toward one another's ears, speaking with mouths hidden behind a fan or a hand, did not bring any joy, or smiles of warmth, to their faces.

It was Colly who put it into words. "They don't want to come to the attention of *el Capitán.* I think the soldiers fear him, too."

"What about the General?" Max wanted to know.

"I don't hear any talk about the General," Colly reported. Tomi guessed Max's next question, the one Max didn't want to ask, and told him, "They despise the King, who's hiding behind his palace gates and his guards. They pity the Queen. Before she became sickly, they say, she was kind to her servants, and very beautiful, but what good did her beauty do her? And her kindness is powerless against the soldiers. That's what they say."

On their third day in Andesia, Max was watching the parade, and enjoying it, and fretting about his parents, willing himself to be patient. He knew that until the embassy came into the King's presence they couldn't begin to think about a plan, and he knew also that until Balcor returned they wouldn't be allowed an audience with the King. He had to wait. He could do nothing but wait.

He was no better here at waiting than he had been at home. In fact, he was getting worse, especially now that there was no solutioneering to distract him, now that his parents were so close and so inaccessible, now with not even a plan to be making. He could only study Captain Malpenso's easy seat on his long-legged, restless gray horse, as his troops paraded in front of him. But what did he care about the man's skill on horseback? And this performance, he bemoaned silently, was the high point of his day.

"¡Pelotón!" came the order. Three hundred soldiers stopped moving and stood to attention. *"¡Marchad el paso!"* they were told, and six hundred booted feet beat out the rhythm, without moving forward. *"¡Derecha ar!"* they were ordered.

All heads turned to the right, where the hawk-headed Captain sat astride the gray. Silver spurs shone against the stallion's flanks, ready to dig in. The bit pulled tight against the horse's mouth. *"¡Saludad!"* The soldiers, straight row behind straight row, saluted and the drums fell still.

Into that silence came a distant thundering of hooves. The soldiers did not look away from their Captain, but the people on the dais, and the crowd around the sides of the parade ground, all turned toward the sound.

"¡Al frente!" came the order. "Eyes center!" Then, *"¡Ya!* Forward, march!"

The sound of hoofbeats rose up against a background rhythm of six hundred booted feet, marching, the way the voice of a singer rises up over the orchestra. Then a great black beast of a horse galloped into view. It charged onto the parade ground and was pulled to a halt so abruptly that its forefeet lifted from the ground. A man sat tall in the saddle, his black uniform trimmed in shining silver, his black boots gleaming, and their spurs, if such a thing was possible, even larger and more cruel than Malpenso's. The Captain might wear a metal helmet topped by a spike, but this man had a shako on his head, a tall black column out of which rose a thick black plume. He raised his right hand, greeting the Captain with a salute.

"¡Pelotón!"

The army stood like rows and rows of wooden soldiers.

Malpenso, motionless, let the seconds tick slowly by.

The audience waited, silent.

This had to be the General, and this was the choked silence of fear and hatred combined. Choked, and choking, too.

The Carrera y Carreras were clearly waiting. But waiting for what? Even Mr. Bendiff seemed uneasy, although neither the General nor the Captain had turned to look at the dais. Beside Max, Ari was alert, like a hunting dog with his nose stretched out toward the quarry, quivering. Max recognized his own feelings from countless evenings backstage at the Starling Theater: the curtain was about to go up, the audience

waited in silent darkness, the actors were in position on the lighted stage, the drama was within a breath of starting—and how it would fare, for good or ill, would soon be determined.

After what felt like a full minute, although it could never have taken so long, Captain Malpenso raised his right hand to return the salute from his commanding officer. The General spurred his horse forward until he halted beside his Captain, dwarfing him. Captain Malpenso gave his next order, *"¡Presenten armas!"*

Now Max could see Balcor's square, broad-cheeked face and the round dark eyes that seemed more sad than fiery. The General sported no mustachio and his mouth was a straight line, not smiling, not frowning, under a broad nose. The face did not match the proud military bearing and the great beast of a horse, or the high plume that rose like cannon smoke above the tall shako. The General watched his troops on parade with an intensity that surprised Max, since the parade was a daily exercise and he must have seen these same performances untold times. His black-gloved hands rested on the high pommel of his saddle and the horse was as motionless as its master. Behind this whole scene, like the backdrop of a stage, three jagged gray mountain peaks sliced into the blue sky.

For the entire last half hour of marching and wheeling, one rank moving around the other and then itself being encircled, of presentations of arms, and rifle drills, and quick commands to fix bayonets and load rifles, Max watched General Balcor. The tall figure remained motionless, as if it were already a statue in the public square, both man and horse carved in black marble. The eyes did not move from the lines of soldiers, not even when all three hundred swords were drawn out of their sheaths and raised high, as practiced as a corps de ballet, to shout, *"¡Muerte! ¡Victoria! ¡Muerte!"* Not even the blinding reflections flashing from those swords raised into bright sunlight diverted the General's attention.

When the parade ended that day, to the usual extravagant applauding and cries of admiration, there were two officers leading the long double line of soldiers out of the parade ground and back to their barracks. Once the military was out of sight, a silence fell over the crowd. People left the parade ground quickly.

Those descending from the dais were the last to exit, the throng of long-nosed Carrera y Carreras followed by the three outlanders. Max was impatient to get back to the guesthouse and share his opinions of the General, and hear what the others thought. But the great black beast was returning. It was approaching them. Its rider reined it to a halt directly in front of them and blocked their way.

The three visitors looked up at him. They removed their hats. The General did not remove his.

"I will arrive at your lodgings in two hours," Balcor told them. "I hope you will be prepared to receive me?"

Ari, the Ambassador and the next Baron Barthold, answered for them all. "You will be most welcome, General. May I present myself?"

"I know who you are, Baron," General Balcor answered.

"And you, I think, will be *Señor* Hamish Bendiff, representing your country's commercial interests, and this"—his glance turned to Max and, unaccountably, lingered—"this is the young . . . Secretary. Who is also a gentleman." Was that doubt Max heard in his voice?

Max didn't know how to respond. Then he remembered *The Queen's Man,* how the spy-hero of that play had greeted the King's untrustworthy younger brother, and he bowed deeply from the waist, and, rising, looked into that face—that sorrowful face? that proud and hungry face?—to say, "Sir." Then he stepped back, so the General could speak privately with the two men.

But the General had nothing more to say. He turned his horse and trotted off to the stables.

The entire rescue party gathered in the dining room of the guesthouse, regardless of what the two servants might think. This was too important an occasion for anybody's opinion to go unheard. Suela and Devera were busy in the kitchen, preparing a stew of yams and chilies for the supper of those who were left out of the nightly feasting. Max reported what General Balcor had said to them, the promise—or was it a threat?—of a visit. This had even Mr. Bendiff on edge. "I can't make sense of him," Pia's father complained. "There's all that tyrant stuff—that warhorse, the uniform, and the total silence all around him. The arrogant way he announced that he will call, when he knows we've been twiddling our thumbs here for days. But I've never seen sadder eyes." Mr.

Bendiff was puzzled. "His face doesn't match anything else about him, including his reputation."

Grammie's mind was clear. "He's our only way to reach the Queen."

"Remember my name, everybody," Max said. He was convinced, for some reason, that a name would protect him, and he was convinced also, he realized, that he needed protection. "Alexander Ireton, Alexander. We have to be careful."

Ari observed, "The General doesn't have the face of a bad man. Not like Malpenso. Do you think?"

But Max knew better. " 'There's no art to find the mind's construction in the face,' " he recited. "It's Shakespeare," he reminded them, and then realized, "It's *Macbeth,*" which in turn recalled to him that *Macbeth* is a play about the murder of a king, and the question burst out of him: "What is it about kings that makes people want to murder them? It's not just *Macbeth,* it's in *The Queen's Man,* and even King Teodor has guards."

"Think of how many Roman emperors were murdered," Grammie added.

Ari took a look at Max's face and decided, "Let's not." He took a long, considering breath. "Here's what I think," he said. "All we can do right now is wait for the General to show up to say what he has to say. I suggest a round of poker."

"Good idea," said Tomi, and Colly said, "I'll get the cards," as he dashed out of the room and up the stairs. Tomi arranged chairs around the table.

They were deep in the game and Colly had just spread a

flush down in front of him, reaching out to gather in Max's chips, when the front door of the house was thrown wide and soldiers marched in, their boots loud on the stone floor.

Ari rose from the table, pushing his chair back, drawing himself up to his full height. "What is the meaning—" he began, and General Balcor stepped out from behind the soldiers and stood in the doorway of the dining room, a full hour earlier than expected.

Mr. Bendiff also stood up. Grammie and the others followed suit.

"—of this intrusion," continued Ari, a Barthold in outrage.

The General did not apologize but he did explain. "My business needed less time than I'd thought." He spoke to the soldiers: "Dismissed," and they turned on their heels to march smartly away. The house door closed behind them, and only then did Max see what had been hidden from him before: General Balcor was *not* a giant of a man. If anything, he'd be described as short and stocky, not at all built to the elegant lines of the Carrera y Carreras and also not to the rapier sharpness of Captain Malpenso. He was several inches shorter than Mr. Bendiff. He was not, in fact, much taller than Max.

"I will take advantage of the presence of your entire party to hear the names of all. You will introduce me," he said, but before Ari could speak, he clicked his booted heels together and bowed. Then, "*Señor* Hamish Bendiff," he said as he stripped the glove from his right hand and extended it to Mr. Bendiff, who took it, murmuring, "General."

"My Secretary, Alexander Ireton," Ari said.

The General didn't offer a handshake, although Max felt himself being looked at closely. "He seems young," the General remarked.

Ari did not answer this observation, as if it was too irrelevant to confirm or deny. "My housekeeper, Mrs. Sevin," he said, not even stumbling over the name.

If Max had been the director and Ari his lead actor, he would have interrupted him to shout out, "Well done!" He himself had only just remembered, and too late, that it was *her* name he had used when he wrote to the King, his father. This was also the name the King had used in writing a response that must have been read by General Balcor before the letter was given to Stefano to be carried to Cúcuta and mailed to Queensbridge.

"Señora," the General said, with neither handshake nor bow.

"General." Grammie bobbed a brief curtsey. She kept her eyes cast down. A housekeeper did not look a tyrant in the eye. "Come along, boys," she said to Tomi and Colly. "Let's return to the kitchen."

"Not quite yet," the General said. "I like to know the names of every foreigner in the country for which I have such—" and here he hesitated, at last saying, "responsibility."

"Colly," Ari said, and Colly bowed his corn-colored head in acknowledgment, then it was "Tomi," who also bowed his head. But except for that brief second, Tomi did not look away from the General's face. He wanted the man to know that he was not cowed, not one bit.

"Also in the party, although not here at the moment, there is the artist. Joachim," Ari said. "He goes out to the countryside and records what he sees there, plants and animals, insects, vistas."

"So I have heard," said the General. He looked for what felt like a long time at Tomi, and then at Colly. After that, "You may go," he said, waving Grammie away from the table, waving the two servants after her, and Max stepped around to join them. He wanted to be out from under this man's eye.

"The Secretary will remain with us, I think," General Balcor observed.

Max transformed his exit into the job of gathering up the cards and chips, putting them into a drawer.

"You are most democratic with your party, I see," General Balcor announced.

"I am," Ari agreed, and he waited.

"I hope you are comfortably accommodated?" the General asked.

"Quite," Ari said. "Except in the matter of an audience with the King," he added. And he waited.

"The servants are satisfactory?" the General asked.

"Yes," Ari said, "although I think Mrs. Sevin would appreciate a boy for the woodpile and the waste buckets." He waited.

Max understood that Ari expected to hear, eventually, the

reason why the General had fallen down upon them as he had. He understood also that by suggesting another servant in the house, Ari was letting the General know they had no fear of spies.

"And you, *Señor* Bendiff, you are being shown what you need to know of our city and our people?"

"The Carrera y Carreras have been most generous with their time," Mr. Bendiff answered.

"They were instructed to be so. It is good that they comply," the General said. Then, at last, he got to the point. "The King will greet you tomorrow, at two in the afternoon. I will arrive here at half after one to escort you into his presence. Unless you object?"

"Why would I object?" Ari asked. "I will be pleased to present the greetings of King Teodor the Third and my own credentials to the King of Andesia."

General Balcor shook his head. "This is not the formal reception," he said. "Only the King will be present tomorrow. There will be no presentation of documents or of royal greetings, although expressions of goodwill are appropriate."

"I see," Ari said. "And the formal reception?"

"That is up to the King," General Balcor answered. "The King will determine if that is what he wishes."

"Of course," Ari agreed.

His business concluded, General Balcor drew the glove back over the fingers of his right hand and pulled it taut. Max looked at Ari. There was a question he wanted to ask, but he couldn't. A secretary did not question the General. But Ari knew what Max wanted to know. "If not tomorrow, then at the formal reception may we hope to be welcomed also by Her Majesty, the Queen?" he asked.

General Balcor hesitated. Then, "Unfortunately," he said, "Her Majesty has of late been unwell, and has kept to her own apartments. Certainly if she feels up to it, His Majesty will allow her to greet her own . . ." He turned to Max, as if Max might give him the word he was searching for.

Max couldn't look at either Ari or Mr. Bendiff. It was all he could do to keep his own face wiped clean of any alarm, to keep his hands from clutching one another in anxiety. What if they had been seen through? Or even were merely suspected? In this country, it seemed, they could be thrown into prison at the whim of the General, or the Captain, or the King, and left to rot.

". . . countrymen," the General at last concluded. "Gentlemen, farewell."

He left as abruptly as he had arrived. For a long time, the three who remained in the room looked at one another in silence. Tomorrow, Max told himself, tomorrow he would see his father. But what was wrong with his mother? She was never ill, never missed a performance. And how would he tell his father what plan he'd made for their rescue when he still had no idea what that plan could be?

12

The Rescue

• ACT I •

SCENE 1 ~ THE CUE

Max did not see the splendor of the high halls through which General Balcor and Captain Malpenso led them, not the murals of gods and goddesses on the walls, not the life-sized portraits of unlikely ancestors, not the gilded sofas and chairs and side tables. He did not gasp in shock or admiration, as Mr. Bendiff did, or sniff in distaste, as Ari did, at the waiting room, where the walls were entirely covered by smooth silver panels. Neither had he felt the rain through which they hurried on the short walk from the guest-house doorway to the high gates, across a courtyard, and into the palace. Nor had he noticed the lines of soldiers through which they walked, or wondered, like Ari, if they were there to protect the King, or thought, like Mr. Bendiff, that their weapons were in service to the General.

Max floated through the corridors as if in a dream, carried along on a cloud of eagerness (he had found his parents!) and anxiety (what should he say?) and excitement (every step brought him closer!) and worry (how would he know what to do?). He could barely remember to put one foot ahead of the other.

King Teodor's embassy to Andesia had dressed formally for this meeting, Ari in uniform, a sword at his side, Mr. Bendiff in top hat and tails. Just in case, Max carried the leather folder in which Ari kept his credentials and King Teodor's letter of introduction. He wore a dark suit that Grammie had ironed that morning, over a shirt so white, its collar so starched, that he felt as if he, too, were in military uniform, and the sword at his side confirmed that feeling. Max walked alone at the rear of the small party and could not catch his breath.

Max had had stage fright. He knew what that was and how to manage it. But this was a different kind of fear. Everything depended on this meeting and he had no idea how it would go. Also, he was sharing the stage with nonprofessionals, two of them the enemy, and he had no script to follow. He did not allow himself to worry about the odds that this would turn out to be a comedy, with a comedy's happy ending, and not a tragedy, which ends in death.

Not death, surely, Max said to himself, floating to a halt behind his companions.

When they halted, he looked up, looked around him, and saw that they stood at the end of a wide, high-ceilinged room, lit by a row of tall windows, down which raindrops ran freely. Straight-backed chairs lined the walls and their red velvet seats glowed warm against the gray afternoon. The stone floor was covered by a thick red-and-silver carpet that led up to—his eyes followed it past the General's booted feet and Ari's legs—a dais on which stood two silver thrones. Empty.

The silence inside of Max echoed, and rang, and made it impossible to hear, or think.

From stage right, the King of Andesia entered. He strode up to the larger of the two thrones, a tall man, regal in a white uniform and long red robe, a silver crown gleaming on his dark head, his face—

Max stared at his father's face. He could not move, and he knew he should not move, and he did not move, but his eyes drank in William Starling's square jaw and dark, expressive eyes, his heavy eyebrows and wide forehead, his mouth that did not smile in welcome.

Why did his mouth not smile? Max wondered, and then—as if only with his father there in front of him could he do it—he woke up. He saw the luxurious splendor of the room, the thrones—could they possibly be solid silver?—each with those three peaks rising from the back, and a dozen soldiers lined up three deep, Malpenso at their front. The General stood beside Ari, ready to introduce the Envoy. Max saw his father's unsmiling kingliness and the theatrical grace with which he seated himself on the throne with a swirling of red robe, and then rested gloved hands on thighs, waiting for General Balcor to speak.

He saw the absence of his mother.

He saw the expression on his father's face, on the King's face, as he waited for the General to speak, and give him his cue.

Where was his mother?

He saw that the King did *not* look at the three figures preparing to be formally introduced by the General.

He saw clearly that he, Max Starling, Solutioneer, could *not* act, not now, not in any way. He could not say anything or ask anything or do anything. He was Alexander Ireton, Private Secretary to the next Baron Barthold, and invisible.

Max watched everybody, but especially the King and the General. He watched everything and listened carefully to the exact words spoken by the two principal actors in this scene. That there were only three major roles was obvious—the King, the Envoy, and the General, who was shorter than the foreigner by a full three or four inches but every bit as imposing in full uniform. All the others in the room, the Captain with his troop of soldiers, Mr. Bendiff, a commercial personage, and the Secretary, a nonentity, had only the most minor roles. Max knew that his own group's appearance was false, and he knew as well that this King was no real king, and wished only to escape his throne. He wondered if Balcor and Malpenso were only what they seemed, and doubted it. And this made him wonder about the soldiers, their appearance of solidarity and strict hierarchy, of obedience to their

Captain, who was obedient to their General, who appeared to obey the King's wishes. Was there anyone in the room who *wasn't* acting?

General Balcor stepped forward, to stand in front of the seated King. "Your Majesty," he said, bowing over one extended leg, like a practiced courtier.

"General Balcor," the King answered. "A good afternoon to you. We are glad to welcome you back in Apapa and are ready to meet this embassy, which has traveled from such a distance to do us honor."

The General wasted no words, but set right to his task. "I present first Andrew Robert Von Bauer Cozart, the Baron Barthold, who has come in embassy from Teodor the Third, King of your native land." Ari stepped up beside the General and bowed over an extended leg, following Balcor's example. The King remained seated but studied Ari's face.

"We did not remember that your family found favor with the royal house," the King said, and thought. "We have also not heard that the old Baroness is dead." Having cast doubt on the embassy Max had worked so hard to create, the King looked to the General, as if asking for advice, or maybe to warn him.

Balcor took only the briefest time for thought before he said, "The Baron asks to be permitted to make a formal presentation of his credentials, to offer you a personal letter from King Teodor, and to explain to you his mission in Andesia."

This apparently satisfied the King of Andesia. "Granted," he told the General. He turned to Ari. "We will receive you the day after tomorrow, at this same hour. If all goes well, your reception will be followed"—he glanced at the General, as if for permission—"by a dinner, during which we will hear from you the particular messages Teodor has sent me."

Did his father think Ari carried the blueprint of an escape plan? The promise of an army? What did William Starling, spy, expect from his King?

"In the name of my King, I thank Your Majesty for this hospitality," Ari answered, and he bowed again. "I am honored to be so welcomed. May I hope, at that time, to be presented also to Her Majesty, of whom I have heard so much good?"

At a nod from the General, the King answered with evident pleasure, "We would be pleased if our Queen is able to join us, and it is an hour of the day when she most often feels well enough to leave her chamber. So we can all hope she will be there. She will be eager to hear the news from our former home."

"I have heard, and been saddened to hear, that the lady is unwell," Ari said.

"She bears it bravely," the King answered, accepting the younger man's sympathy without self-pity. "As with all else of this world, it cannot last forever. There is comfort in that."

And what did that mean? Max wondered. Was his mother fatally ill? This was so alarming a thought that he almost missed the King's request.

"We would ask, General, to be introduced to the other members of this embassy."

"Of course, Sire," the General answered. "I now present *Señor* Hamish Bendiff, a citizen and subject, with skills in the world of commerce, where he has many times distinguished himself."

"Mr. Bendiff." The King welcomed Pia's father warmly. "We know of you from our sojourn in Queensbridge. We are glad to welcome you to our poor country, and even more will we welcome any advice and counsel you might give us that might lead to an increase in the well-being of our people."

"Your Majesty," Mr. Bendiff answered with a deep bow. "I will be happy to share what I know, which, while not in itself so significant, might prove useful."

"Then look carefully about you, if you would," the King said. "Any means of allowing our poor to escape the confines of their poverty will be, we assure you, most attentively considered."

That, at least, sounded like something William Starling would say, and Max looked at General Balcor, to see how it was received. He could read nothing on that face.

"Is the gentleman being given free and full access to whatever he wishes to see?" the King asked General Balcor, in such round and regal tones that Max felt stirrings of alarm. William Starling was enjoying this role, with its red robes and its royal *We.* He didn't seem much worried about his Queen, or his son, either.

"He is, of course," the General answered. "Of course he is," he repeated, perhaps with displeasure. "Everyone hopes that good will come to Andesia from this embassy. And there remains to be introduced"—and here he seemed to intensify his watch over the King—"the Secretary . . . ?" There was a pause.

Ari leaned over to murmur to the General, and the General added, with his attention still fixed on the King's face, "One Alexander Ireton."

Max bowed, low, from the waist, and felt the General's attention. Not until he was upright did he meet the King's eyes. His father's eyes. "Your Majesty," he said, a young man swollen up with pride at his place on this important occasion.

At the sight of his son's face, the King rose. Abruptly. He was seated and then he was on his feet. It was as if the throne beneath him had burst into flames.

Max did not know what to make of it. Neither, apparently, did General Balcor. "Sire?" the General asked. "What is it?"

But the King spoke only to the Secretary, as if there was no one else in the room to hear his words. "I did not expect to greet you here for many months," he said, full of royal anger.

And Max knew exactly where he was. He was in the second scene of the third act of *The Queen's Man,* in which the King's traitorous younger brother returns from a successful war, with plans to overthrow his brother and take the throne for himself. He knew his line.

"The winds blew fair for me," he answered coolly, swollen now not with pride but with arrogant confidence in his cleverness, a young man with every intention of taking the prize.

General Balcor intervened. "Do you know this . . . Secretary?" he asked, with just enough hesitation before the word

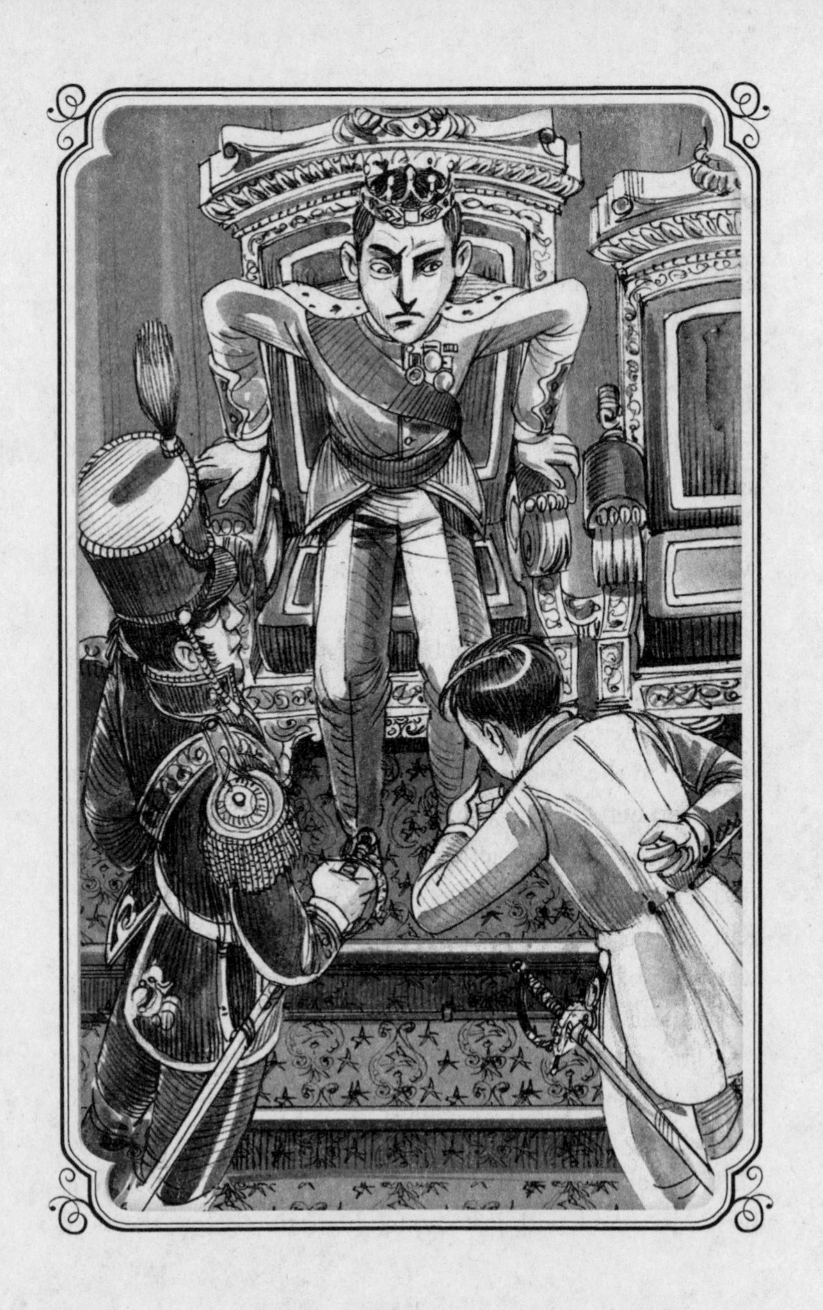

to make Max wonder if he had been discovered—discovered as only a boy, discovered as his father's son, discovered as a member of an embassy traveling under false pretenses, he didn't know which. Just discovered: and if so, in danger of his life, of all their lives.

"I know him too well," the King answered. *He is not welcome here,* his voice conveyed clearly, to all of them. "I know him to be a coward, and a fool, and a conniving opportunist, for all that I also know him to be my mother's son."

The room vibrated with silence. Ari and Mr. Bendiff both turned to Max, but Max looked only at the King.

The General said, "I did not know there was a brother, Sire."

Captain Malpenso stepped forward to ask, "Do we take him to the cells?"

"The man is not dangerous," the King said scornfully, at the same time that Ari pointed out calmly, "He stands under my protection."

"No need of prison," General Balcor decided, "not when the Baron claims him. As long as his presence does not disturb you, Sire?" he asked.

The King of Andesia had returned to his throne and assumed a carelessness that was obviously false. "We are in no danger from such a creature. We are only surprised to see him in respectable company—no offense intended to you, Baron."

How did he expect Ari to answer that? Max wondered, but he recognized the dramatic skills of William Starling, building the tension of a scene.

Ari only repeated what he had said before. "He is my Private Secretary. I am the Envoy of my King."

"That will be enough," the General assured the Envoy. "Have no doubt of it." To his King he said, "Let us make our farewells," and he bowed.

Ari, Mr. Bendiff, and Max also bowed, although Max carefully did not bow so deeply as to take his eyes off the King's face, an insolence for all present to see. They followed the General out of the throne room and back into the long corridor. Some of the soldiers came behind while others remained with the King.

Max did not take in the details of this corridor on the return journey, either, but for entirely different reasons. He was thinking furiously about what his father had told him, and acting furiously like a traitorous younger brother ambitious to seize the throne, and at the same time planning furiously for the next scene.

13

The Rescue

• ACT I •

SCENE 2 ~ MAX'S PLAN

In that small city, word spread quickly—but who spread it?—that the Secretary was no less than the King's brother. Despised and unwelcome, perhaps, but still, the brother of the King. Moreover, everyone knows how the wrongs done between brothers give rise to long-lasting hatred, even vengefulness. The Carrera y Carrera cousins understood this; they understood also that in such quarrels, no outsider can know who is in the right. On the whole, Juan Carlos advised his family to welcome the news. If nothing else, it made this Alexander Ireton a more significant guest at their table. As the King's brother he was, among other things, next in line for the throne. That evening, they welcomed him into their hacienda with warm attentions.

Max was no longer free to stand at the back of the drawing room or sit silently at the bottom of the long table. Just at the time when he needed to think with as much concentration and speed as he ever had before, in his whole life, Max had to be flirted with from behind a fan. He had to be flattered by all three of his hosts. He had to be included in the conversation at the head of the table, during the usual meal of the usual roast alpaca and yams with a chili-jicama relish Mr. Bendiff couldn't get enough of, the usual French wines, and the usual condensed milk pudding for sweet.

Like all other men who grew up together, like brothers, in fact, the cousins seemed to be able to act in unison at the same time that each tried to outshine the others. So that, during the long evening, Juan Luc and Juan Antonio made it clear that Juan Carlos was not the practical businessman they were, that his silver mine had yielded less and less income for years and he'd made no plans for the future, although they granted him a daughter who would marry well, and also granted him a superiority in sophistication. At other times, Juan Carlos and Juan Antonio were not at all interested in Mr. Bendiff's questions about the alpaca wool the natives wore. Only Juan Luc was willing to discuss the number of beasts an acre could feed, and the recipe for the spicy sauce, too, revealing himself to be little more than a merchant at heart, as his cousins pointed out. Max noticed that Juan Luc and Juan Carlos did not bother to disguise their pity for Juan Antonio, who had no sons to inherit his name and no suitors for his two daughters, and had let himself grow fat from his disappointment.

Max had to be included in all these conversations. Even Elizaveta occasionally smiled in his direction, and once leaned across Captain Malpenso to ask Max if he found the girls of Andesia as charming as those of his homeland. "Certainly *you* are," declared the Captain, as if Elizaveta had spoken to him, not the Secretary, and she drew back into her seat, away from the soldier, and insisted, "*Señor* Ireton, *do* you?" although it seemed to Max that she was more interested in *not* talking to Malpenso than in hearing his opinion.

However, "Charming?" Max echoed politely, and, thinking of Pia, wanted to laugh out loud. It was the grin of a thirteen-year-old boy that spread over his face, he knew, and he erased it immediately. But in fact, Elizaveta's restless glance had returned to Ari, whom she asked, "Did you know who he was?" and Max could see that Ari did not know how to answer that question, so he knocked over his glass of wine.

In the ensuing confusion of apology and gracious acceptance, Max tried to signal to Ari that they should leave as soon as possible.

Once back in the guesthouse, Max gathered everyone together in the sitting room. The others each took a chair, but Max was too agitated to stay still. "It's *The Queen's Man,*" he told them, looking down at the six faces that watched him. "Gra—I mean, Mrs. Sevin knows it, but I'll summarize it for the rest of you." He paced, and told the story.

"It starts in a garden. A young noblewoman is asking her old Nurse for advice about which of three suitors she should accept. Two are of royal blood, one the eldest son and heir to the throne, the other his younger brother. The third is a fine young man of noble birth. All three are possible matches for her. The Nurse asks if she loves any of them, and she does, she loves the eldest son. Except—which is the point of the scene, the *except.*" He remembered, "My father calls scenes like this the 'excepting scenes,' because without them the action of a play won't start . . ."

Max was momentarily distracted from his tale-telling by the unwelcome memory of the way the King had watched the General—his jailer? adviser? prime minister?—during the interview. It felt suddenly as if the mountains had moved closer, closing in on the embassy, to trap them. He felt sharply, as sharply as he might feel his fingers burning on a pot handle, his own ignorance. There was too much he didn't know. He turned his back to the listening people and looked at the shuttered and barred windows of the room, beyond which stood soldiers to keep them safe (but from whom?) or to block their escape (again, from whom?), and beyond the soldiers rose those mountains.

But if this was a trap, wouldn't his father have warned him? Hadn't his father called for help? Could Max have misunderstood everything?

"Wake up, Eyes!" Tomi urged, more loudly than was necessary.

"I know the story, I can tell it," Grammie offered.

"No," Tomi advised. "Let him tell it. He'll have a plan."

Tomi was right, and he'd been right to shake Max out of his nightmare. How did Tomi know so much about him? Max wondered, with a curious glance at the stocky boy, who never seemed out of sorts or out of hope. Was he going to end this rescue mission with a friend as well as parents? At that question, Max felt his spirits rise.

He picked up the thread of the story. "The first *except* is: The young woman knows that the younger brother is eaten up with jealousy, about everything having to do with his older brother, and also that he is capable of doing anything, however wrong, to get what he wants. So if she agrees to marry the one she loves, that may be what causes his brother to attack him, destroy him somehow, maybe even murder him. The nobleman, on the other hand, is noble in nature as well as birth, and he is truly devoted to her. He would make her a good husband, and marrying him would keep her true love safe. *Except,* she doesn't love him. Although she feels real friendship for him, and pity because she can't answer his feelings. *Except,* the surest way to know what might threaten her beloved would be for her to marry his younger brother—who makes her skin crawl. In the opening scene, she is asking the Nurse what the right thing to do is."

He had everybody's attention now, although Mr. Bendiff looked a little impatient, as if he wanted to ask, *What's the point of all this?*

"What the Nurse says to her is, 'To marry for fear or for pity, that's a great wrong; 'tis best to marry only for love, since a wrong can give birth only to greater wrongs.' So the Nurse advises her to marry the older brother, the one she loves, the King-to-be."

Colly wondered, "Couldn't she just not marry any of them?"

Max laughed. "Of course she could, but then there would be no play. At the end of act one, she marries the older brother. At the start of act two, which takes place not long after, the old King dies, her husband assumes the throne, and she becomes Queen. The third suitor, the nobleman, becomes the Queen's Man, and protects her from the younger brother, who spreads rumors that she's unfaithful to her husband, and claims that she is scheming with him to make him King, with her as *his* Queen. He's the King's only brother, and the King will not see how dangerous he is until, in a blind fury at a banquet, the brother draws a knife on the Queen, who by then is very pregnant with their first child. The Queen's Man swats the knife out of his hand, and at that point even the King acknowledges the danger."

"But of course it's his brother," said Colly, so swallowed up by the story that he leaned forward in his seat, to hear as soon as possible what would happen next.

Max told it more quickly. "At the end of act two, to keep his wife safe, the King makes his brother a general and sends him off to a distant war, with the idea that he will be gone for years. In act three, the brother returns unexpectedly. He finds out that the Queen has had a son, which means that now one more person stands between him and the throne. He tries to kill the child, but the King catches him at it, stops him, and accuses him of treason. The brother, because he is of royal blood, has the right to a trial by duel, against someone of noble birth. The King has to accept the challenge. He doesn't want to, but the younger brother has forced his hand. So the Queen's Man steps in, to fight the duel with the brother, because if *he* loses and the brother goes free, he'll still have been unmasked before everyone. And if he wins, the Queen and her son will be safe. But if the King fights and loses, the brother will rule as regent, so the child will be at risk, and the Queen, too. Even if the King fights and wins, he'll have killed his own brother. So. At the climax, there's a duel in which the Queen's Man kills the younger brother."

"That's the end?" Colly asked.

For Max's purposes it was, but he understood Colly's curiosity. "There's a final scene," he told the boy. "The denouement. The Queen's Man goes to see the old Nurse to tell her he's emigrating to Brazil, because now the Queen is safe, and her son, too. Moreover, the King wishes to be the one who protects her, as he should be. 'I've done all I can,' the Queen's Man tells the Nurse as he's exiting the stage, 'I've done my best.' And she answers—it's the last line of the play—'What more than his best should a man ask of himself?' "

Colly nodded, satisfied.

Mr. Bendiff, however, was not. "What does this story have to do with getting your parents out of Andesia?"

Of course Mr. Bendiff hadn't understood the cue. Max shouldn't have expected him to recognize the King's line, and what it meant. "In the play," he told Pia's father, "when the younger brother shows up in court when he's supposed to be hundreds of miles away with his army? The King uses the same words my father said to me today, 'I did not expect to greet you here for many months.' "

"And?" Mr. Bendiff asked.

"And I answered him with the younger brother's line, 'The winds blew fair for me.' "

"I get that," Mr. Bendiff said. "I remember you said that, because you know perfectly well that the *Estrella* was a steamship, not a sailing ship. But what does it have to do with us forming a plan?"

"It *is* the plan," Max told him. "Because of the duel. My father was showing the General that there is bad blood between the two of us."

"He's going to fight a duel with Ari?" Mr. Bendiff asked.

It was becoming clear to Max that the kind of imagination necessary to be a talented businessman was not the same required for a playwright. He hoped Mr. Bendiff would be a good enough actor not to give everything away.

"A duel with me," Max said. "We've done it before, onstage, so he knows I know how. Only this time, I'll kill *him*. Or it'll look like I've killed him," he corrected himself, "and then you and Ari will insist on taking me back to Queensbridge to be tried under our laws. But really we'll be making our escape."

"What about your mother?" Grammie asked. "If you think I'm leaving without her . . ."

"Nobody would think that," Joachim said. "I could slip out and find her while all this is going on, couldn't I, Max?"

Max had thought it out. "She isn't of royal blood herself. She just married it, and she'll want to return to her own people. They'll be glad to have her go, that's my guess."

Ari had been thinking. "What about your father? How do we get him away? If he's supposed to be dead."

"We could fill a coffin with stones, pretend he's in it, and then sneak him out into the countryside under cover of darkness," Tomi suggested.

"Or we could put him in the coffin," Colly offered. "With airholes, of course, and leave Andesia openly, carrying the coffin on a wagon draped with a silver cloth or something else royal, and the Queen would ride with us, on her own mule, with a silver saddlecloth."

Unlike Mr. Bendiff, Colly did have a dramatic imagination.

Max knew the body would present a problem, but he was hoping that the solution to that problem would become apparent, once there *was* a body. "A false coffin isn't a bad idea," he said.

"We'll have to do this during the reception," Ari said. "With everybody watching."

"That's the point of it," Max said. "That's why my father cued me with that line."

"It seems risky," Joachim observed.

"Yes," Max agreed.

"What if you're caught?" Joachim asked.

This, Max had thought hard about. "Ari has King Teodor's letters to protect him, and you, too, Mr. Bendiff, because Teodor sent you as well. Grammie, Tomi, Colly, and Joachim are all servants. They can't be blamed."

"I'm the party's artist," Joachim pointed out.

"That wasn't an official appointment, and besides, artists are a little loony, you told me everybody thinks so, in every society. People don't think artists are dangerous. I'd be the only one in trouble," Max told them. "I think the rest of you would be safe, although you'd probably be thrown out of the country."

"But there's a little butter-yellow mountain flower . . . ," Joachim protested, which as far as Max was concerned just proved the point about artists.

Then Joachim fell silent, as silent as everyone else, thinking, until Mr. Bendiff, who had been huffing a little, shifting himself in his chair the way people do when they're waiting to see if anyone else is going to speak up, finally objected. "I don't see it, and I haven't heard anybody else's ideas . . . Not that I have one myself, yet, but I could, I'm sure. Are we supposed to just let this . . . this estimable young man, I grant you that, but are we going to let him move us around like chess pieces? Is that wise? When there are three grown men in the room, and a woman with a lifetime of experience, too?" He looked around at all the faces in that shadowy room and, being a person of some experience himself, saw immediately that nobody else had the same doubts. "I guess I have to trust you to know what to do," he said. "I hope you're right."

"I hope so, too." Max's voice rang with sincerity, because it was so very true. He could only hope to have it right, but because that was all he could do, he hoped all the more fervently. Then he did sit down, to set out the details of his plan.

"We have a day and a half. Everything will have to be ready at the time of the reception the day after tomorrow." He gave the orders: Grammie was to have chickens to slaughter so that on the morning she could fill a small, flimsy sack with fresh blood. Max would take one of the gold coins he'd hidden in the waist of his trousers so that Joachim could hire a wagon from a farm outside the city. "We don't want word of a family's sudden riches to reach Apapa before we're safely away." Tomi and Colly had the job of gradually gathering stones to equal the weight of a man.

Ari's part was to continue acting the proud Ambassador, and when the time came, to do anything he could to heighten the tension that would lead to the duel. "Then, when my father is lying there dead," Max told Ari, "you need to hover over the body and make sure no one gets close enough to see that it's an act. He's a very good actor, and people have always believed it when the Queen's Man kills the brother—there's that gasping sound from the audience, that's how I can be so sure," he told Mr. Bendiff. "But this isn't a play, people don't know they're the audience, and also they'll be closer to the body than they would be if it was on the stage. Afterward, it's going to be up to you to do your full Baron Barthold act."

Ari nodded. "What if the General doesn't listen to me?"

"If he thinks it'll work in his favor, he'll listen," Mr. Bendiff said. "That's human nature. But what about me?"

"Your job is to involve the Carrera y Carrera cousins in business proposals," Max said. "Believable ideas, I mean, and profitable, especially for Juan Carlos, if what we hear about the silver mine producing less is correct. We need the Carrera y Carreras to not want to upset the embassy and risk losing possible profits. If they're a little confused about which side they want to be on, about who to back, that will work to our advantage. Anyway, that's what I think," he added, because Mr. Bendiff would know more about anything to do with business.

"Well," said Mr. Bendiff, "I guess I might be wrong to doubt you, young man."

"Thank you, sir," he said. Maybe later, once they were safely beyond the boundaries of Andesia, if they did get that far, he would take a minute to enjoy the memory of Hamish Bendiff's benediction. Now, however, he had other things on his mind, not the least of which was his loss of invisibility.

The Rescue

• ACT I •

SCENE 3 ~ DANGER! DANGER!

Alone, Max sat on the edge of his bed. He couldn't do anything to make things happen more quickly, he knew. He had to wait—wait again! wait more!—through the entire next day and most of the day after. He sighed, stretched, and stood up to fetch a freshly laundered nightshirt from the basket of clean linens the servants had left beside Ari's bedroom door. It was not until he had the nightshirt in his hand that he saw the snake.

The creature was curled on top of a pile of handkerchiefs that had been under the nightshirt. It was an elegant thing, bands of bright yellow and sharp black and a deep, bloody red. Disturbed by the removal of its cover, the creature unwound—

Max leaped backward, up onto the low bed.

—and its head swung toward him in what could have been irritation. Or attack.

"Ari?" he called, but not loudly. He heard the movement beyond the door cease and knew that Ari had caught the urgency in his voice.

The words rushed out of Max. "Don't move fast bring your sword there's a snake."

"Where?" Ari's voice was surprisingly calm.

"In the basket of linens just by your door."

Max was transfixed. The snake had raised its head now, to watch him, and he was almost enchanted by its sleek beauty and its attentive stillness. He could understand how any small creature, any field mouse, could be hypnotized by this snake. He had his attention so riveted on the sleek, swaying creature, the darting fangs, the slitted eyes, that the first he was aware of Ari's presence was the flash of the blade, falling, to cut off its head.

Max's knees gave way. "What—?"

Ari stepped over the basket to sit down beside Max on the bed. Eventually, "That's a coral snake," he said, and his voice shook. "They call it the twenty-minute death."

"I don't know anything about snakes," Max whispered.

"I looked them up," Ari said, taking a deep breath, and then another. "I looked up poisonous snakes, and poisonous insects, too. I wanted to know the dangers," he explained.

"You saved my life," Max said, shocked, since it just then came home to him that he might have lost that same life, not two minutes earlier.

At that, Ari smiled quietly. "Then we're even," he said.

For a while, neither of them spoke, until Ari asked the very same thing that Max was unwilling to say out loud. "How did it get there?"

"And why now?" Max asked, since they seemed to agree that the snake had not slithered up the stairs on its own and then, tired by the effort, decided to take a nap in the convenient basket.

"Was it for me?" Ari wondered.

"Who would care enough about me?" Max asked, and he hoped he was right.

"You are the King's brother," Ari offered.

"But I'm not a threat to anyone. Though—why would anyone want *you* dead, either? You're a useful connection for them. Unless it's not the Carrera y Carreras, unless it's the General. In which case . . ." But Max wasn't sure what that case was.

After a while, "It could be a coincidence," Ari suggested.

"It could have crawled into the basket when Suela or Devera was taking the laundry off the line," Max tried.

They both doubted that. Neither one spoke his doubts aloud.

"We'd better be vigilant," Ari decided. "There was that cake bomb and— Have you wondered, Max—because I have—about the Queen's poor health? The kind of day-after-day poor health that slowly gets worse and never better?"

Yes. He had been thinking that. "Is there arsenic in Andesia?" Max asked unhappily.

How could he wait another day and a half if someone was trying to poison his mother?

"The world is full of poisons," Ari announced, equally unhappily.

And why wasn't the King protecting his wife?

"For that matter, we could have been poisoned at any one of these dinners. We could have been poisoned tonight," Ari concluded.

"Do you think we were?" Max asked.

Was it fear or poison contracting his stomach?

"Actually, no. I don't. If they wanted us dead, they'd have slaughtered us on the journey into Andesia. The soldiers, or Stefano and his men, and they'd have blamed it on robbers. But now they've taken our measure . . . and with this snake . . . and there's another dinner tomorrow . . . I'd better tell Hamish—just in case."

"Just in case," Max agreed.

Left alone with the limp body of the snake, he didn't move from the bed, but stared at the one small, shuttered window and felt, although he couldn't see them, the presence of the three peaks that hovered over the small city like great-winged, carrion-eating condors. The twenty-minute death. Twenty minutes, he thought. Twenty minutes and then—

Now he really was afraid. There was no eager excitement to it, not any longer. His legs wanted to run, run fast and away, and he didn't care *who* he left behind.

Except, of course, he did care, and he couldn't run. All he could do was be as careful and smart as he had it in him to be, and to make use of all the wariness and intelligence of the people he was traveling with. If they couldn't pull the rescue off together, it couldn't be done. This was not something that was up to just the Solutioneer. Mister Max, on his own, could never do it.

Reluctantly, they woke the rest of the party to warn them, although they all agreed Grammie and Joachim and Tomi and Colly were unlikely to be the objects of an attack. Probably, they decided, Ari was the target. He was, after all, the official leader of their party, its most important member. If Ari were to come to grief here, no other nation would send an embassy for a long time and Andesia would remain as isolated as somebody wished.

But who longed so desperately for the present isolation to continue? Balcor? Juan Carlos? All three Carrera y Carrera cousins? It might even be the people themselves, although, "Probably not," Max decided. No one would want to continue living like that, slaves in the mines, servants in the homes of the wealthy, subsistence farmers, or outlaws hiding out in the mountains, and always under the rule of a foreign army.

"It is, however, Balcor's army," Ari pointed out, "and his mother was Andesian."

"Could Balcor have family left in Andesia?" Tomi asked. "Who *was* his mother? One of the people or a Carrera y Carrera?"

Colly wondered, "How did she come to marry a Peruvian? Did she want to marry or could she have been forced into it?

By the royal family, maybe, or one of the Carrera y Carreras. What if someone wanted to get rid of her?"

"And what if she has relatives, who want to revenge the wrongs done to her?" Tomi asked.

"You mean by killing the old King? Then starting a rebellion and shooting at the new King, trying to kill him, and with that bomb, too," Colly suggested.

"Or is Balcor himself behind it all," Mr. Bendiff wondered, "so that he has an excuse to stay on and rule here?"

Grammie had an opposite idea. "Someone could think that if the embassy has to flee Andesia, Balcor will be replaced."

"Who'd replace him?" Joachim wondered.

It was Mr. Bendiff who raised the most practical and immediate question. "Who put that snake in your room?" he asked.

That puzzle at least was solved in the morning when, after stoking the fires and opening the shutters downstairs, Devera and Suela disappeared together out the front door, without touching the body of the snake where it had been laid out at full length at the foot of the stairs. They went out through the front door, and the soldiers did not stop them.

Despite the night's disturbances, in the morning the businessman, with the Envoy—and his Secretary, too, of course, because records must be kept—met with not only Juan Carlos and Juan Luc but also Balcor and his Captain. Neither the Captain nor the Secretary spoke, and their opinions were not sought. Balcor offered little, but he was always ready to protest when the discussions became overly unrealistic (Mr. Bendiff's vision of Apapa as a tourist center for hikers and mountain climbers, with restaurants and hotels and a streetful of shops offering special clothing and equipment for the exercise enthusiasts) or personal (Juan Carlos's insistence on the importance of elegance and sophistication). Balcor was interested in Mr. Bendiff's enthusiasm for the alpaca wool every farm produced, despite Juan Carlos's objections ("It doesn't have the weight of sheep's wool or the elegance of silks") and Juan Luc's protests ("If the women are carding and spinning, the men will have to work the fields and watch the herds, and who will work in the mines?"). Only Mr. Bendiff was enthusiastic about the chili-jicama relish, but he spoke convincingly of the ease of production, the means of packaging; he had many ideas about how to label the jars and where to offer it first, so word of its excellence would precede it into the marketplace. "This is something I know," he assured Balcor, who answered, "I believe you do."

Mr. Bendiff continued, "The people don't have to be so poor," and did not go on to say the natural next sentence, *The Carrera y Carreras don't have to be so rich.* That thought was unspoken, but everybody at the table heard it. At which uncomfortable point, Ari suggested, "Isn't it better for a country's economic well-being to have more than one source of income? If there is more than one product to bring to market, it seems as if everyone is better off, with more jobs and more ways to earn."

As the meeting broke up, the Carrera y Carrera cousins

said that, since it was a fine spring day, after the midday parade they would like to offer Ari—and the King's brother must come, too—a ride up into the hills. Captain Malpenso would ride with them, to ensure their safety. The businessman and the General had already agreed to talk more about the methods for setting up international trading partnerships, so they were not available. But the cousins were most eager to show the Envoy, and the King's brother, too, of course, the beauties of the countryside. Max didn't dare admit that he had never been on a horse. For a King's brother, who had claimed to be a gentleman, horsemanship was an essential skill. "Just do what I do," Ari advised. "Clamp with your thighs, hold the reins loosely, and don't be afraid. That's the most important, not being afraid."

Max was too anxious to even laugh. Besides, Ari wasn't joking.

Captain Malpenso brought out a large bay stallion for Ari, and Max could only be glad that he didn't have to try to manage such a huge animal. His own mount was a small, rather skinny gray mare, which was a relief.

Ari, however, wanted to claim the mare for himself. "She pleases me—I admit it—she reminds me of the pony I first learned to ride on. You know how boys are, I loved that little pony."

Malpenso asked, "Is the bay not a worthier mount for a Baron?"

"We wouldn't wish to be seen as failing to show honor to your King's Envoy, not in any way," Juan Carlos added.

Ari was determined. He took the little mare's reins in his hands, while holding her muzzle so he could look into her large, dark eyes. "Gaby, her name was," he told Juan Carlos. "Short for Gabrielle. Really, I would so enjoy it," he insisted.

Gabrielle? But before Max could try to ask Ari—how would he do that?—what the secret message was, if there *was* a message in that odd statement, he was told to put a booted foot into a soldier's cupped hands and thus was tossed up onto the back of the stallion.

He concentrated on acting confident. He might be a clumsy rider, whose skills could not live up to his boasts, but he had to appear confident. All eyes were on Ari, in any case, as the Envoy swung an easy leg over the back of the mare and settled himself into her saddle.

Max clamped his thighs tight and made sure his boots were securely in the stirrups. He held the reins low, as the others did. He hoped no one was watching him.

And they weren't, because as soon as Ari mounted, the skinny gray mare began to hop, and sidestep, and pull against the bit. "They'll like a good gallop," Juan Carlos promised as the stables were left behind, and the barracks, and they ascended the first gentle slopes of the hills.

The mare didn't wait for the others. As soon as they were beyond the corral, she took off, Ari leaning over her neck, but whether to cling there or to maintain what control he could, Max had no idea. He hoped his friend really did know how to ride, as he watched the mare—with Juan Carlos on her tail, although his mount couldn't match her speed—round the top of a slope. Max didn't know whether to be more impressed by Ari's horsemanship or frightened for himself. If Max had been on that horse . . .

Luckily for Max, the big bay was a lazy mount who never wanted to go faster than a slow, rocking canter. For a time, the Captain tried to bring the horse to life by riding close beside Max, urging the bay to follow the example of his more lively mount, but it was no use. When Ari eventually came back into view, the mare now sweaty and breathing hard, he greeted them cheerfully. "She may look like my old Gaby, but she certainly doesn't have her gentle spirit!" he cried. His cheeks were pink and his mouth carried a smile, but there was hardness in his eyes as he led the party back to the stables, dismounted, and waited for Max to join him. He thanked Juan Carlos—"And you as well, Captain Malpenso, for a most enjoyable outing"—but once safely back inside the guesthouse what he said to Max was, "It seems to be you they're after. That mare wanted to kill me."

Max didn't argue. "Do you think Balcor has guessed who I am and what I plan?"

"Balcor wasn't even there."

"If I wanted to arrange a perhaps-fatal accident for someone," Max remarked shakily, "I'd be sure that I was far away when it happened."

"I'm glad we're coming to the end of our time in this place," Ari answered.

"Because why bother to dispose of the King's brother unless you plan to get rid of the King, too," Max said.

15

The Rescue

• ACT II •

SCENE 1 ~ THE PLAY'S THE THING

When he entered the palace for the second time, Max did notice the ornate furnishings, the third-rate paintings, and the vast decorated ceilings. When he actually saw the anteroom, lined from floor to ceiling with silver, he didn't know *what* to think. Except that, of course, he knew exactly what he thought of it. The final, high-ceilinged chamber in which they awaited the King—and would the Queen accompany him? was Max about to see his mother?—was lit by windows so tall that even the mountains couldn't prevent their view of the sky.

King Teodor's embassy waited at the front of a small group of people that included everyone worthy of invitation: all the members of the three Carrera y Carrera households, including the doctor and with the exception of Juan Antonio, who as usual was needed to oversee the mines. Stefano was also present, with his wife and daughters. There were soldiers, too, too many soldiers, all standing guard at the doors, the wide doors through which the visitors had entered, at one end of the long throne room, and a smaller, carved wooden door to one side of the two thrones, which waited at the opposite end. Max stood at Ari's shoulder, watching that carved door, waiting, and reviewing in his imagination what would happen soon, and what needed to happen immediately afterward, and what they had to wait for the dark night to get done. He patted his jacket and felt against his chest the sack of chicken blood. He reached his hand down to take the hilt of his sword. He looked over to Mr. Bendiff, who stood between Ari and Juan Carlos, prepared to be an entirely innocent, entirely shocked bystander.

Grammie was a servant and couldn't be at the formal reception, to see with her own eyes her son-in-law and—as they all hoped—his wife. She wouldn't be able to aid and abet Max's plan. This worried her. "I should have come as the Baroness. I'd be a good Baroness, and if I had I'd be right there, to do whatever I can, and we might have that kitchen boy we've asked that Juan Carlos for, as well. Oh"—and she had wiped her dry hands on her apron—"never mind me. I hate being left out, especially now, when I might be of some use for more than my chicken-slaughtering skills. Ignore me, Max," she said. "I'm just . . . anxious, and I . . . This *has* to work."

"You would have made a great Baroness," Max told her. "You would have been brilliant."

"But then who would have kept the house, and cooked?" Grammie asked, and he knew he had said the right thing.

Now if he could only think of the right thing to say to the King, so that everyone would believe there was reason for them to draw their swords . . . Once again, Max reached down across his hip to touch the hilt of the sword he had put on for this very formal occasion. He was well-rehearsed, Ari had seen to that; but Max knew from experience how different a rehearsal was from the actual performance.

And this performance would be more difficult, because he and his father would be improvising the scene. He'd have to figure out how to cue his father, too, so that the scene would play out as it had to, with the body of the King lying in a puddle of blood and Alexander Ireton, through the use of Ari's diplomatic skills, taken into the Envoy's custody to be locked up in one of the guesthouse bedrooms, probably in chains, then carried back to Queensbridge for trial. Max wished he could have gotten a copy of this script to his father, but that was impossible. At least he could be sure that his father knew a play was being performed, and Max knew what a skillful and practiced actor William Starling was. Of course he could be trusted to play his part well.

The carved door swung wide. Led by Captain Malpenso, four soldiers entered, to take up positions behind the thrones. The Captain stood stiffly beside the King's throne, looking over the gathered guests the way a hawk on the hunt looks down at a family of rabbits, to select its dinner. Two footmen in green and silver livery, their bearing so erect that Max knew they, too, were soldiers, rolled a crimson carpet out from the carved door to the shining thrones, then stood at attention, one behind each throne. At last the King appeared, his Queen at his side, and the assembly shifted on its feet and inched forward. The royal couple walked along the carpet at a stately pace.

General Balcor followed them in, but nobody paid him any attention.

Oh, but they were splendid, the King and Queen of Andesia. The royal couple was young and handsome. Her silver tiara sparkled with gemstones, and on his crown each of three peaks was topped with a pearl that shone white against the gleaming silver. His long red cape was lined with ermine. His red military uniform bore silver buttons, the sword at his side was sheathed in silver, his boots had a polished glow, and his face . . . his face held solemn majesty. The man was every inch a King. His Queen, too, was regal, in a gown of white silk embroidered with silver threads that was styled high at the waist in the medieval manner, so that it bellied out in front of her. Their smiles were full of confidence, as befits a Queen and her King.

Max watched the royal pair, who stood smiling in the way that he remembered so clearly, the stars of the performance taking their bows, and joy rose up in him, a joy that was so warm and bright that he struggled to keep it from his face, out of his eyes. There was no time for joy, now, nor for celebration and relief: Their hands were clasped between them in a signal that Max recognized—*trouble.*

He took a deep breath. *Curtain going up!*

The assembled guests sighed at the magnificence of their monarchs, and a few gloved hands applauded.

The King stood in front of his throne, his Queen at his side, and waited. When the entire room had quieted to an expectant silence, he spoke. "My people," he called out, in a voice that carried down into the farthest corner of the long room. He looked into the small audience, but his gaze didn't settle on anyone in particular as he made his announcement. "On this auspicious day, we ask you to join in the happiness of your Queen and ourselves: We are pleased to tell you that in not very many months there will be a child."

The burst of air that emptied Max's lungs was not admiration. It was shock. And sudden understanding. And the recognition that he had been given the insult that would provoke the King into a duel everyone present would believe in. This was indeed *The Queen's Man.*

But could his mother really be pregnant? Had the sickliness of which everyone spoke been not a matter of poison but of pregnancy? Or was this a costume of pregnancy, a strategically placed pillow?

Max set about adjusting his script. The question of pregnancy could be settled later, but right now, he had a duel to incite. Besides, his father was speaking his first lines and Max had a cue to listen for.

Responses in two languages came quickly, and the overwhelming tone was that of rejoicing at good news. King Teodor's representatives clapped their hands quietly, as behooves strangers who happen to be present at private celebrations.

After a minute, the King held up his free hand to announce, "Be the child a male or a female, it is the heir to the throne of Andesia our Queen carries. We so declare it."

Later, Ari would report to Max that some were surprised to hear this, but at the time Max was too shocked to hear anything. Neither of his parents so much as glanced at him. It was as if they didn't know he was there, or as if they didn't recognize him. He willed them, either one of them, to just look at him. But he was the unwelcome younger brother, and both King and Queen refused to see him.

Juan Carlos stepped forward. "Majesty," he said, with a low bow, "our happiness at your news is large. But I must tell you: Never has there been a female heir in Andesia. General Balcor, is that not so?"

The General bowed his head, slightly. "It is so," he answered, and nobody asked how he had become so knowledgeable about the history and traditions of a nation his army had only recently occupied.

King William of Andesia was not dismayed to hear this. With a benevolent smile on his mouth and in a voice rich in royal wisdom, he proclaimed, "Into the history of every nation will come a time of change." He handed his Queen into her throne. Seating himself beside her, in his own silver chair, he went on. "Just as this welcome delegation is also a change, opening a doorway between Andesia and the great world beyond." As he said this, with a voice full of welcome, he looked at Ari, where he stood at the front of the gathering, General Balcor beside him, and he looked at Mr. Bendiff, at whose elbow Juan Luc waited, and then—*finally*—his eye fell on Max.

Fury, an overwhelming fury, burned in the King's eyes and stiffened his jaw, brought heat to his cheeks and pulled his body up, out of the throne. He took two steps forward, and threw his long cloak back to free his arm.

Max knew that furious face and those two threatening steps forward. The action was under way. He met the King's glance with a mocking inclination of his head, and a smile.

"What is that man doing here?" the King cried. He raised an arm to point at Max. "In our presence. In the presence of our Queen. When he was so clearly unwelcome!" the King raged.

Max had never played the role of the evil younger brother, but he had watched it being performed; he had cued the actor, and he knew his lines. He put a hand onto the hilt of his sword and stepped out from his position behind Ari.

Ari ignored Max, and answered, "Alexander Ireton is here as my Private Secretary. My trusted Private Secretary," he declared, a portrait of one of the old Barons Barthold come to life, with the Barthold arrogant lack of interest in anyone else's opinions or feelings.

"This is not a man of whom the word *trust* can be spoken," said Max's father, the King in his castle, in front of his throne, with his soldiers around him.

"He is in my service," answered the Baron Barthold, unimpressed and uncowed.

Max interrupted, deliberately insolent to both men. "I think the Queen at least will be glad to see me. I think she might be very glad indeed to, at last, see me again. Is this not so, my lady?" and he glanced carelessly at the woman still seated on her throne, without really looking at her, because his attention was on the man in front of him. Max saw that his father had understood where in the scene they were. The King set his own hand on the hilt of the blade that waited at his side.

"My Queen is nothing to do with you, and she never has been," the King snarled, and turned to Ari. "No decent person would have to do with him."

"Sir, you insult me," Ari said, in the voice of a powerful man whose pride has been touched. His hand went to his sword, so that now there were three of them, ready to set to it.

The assembly had begun to understand that some deep and serious quarrel was afoot. The King sensed this and looked at his people, and his soldiers, and his General. It was Balcor to whom he spoke. "This is a private matter, General, between me and this . . . *brother.* It is an affair of honor. Let no man interfere."

By now the Queen, too, had risen from her throne, her hand placed protectively over her belly. Or her pillow, Max thought, as a nervous excitement bubbled up in him. He took a deep breath, to steady himself. He turned to reassure the Envoy.

"His insults are for me alone, Baron," Max said, speaking from deep in his diaphragm, as if he were projecting his voice from a stage.

General Balcor came up close beside Ari, and spoke into his ear, and placed a restraining hand on his sword arm.

Max turned back to the King, his father. "I would be the better man for the throne that has been given you. We both know that. My head is more worthy of a crown. The Queen," he sneered, "will agree, if you dare to ask her which of us is the more courageous, the wiser. Ask your Queen which of us is more of a man."

The King swept off his long robe and stepped off the dais, drawing his sword out of its shining scabbard. Max stepped out to meet him, as if they were two dancers preparing to join hands and move to music.

"You would still defend the . . . lady?" Max asked, in such a way that anyone hearing him had to know that he thought she was not one bit a lady. "You still deny what all the world knows?"

"What the world might think it knows is only because of your poisonous tongue," the King said. "You dog's dinner," he added, in a voice that rang out in every corner. "You perfidious pip-squeak," he said as the two circled, each watching the other's face and sword arm. "You ever were our father's shame," he pressed, "ever our mother's misery."

They had rehearsed such swordplay for many hours, and Max had his own sword out, his own line ready on his lips.

"To think that you"—he studied his father scornfully—"would be king of anything more than your nursery toys."

Each knew his steps in the fight. Their audience watched the two swordsmen cross blades, step back, circle one another slowly, each all the while attentive to the expression on the face of the other, as if they could read in the eyes when the strike would be made and from which direction it would come. Thrust and parry, two steps forward, thrust and parry, four steps back. Step and lunge, step back. The sharp blade swept close to an arm, and the watchers gasped. The duelists moved forward, coming closer, until they stood not two inches apart, one sword blocked and held by the other. Max angled slightly, just slightly, to show his father the bag of blood resting against his chest. "Take it," he whispered, then spoke to be heard by everyone, "Foolish move, brother. You always were the weaker, of mind and skill," and to keep the eyes on himself, he maneuvered his father around so that the King's back was to the watchers and only the Queen could see what was happening.

But his father did not take the sack of blood. His father stepped away, rotating so that now it was Max the watchers could not see. "Stick to the script," William Starling murmured, and the King cried out, "Now, vermin! Die!"

In the play, this was the cue for the brother to take two steps back, hold his own sword out before him, and lunge, so that when the Queen's Man shifted his stance, the villain impaled himself on his adversary's blade. But that was not the

script Max had written for this occasion, so he moved back, sideways, and parried his father's stroke. "I think *not,*" he grunted, as if with the shock of the two blades meeting. "It is *you* who will fall," he explained softly, once again showing the sack of blood attached to his shirt.

"Fool!" his father cried, and lunged as if he meant to drive his sword straight into Max's heart.

At that moment, the Queen cried out—

And Max looked back at her, *What?*

—A woman's voice shrieked, *"¡La reina!"* and a man observed, "She's fainted!" and someone else, another woman, cried out, *"¡El bebé!"* and his father's sword pierced the sack of blood.

Max had no choice. He was flummoxed. He was helpless. He was furious. He crumpled to the ground, facedown, positioned so that blood would ooze out from under his chest in the direction of the watchers. He had his face turned away from them so he only heard them gasp, *"¡El secretario!"*

"Is he dead?" was asked repeatedly in two languages.

"Has the King killed the Secretary?"

From where he lay, Max could see only his mother, sunk down into her throne with her head folded over her chest and her hands clutching at the carved silver arms. Her tiara clattered down onto the marble floor, and then two women came and bent over her. Max couldn't turn his head to see more clearly what was happening to her. Also, he had to keep his gaze a blank. Any soldier would know the living from the dead.

While Max was stretched out on the ground, and unable to move, something happened behind him. He heard steps pounding forward purposefully. A man cried out, "Enough! Of these murdering kings, enough!" and there was the sound of a sword being drawn. What man? Whose sword? Immediately, there came a sharp, metallic blow and something bounced, clattered, on the floor. But it didn't ring like a fallen crown.

"Leash your dog, Carrera," someone ordered, and Max recognized the General's voice. What dog? What metal thing had fallen to the ground? Where was the King and what did his father expect him to do now?

That last question was easy: Play dead.

But what about Ari and Mr. Bendiff, whose parts had been entirely rewritten? What did his father think he was doing? Max thought angrily. Summoning Max, asking for help, and then not doing what Max told him.

"Clear the room!" Balcor's voice ordered, loud enough to drown out all the others. "You, too, Doctor, your services will not be able to help this young man. You, *Señora,* take the Queen to her apartments and call her servants. Her Majesty must be attended to. If these fools have set off a premature birth . . ." The voice did not finish the threat.

Why did the General want the room cleared? What was he going to do that he wanted nobody to witness?

Ari said, "I will stay here, with what is left of my Secretary," and it was a voice not to be gainsaid.

"I will stay with you," Mr. Bendiff announced.

"You, no," the General said. "You . . ." He hesitated.

"I stay," Ari announced, iron and steel.

"On your own head be it, but you, *Señor* Bendiff, will witness that he stays of his own free will."

"Dead or alive, the young man is here under my protection, Hamish," Ari said calmly. "You might begin to pack our bags, however, since I sense that our visit here draws to a close. And you might see if there is a coffin to be had—send the boys to ask."

General Balcor gave his orders to the soldiers. "Escort the foreigner out of the chamber. See that he gets back to the guesthouse undisturbed." Or at least, Max assumed those were the orders, since he recognized only two or three of the words.

There was movement behind Max, there were many footsteps walking away and voices murmuring, but he could see nothing of what was happening. He concentrated on gazing blankly and on shallow, imperceptible breathing. His father's boots moved into view. The King seated himself on his throne again, and now Max could see how the silver, triple-peaked crown glowed in William Starling's dark hair. He paid no attention to Max. He seemed interested only in something, someone, standing behind the body. Probably Ari. Probably his father was wondering if Ari would be an ally or a foe in getting free of the General, and Max wished he could cry out to promise him before he made some terrible mistake, "Ally!"

From the far end of the room, the General spoke to his Captain, not in Spanish. "Malpenso, wait outside with four men. I'll need them." Then came the echoing sound of the great doors being closed.

Nobody spoke.

Booted footsteps were returning down the long, marble-floored chamber toward the dais; he could hear them, and his father's legs straightened as he stood up, ready.

Clap, clap, clap: One pair of hands clapped slowly.

Clap, clap, the sound coming closer, the footsteps coming closer.

Max saw the angle of the bloody sword change, as if his father was preparing to use it again.

The footsteps stopped just before they came to Max. *Clap, clap, clap.*

The Rescue

• ACT II •

SCENE 2 ~ BALCOR'S PLAN

The clapping stopped.

Nobody spoke.

Max looked in the direction of the King's boots, with an open-eyed dead gaze. He stared at his father's boots, which shone like the polished marble floor. His father's brand-new and very fine boots. Max lay motionless and watched those boots and was furious.

He was, however, an experienced actor. He had been solutioneering for weeks and weeks, too, which also helped. So he did *not* jump to his feet to demand of William Starling, "What were you thinking of? I *told* you to take the blood and die. Can't you ever let anyone else direct? I had a *plan,*" he wanted to yell, right into his father's face.

It would be useless, he knew. He knew his father. William Starling would either match Max's fury with a cold fury of his own, because it makes better drama when there are equal opposites onstage, or he would turn it into something comical, and Max could think of at least two ways to do that, comical and therefore ridiculous and not to be taken seriously. Max knew his father too well, and he was too much the experienced actor and Solutioneer to give way to his feelings, but all the same, he was deep-down angry.

He had no idea what his father had in mind, or what it had to do with *The Queen's Man.* He had no idea what might happen next, now that what he had arranged to happen had been rendered impossible.

A boot nudged against his ribs.

Max did not respond.

The book kicked at his hip, not gently.

The King spoke. "It was a duel, General," he said, in a voice that combined confidence in the rightness of what he'd done with apology for having done it. "My quarrel with that man—not a good man, not an honest man—goes back—"

"But not a bad actor," the General interrupted. "For a boy."

Silence spread like spilt milk out from the group of three standing men. Max could almost hear his father's brain working, the gears separating, then joining up in a new position, spinning. He could have laughed. It served his father right. If he hadn't been playing dead, he would have laughed . . . And if the situation hadn't been so serious, he knew, his father might well have joined in.

"You might as well get up, young man, and let me look at the damage you've done to the floor," General Balcor said.

Max rolled over and stood, blood on his shirt, his eyes on the General and not anybody else. Balcor said, "I think you will be the son, Maximilian, although I did think you younger." Before Max could respond in any way, the General turned to the two men. "How could you think I didn't remember about the son, William? How could you think I would not see through those ridiculous messages you sent? How great a fool do you think I am?"

"Not a fool," answered William Starling, in the voice of Lorenzo Apiedi. "A tyrant."

Max had to admire his father.

"But you"—Balcor turned to Ari—"you I did not expect. You are not an actor, I think, and you may well be a Baron."

"I am," Ari answered, without any apology or excuse or explanation.

Max had to admire Ari, too. And now Max wondered: Could he admire himself, Max Starling? He hoped so.

"I'll see those credentials," the General said. He held out his hand and Ari passed over the leather file that held Teodor's letters. They all waited while the General read, slowly, then closed the file and returned it to Ari. "I think *Señor* Bendiff also is not an actor?" Balcor asked.

"No," Ari answered, calmly.

"You are, then, a genuine embassy. Interesting," Balcor said.

"Is she really going to have a baby?" Max asked his father,

as if General Balcor was not even in the room with them, as if even if the General *was* in the room with them he was not someone to worry about.

"What do you think?" William Starling answered.

"I don't know *what* to think," Max said, impatient with this *acting.* "It's also possible—isn't it?—that the rumors are correct and she's being slowly poisoned." His father received this news with a thoughtful nod. "There was also," and here Max turned to the General and looked the man in the eye, perhaps accusing him, "a coral snake put in our rooms, hidden in a basket of clean laundry." Now he, too, became Lorenzo Apiedi, with a gallant, careless smile. "Which I thought was intended for the Baron, but afterward, when there was the matter of a horse . . ." That story he let Ari tell.

"A half-broken, hard-mouthed little mare was brought out for an unskilled rider. Which is to say, for Max," Ari said. "Except, of course, I have had experience of horses and claimed her for myself. It would seem that someone was unhappy to find the King had a brother to add to the line of succession."

The General said, thoughtfully, "That news had not reached me."

William Starling had not heard it, either. "If these are attacks, and one cannot think of them as anything else, one wonders," he said, speaking slowly, the Absentminded Professor thinking aloud, "*who* is behind them. And what that person is after, specifically. Although, in general," he went on in a vague, thoughtful voice, "it's clear that profit and power are on the table here."

"You will have your suspicions," the General said to the King.

"One knows history," the rather boring Absentminded Professor responded. Then King William of Andesia boldly looked his captor in the eyes. "It is not unheard of for a man, a gifted soldier, to lead a liberating army into a nation which has been ground down under the heel of tyranny, and, when the events have played themselves out, for that man to become the . . . Governor, or President-for-Life, or even himself the King. And if that soldier had himself some ties to the land . . . if he was—say—himself the son of a native-born woman? After enough disaster, it would seem natural for him to be asked to assume the rule. Natural, also," William Starling concluded, now accusing, "for him to be ambitious to rule."

"I see," said the General.

"Revenge, as well, might come into the play," William Starling added carelessly. "If a gifted soldier felt slighted, dishonored, for reason of his mixed blood." Now he played the Queen's Man, so cool-headed and quick-handed, no one could get the better of him, not with words or the blade, a man fearless for justice and his Queen, the perfect knight.

"Revenge for a childhood of humiliations, a lifetime of insults?" the General asked, almost cheerfully. "I can well imagine that it might." He seemed in no hurry to end this interview, and ignored the commotion going on beyond the closed doors.

It was Ari who insisted, "You will have a plan."

"I do. Given this turn of events, I believe I do. Since you are all a part of it, I will share it with you, although it is so simple that you can grasp it easily, dramatist that you are," to William Starling, "and diplomat," to Ari.

Maybe, Max consoled himself, there was some advantage to being too minor a player in the scene to claim anyone's attention. Such minor characters take no part in action or dialogue, which leaves them free to pay close attention to every word spoken by each of the principal actors, to note every facial expression, follow every gesture, and learn everything there is to learn.

"I plan," the General said, "for there to be in Andesia what has never before taken place: a trial. There has been a murder—"

"A duel," protested the King. "A fair fight."

The General made a dismissive gesture with his right hand. "There has been a death, a death caused by another man's sword. Now there will be a trial, as there would be in any civilized nation. There will be a public trial and the people will see that when there is law, even the King is subject to it."

"Can there never before have been a trial?" Ari asked.

General Balcor, commander of the occupying army, raised his shoulders and spread his hands, palms up. "Before the mines, before silver and copper and wealth, the people lived in small villages. They traded goods and skills among themselves. When there is nothing to gain by it, why would anyone steal? An alpaca cannot be hidden as can gold coins, in the waistbands of skirts or trousers," the General pointed out.

What *didn't* the General know? Max wondered. And just what was the General's purpose, that made a public welcome of this embassy suit him? If Balcor had known all along who Max was and that they traveled with a supply of gold, why hadn't he spoken out, to unmask them?

"When the wealth of the mines came to Andesia," Balcor continued, "it was followed by bands of robbers, their leaders ruthless men who accepted tribute from the mine owners and ruled Andesia by sword; in not much time, a robber captain proclaimed himself King, to rule over Andesia—until the next robber band invaded the city. There is no law in Andesia except the law of the sword, the law of wealth to purchase swords."

"You will put me on trial," said William Starling.

Ari had been thinking along different, more Euclidean lines. "If," he began, and he had General Balcor's full attention, "there is no wealth to be traded, there is no need of formal agreements between buyer and seller, and thus no need of law. If there is no inequality between one man and another, more than nature makes, then there is little room for ambition to grow to monstrous size, and thus no need of law to govern one man's treatment of another. But if there is wealth and ambition and no law, then who is strongest, or wealthiest, or even the most cruel, can do as he will without fear, and who is weakest and poorest will exist at the mercy of the strongest, and live in fear. He will live without the law's protections. Those people—all of them—will live by the will and whim of a King, or a Tyrant, or a General. They will live as slaves, as creatures, not the men and women they are."

"You understand me," the General said.

"You will put me on trial," William Starling said again. It was not a question.

"But if," Ari continued, "there is law, and if even the most powerful of men, even a King, is subject to the law, and if all the people see the strength of the law, then all will learn that greed and cruelty can be contained, and thus, inequalities in wealth and power will begin to be lessened. Am I correct?"

"You are correct," the General answered.

"I am to go on trial, then," said William Starling, who no longer sounded as bold and sure as Lorenzo Apiedi, nor like a King in his throne room. "Who will judge me?"

"I will," General Balcor answered. "I will put you into prison and bring you to trial and be your judge."

"For murder," said William Starling.

"Yes," said the General.

"Which you will declare to be a hanging offense."

"Yes," said the General.

"Who will defend me? If there is no law and no lawyer to argue the justice of my case?"

"I will," Max offered.

"You're dead," the General reminded him.

"I will," Ari said.

"He killed your secretary," the General said.

"I must defend myself," said William Starling.

"Yes."

"There is the matter of these attempts on Max's life," Ari said. "Where murder was planned, and the perpetrator has not been identified. Doesn't the law speak to those?"

"Why didn't you tell me?" his father asked Max.

"How could I tell you?"

"You could have found a way," his father announced.

"I was busy making a plan to rescue you and my mother," Max said. "I was busy being worried about you," he snapped.

"With good reason, as it turns out," said his father, with a laugh.

"Did you order the attempts, General?" Ari asked.

"What do you think?" asked the General.

"I thought I knew," Ari answered, "but now I am not so sure."

The General nodded and did not answer Ari's question but said only, "I do not wish my actor to spend too many nights in our prison, in the care of Captain Malpenso's guards. I can, I think, protect him for a day or two. I hope."

Max's father had grown pale, and Max did not think he was acting.

"So the trial will be the day after tomorrow, which gives time for the soldiers to spread the word and gather the people. You might advise your housekeeper to get rid of those two servants," General Balcor said, and he turned on his heels and strode off, down the long room toward the closed doors.

"What about the body?" Ari called after him.

The General turned back and Max could have sworn he

was swallowing laughter. "The Secretary? Alexander Ireton? I suggest you ask the young man yourself. He seems a nimble-minded fellow," and he opened the doors wide and called out to his Captain, "Malpenso! Take the murderer down to the cells!"

There wasn't much time. Max lay down again, to be dead, but asked, "Is she really?"

"Why else do you think I cued you from *The Queen's Man*?" his father asked.

"For the swordplay," Max said, from his position over his puddle of chicken blood.

"Then why didn't you die on cue?" his father demanded.

Because I had my own plan to save you, Max would have said, had he not been dead. He was getting angry again, as he remembered that by now they could be packing the King's body away into a coffin and Ari could be demanding not only that Max stand trial in his own country but also that the King's body be carried to his native land for its burial, with the Queen echoing Ari's request and insisting that she had to accompany it. His father had ruined everything, and now Max had no idea what to do.

It was possible, he knew, that General Balcor had schemed to bring William Starling to Andesia to be the final straw—that is to say, the final King, who proved to everyone the necessity of creating law in Andesia. That was certainly what the General seemed to be saying he wanted. But it was also possible that the General had done this so that he himself could become King.

Soldiers marched up the long room, boots loud on marble.

But the General, Max realized now, hadn't known that Devera and Suela had already left the guesthouse the day before. If they weren't working for the General, who *were* they working for? And why would *that* person, whoever it was, want the King's brother dead? He took a breath to ask these questions.

"Dead men don't breathe," Ari told him.

Suddenly everybody was telling Max what to do.

"I'll carry you out," Ari said. He bent over to lift Max into a fireman's hold, laying Max across his shoulders and gripping an arm and a leg.

General Balcor had flung open the doors, and the people gathered there drew back in shock as the handsome, redheaded Envoy, stone-faced, carried his man out and away, down the wide corridor. They turned quickly back in order not to miss Captain Malpenso leading the prisoner off in the opposite direction, the King, crownless and surrounded by soldiers.

17

The Rescue

• ACT II •

SCENE 3 ~ THE DEFENSE PREPARES

Max lay limp across Ari's shoulders, limp and lifeless, with empty, staring eyes and ears forever stoppered now—soldiers marched ahead of Ari and behind him; soldiers know death—as the Envoy walked wordlessly along the palace corridors, across the courtyard, and into the roadway, a gentle rain falling on them all, and the final few steps to the guarded guesthouse door and inside.

Max lay limp and lifeless, but his brain battered against its bony prison. *Think,* he needed to think, he needed a plan, a whole new plan.

When Ari lowered Max from his shoulders, "This isn't what you said would happen," Mr. Bendiff greeted him.

"It's not what any of us expected," Grammie agreed.

"What is *wrong* with your father, Max? What has he gotten her into?"

"What do we do now?" Tomi asked.

Max shook his head. He had no idea. He was so . . . foiled by his father, and trapped by what his father had done, and so angry, too, that he couldn't think. But he had to think, and think in some entirely new way. He needed to be alone and quiet, to think.

"We have a day and a half to figure that out," Ari pointed out.

"What about Mary?" Grammie insisted.

"She's pregnant," Max announced angrily. The information silenced his grandmother.

Max needed, first, to learn as much as he could about what was going on. About what the person behind things was after. If he could figure *that* out, he could figure out who that person was.

Was the object of all this the throne? The mines? Or was Balcor the invisible playwright-director and the law his real objective? Now Max wondered, and he asked, "Why doesn't the King own the mines? And if he never did, how did the royal house get so rich?"

That, Mr. Bendiff could explain. "Half of the earnings go into the royal treasury. Juan Luc told me it's always been that way, whoever sat on the throne. The Carrera y Carreras keep ownership and the right to work the mines by—it's bribery, really—paying half of what the mines make into the royal treasury."

"You know, Max, what Balcor says about the importance of laws is true," Ari said.

"What did he say about that?" Colly asked. "Do you believe him, Max?"

"I don't know *what* to believe in what Balcor says," Max admitted.

"If he's the one behind it all, and he's also the judge, your father doesn't stand a chance," Joachim observed.

"A duel is between two equal and consenting parties," Ari pointed out. "So it *was* self-defense. But if that argument fails—and it seems as if the General intends it to—we'll have to have someone else to cast suspicion on."

"But there were a dozen witnesses!" Mr. Bendiff protested. "Everybody there could testify."

"Unless they're too afraid to speak up," Tomi said.

Max had an idea. "What if there were no body?"

"That's not an option," Ari warned. "If it comes out that we faked your death, I don't know what Balcor will do. Nobody can find out you're alive, Max."

"We just don't know enough," Colly urged. "We have to learn more."

"Starting now," Tomi agreed. "Come on, Colly. We'll go to the plaza and see if anybody's saying anything about it, and what they know."

"*I* am going to finish my pot of chicken soup," Grammie announced unhelpfully. "Well," she said, in answer to the expressions on their faces, "I don't like waste and I had those chickens . . . We'll have soup for supper, at least."

"Ari and I can talk with Stefano," Mr. Bendiff offered. "I have the excuse of looking over his stock and giving him advice. We don't know how much he knows, and he might know something."

"If we knew how the soldiers feel," Ari said, "that might tell us something."

"I can do that," Joachim said. "With a sketchbook—what if I do portraits? I can go anywhere and nobody really notices me. I'm just a man with a sketchbook."

"What about me?" asked Max. "If I can't leave the house, what can I do?"

"Start packing us up," Grammie answered unsympathetically, speaking over her shoulder as she withdrew to the kitchen.

The others left the house, Grammie went to the kitchen, and Max turned to the staircase, to start packing . . . and *not* stew about what his father had done and the trouble they were all in because of it. Because he had to think, and hard, about what was really going on, and what solution he could come up with. Preferably one that would give them all the best chance of not dying here in Andesia.

At that thought, his feet broke into a run, his feet pounding on the wooden steps as hard as his heart pounded against his ribs.

Despite the steady drizzle, a few hopeful women sat at the edge of the wide plaza, *chupallas,* eggs, yams, and in one case a few pieces of woven cloth spread out on blankets, ready to be bartered or sold. They hunched under ponchos while a few small children ignored the wet altogether and ran about chasing a wooden ball, or battered one another with sticks. Tomi and Colly approached a woman who was offering three small woven baskets, each holding four eggs. They asked for two of the baskets. The seated woman assured them, barely glancing at them, that Balcor would pay, and then, when her neighbor spoke urgently to her, she looked up with a question.

By that time, the people in the market understood that the housekeeper and her two boys knew a little Spanish, although they didn't suspect how much. The neighbor had said, in a low voice, "Ask them. Ask. They will know."

Tomi and Colly pretended not to have heard. They looked up at the sky, where low clouds hid the mountain heights, and Tomi remarked, "Looks like it'll turn into a real rain tonight," and Colly answered, "Let me do the talking." Tomi had no trouble with that. He was a person who *did* things, not someone quick with words.

"At a nod from her neighbor, the egg seller turned back to the boys, looking up at them out of serious dark eyes. "You go to *tree-ya-la*?" She used the word in their language. "After, will be new King of Andesia and *Señor* Juan Carlos gives everyone a feast. With meat," she concluded. She spoke in very simple Spanish so the boys could understand her.

"Pigs from Stefano's farm," the neighbor added eagerly.

A third woman watched the boys' reactions. "But maybe this *tree-ya-la* is to make a pig from us," she said. "In a corral. Animals?"

Colly shook his head, to say they didn't understand her.

"Pigs for the soldiers to shoot," she explained.

"The soldiers will shoot? Shoot everyone?" Colly thought he must have misunderstood.

"Maybe it happens." Nods, yes, gestures of guns pointing, triggers being pulled, yes, that could happen.

"Not shoot my masters," said Colly. "Not shoot us," he pointed at Tomi and then at himself.

No, shakes of the head, then shrugs because soldiers sometimes made mistakes in who they shot, as everyone knew.

"Will you stay home?" Colly wondered.

Shrugs, glances, one at the other. "If we do not go, they will come to shoot in our house."

"Why?" Colly asked.

He was told, in gentle tones and simple language, as a mother speaks to her child, that soldiers do as they are told. "The King orders and the soldiers obey. Now the King has murdered a man."

"We are unlucky in our kings, we Andesians."

"Unless *la bruja* can bring the dead man to life again?" the egg seller asked hopefully.

"Bruja?"

Tomi defined it quietly. "Witch."

The women nodded confidentially at the boys. "We know. Suela told everyone. She feared to live with a *bruja,* and Devera feared to live alone with foreigners."

The neighbor was more hopeful, or perhaps she didn't want to upset the boys. "Kings will be kings and maybe the soldiers don't shoot. Maybe they guard and after we will feast."

"I have not heard the voices of pigs," the third woman observed. "If we are to feast, where are the pigs?"

When Max came downstairs for a glass of water or a cup of tea, with Ari's trunk half filled with carefully folded clothing and his mind half filled with possible guilty parties and possible lines of action to follow, he called to his grandmother from the bottom of the stairs. "Grammie?" Now that there was nobody but the rescue party in the guesthouse, he could use her real name.

But nobody answered. Grammie wasn't there, and Max was alone in the house. Where had his grandmother gone?

In the kitchen, a pot of soup bubbled quietly on the stove and vegetable peelings lay scattered all over the table. Max cleared up and cleaned off, and waited for someone to return.

Nobody returned.

Max went out to the courtyard and sat on the bench, and waited for someone to return. In the gathering dusk, his thoughts began to argue among themselves. His thoughts were not comforting companions.

Nobody returned, and the air grew cool, so he went back inside. He put a kettle of water on the stove and put tea leaves into the pot, to be ready. He couldn't settle down. He didn't like not being free to leave the house, even if there was nowhere for him to go. He wondered if his parents had felt that way, all these months in their tower, and then he wondered what his father was doing behind the iron bars of a dark prison cell, deep under the palace. And he waited.

When at last he heard the guesthouse door opening, Max almost ran into the hallway, to find out . . . something, anything, whatever there was to be known. What was happening out in Apapa?

"Max?" His grandmother's voice. Before he could say anything, she repeated, "Max!"

"Here," he answered, just like a boy in school, as he stepped into the hall.

Grammie was carrying a large covered pot in both hands, and Max was so relieved to see her that he was almost angry. "I didn't know where you were. It's getting late and you didn't say where you were going."

Grammie went past him into the kitchen. He followed. She put her pot down on the table, and when she turned to look right at him, he saw on her face a happily worried smile.

Unless, he thought, studying her, it was a worriedly happy smile.

"I saw her, Max. I went there. I decided to try and I went and I saw her. The baby is due in May, which explains the sickness. But she also made herself a pillow to look more pregnant so that— It's a *terrible* mess, Max, I don't know how— Where's Joachim, anyway? Shouldn't Hamish and Ari be back by now, to have time to change for dinner? I better put some water on for them to wash up in, and where are the boys?"

Grammie sank down into a chair, unwound the wet shawl from her neck, and said, "I *saw* her, Max, I talked with her, she's . . . she's all right. Upset, worried about him, and very unhappy, but . . . she's herself." Grammie smiled, remembering, then added, "It's a real mess."

Max poured the hot water into the teapot and set out two glasses while Grammie settled down. When they sat facing one another, drinking hot tea, she set off talking again. "She has no idea what your father will do. He planned to insist on returning your body to Queensbridge, that was his idea. I have to say, yours was much better."

"He's an actor," Max said. He didn't know why he was defending his father. But, "I guess the General surprised him as much as us," he admitted. "With this trial. How did you get into the palace, Grammie? How did you convince the soldiers to let you pass?"

"I looked them straight in the eye and told them my soup had special healing powers." Grammie was so pleased with her cleverness that, because Tomi and Colly had come into the room at that point, with Joachim just behind them, she boasted about what she'd done. "I gave them the hairy eyeball, the way I used to treat misbehaving students—one of them muttered, *'Bruja,'* and that's fine by me. *'Sí,'* I said, *'mágico,'* and they backed away. Chicken soup *is* well-known to be good for the sickly," she concluded smugly. After all, she had done what nobody else had been able to do. "It *is* practically magic, how much good it does. I guess soldiers are as superstitious as anybody else," Grammie said. "Which is lucky for me."

Joachim warned, "Don't be foolish, Aurora. You better

be careful. Those soldiers are uneasy and confused. Worse, they're nervous, and nervous soldiers make *me* nervous. Not a one wanted his picture drawn, not a one dared to refuse when I picked him out, and not a one said anything more than *sí* or *no* to me or anyone else. Not where I could hear him. You should stay close to home, Aurora."

Grammie laughed, "It's a little late for that, isn't it? What do you make of it all, Max?"

"Nothing useful," he admitted, but added hopefully, "yet. Maybe Ari and Mr. Bendiff will find out something from Stefano or at dinner."

Ari looked across white linen, through silver candelabra, down the long table at the assembled guests. Candlelight flattered every face, but especially Elizaveta's, and it caught at the heavy silver dessert spoons the way the sun catches at the waves on a lake, making the surface sparkle. The final course of that evening's meal was a cake layered with pudding and slices of canned peaches "from California," Juan Carlos boasted to his guests. "One read of this new preservative process, and our clever Stefano," with a nod in the direction of that merchant, "was able to procure them for me. They are as fresh as if grown in our own gardens," he was pleased to say. "It is very new, very modern." He smiled, including everyone in his satisfaction. "My table offers wines from France, coffee from Brazil, and now peaches from the United States. Even on this unhappy day, how can we not feel fortunate to be the Carrera y Carreras of Andesia?"

Ari watched the reactions to Juan Carlos's boasting. Most of them, men and women, had heard all this so often that that night's claims fell on deaf ears. They continued spooning up their desserts. Except, he noticed, for Captain Malpenso, who smiled and raised a wineglass in a wordless toast to his host, and except also, he now saw, for Elizaveta, seated that evening between the Captain and Jean Luc. Elizaveta's cheeks were pink and her eyes cast down. In modesty or embarrassment? Ari wondered. She raised her napkin to her lips, though she had not even picked up her spoon. She glanced briefly across to where the General had been placed, between Ari and Mr. Bendiff.

Ari had been dismayed to have the General join them for the occasion. What could they hope to learn, with Balcor there? Which was, he thought, exactly why the man had joined them. Hamish, he could see, felt the same way—blocked, thwarted, frustrated.

All during the many courses of the meal, everyone had kept clear of talk about the trial. They had spoken of summer in Andesia, its hot days and cool nights, almost as if the General thought the embassy would not be long gone by then. Mr. Bendiff had involved Juan Luc, Juan Antonio, and General Balcor, too, in a discussion of how to attract tourists, what activities and amenities Andesia could offer. The General was of the opinion that the rigors of the journey between Apapa and the coast made pipe dreams of these ideas, and compared it to Napoleon's unlucky decision to invade Russia. Noticing her interest, Balcor had asked Elizaveta, "*Señorita,* why do *you* think Napoleon, who was a great general, thought he would be able to conquer Russia?"

Before his daughter could speak, Juan Carlos announced, "He could not know that the Russians would flee before him, cowards that they are, burning their own homes and crops, so that he must starve unprotected in a winter. Burning their own cities, too."

"*Señorita,* do you agree with your father?" the General asked.

The young woman shook her head. "I think that Napoleon had forgotten that he was a man, not a divine being."

"Dear child, why should such a great general think he was in danger of defeat by such a people?" asked Malpenso.

This she answered quickly. "It seems to me, *Capitán,* that any general who doesn't imagine a defeat enters battle unprepared. What is your opinion, General?" she asked.

At the question, Balcor bowed his head slightly to say, "I think you are not a child, but a young woman with some understanding of the world, and the men in it."

As he reported later, when the rescue party had gathered together in the guesthouse kitchen, Ari was surprised by all that, and not least by Elizaveta's words. "Her father didn't know what to say. He apologized to both the General and the Captain for her inappropriate behavior. Then, when I told Juan Carlos we would not join him for dinner tomorrow, he became openly displeased. And yet, he knows that, whatever the outcome, we will depart immediately after the trial and must be packed and ready. However, at that point Hamish stood up to make a handsome farewell toast, speaking for all of us, thanking the Carrera y Carreras for their hospitality, which flattered them. He very cleverly— It *was* clever, Hamish, and not accidental, and you know it. He concluded with a reference to our absent companion, so sadly missed, and suggested we toast the poor lad. And that silenced all objections, because nobody had said a word, all evening, about poor Alexander. Not one word."

At breakfast, Max refused to spend another day hidden away in the guesthouse. "You or Colly can take turns staying inside," he told Tomi. "I'm going with Joachim, I need fresh air, I need . . . I want to see something new."

"Won't someone recognize you?" Tomi protested.

"Not in a poncho. Not wearing a *chupalla.* They'll think I'm you or Colly."

Neither Tomi nor Colly wanted to be housebound, but Max had the ultimate argument: "I need to *think.*"

Joachim also wore a *chupalla,* but since a poncho hampered the movement of his arms, he chose his usual loose shirt. He carried his sketch pad and had a shirt pocket full of pencils, while Max had on his back the rucksack with canteens of water and slabs of bread. Joachim peered into the low grass through which they walked and ignored Max until, "Wait—" he said, and stopped in his tracks. "There's one. It'll only take a minute," and he sat down, opened his sketch pad, took out a pencil, and set to work.

Max didn't have a sketch pad. Alexander Ireton was a

secretary, Tomi and Colly were servants, so no matter who Max was pretending to be, he couldn't have a sketch pad. He sat down at a tactful distance and looked around, looked at the sky and the hillsides, the steep mountains and the running rivers, the small city nestled—or huddled? he couldn't decide—in the valley below. The more he looked, of course, the more he saw.

He saw the flower Joachim had been searching for, a single bloom, grown low in the safety of the grass, as if in hiding. Yellow petals surrounded the little dark dot of an eye of a flower that really was the color of butter, summer butter, when the cows feed on lush grasses and their milk is especially rich. Joachim drew it, and made notes on the bottom of the page that Max was too far away to read. Then Joachim moved to a position slightly uphill and started to draw the flower again, from a different angle.

Max breathed in the rain-washed air and felt himself settling down. There was so much to see, so many colors—the stone-gray mountain peaks slicing into a bright blue sky, the sharp green of scrub trees growing up the mountainsides, the browns—so many browns, so different, each from the other—in old dried grass and the mine openings and the roads leading down from the mines and the adobe of the city houses and even, when his eye was caught by a movement, the small herds of alpacas. He hadn't left the city, but he recognized them immediately from Joachim's pictures.

"They look like Sunny," he said.

"I'm working," Joachim answered.

Max fell silent.

He tried to think. They *had* to have a plan to extricate his father from the trap into whose sharp jaws William Starling had shoved them all—and why couldn't his father just let Max be in charge? For that matter, why hadn't he just told Max a long time ago about all those gold coins? What kind of a King did his father think he was?—because Max could have told him, if he'd been asked, *Not any kind.* And what kind of plan could get them all safely out of Andesia now? Max tried to think, but the only idea he had as he waited patiently for Joachim to fold his sketchbook closed was a question. "Did Grammie ever come up here? Did she ever get to leave the city?"

"She'd like it, wouldn't she?" Joachim asked. That seemed to remind him, "We should be moving on, it's been a while. Let's go explain that we don't need the wagon after all and then get home." He rose hurriedly and set off in long strides, going diagonally up across a hill.

But the woman in the high, solitary homestead shook her head, and insisted that the wagon was Joachim's. Glad to understand that this boy with him knew her language, she pushed Joachim around the house to a small wooden wagon, pointed at a mule tied nearby, and even thrust the coin he'd given her back into his hand. She shook her head. "After *proceso,* you will leave. Take wagon. Take mule. Leave Andesia."

Joachim turned to Max. "But we won't need to leave secretly, will we? However things turn out, we'll go with Stefano's wagons. Explain it to her, Max."

Max turned to the woman to tell her that it was all right for her to keep the coin. But before he could say a word, she grabbed his hand in both of hers and burst into tears.

When they got back to the guesthouse late in the afternoon, Joachim reported what the woman had told them. "She wanted to hide her children at the bottom of the wagon, among luggage. She wanted us to take them away, take them anywhere as long as it's out of Andesia. They'll be safer living in the jungle, she says. Her son is four," Joachim told them. "The girl is six."

"Six?" said Mr. Bendiff in a shocked voice.

"Only four?" Grammie asked. "Are you sure?"

"Why does she want to get rid of them?" asked Ari.

"The girl's at the age when children are taken to the mines," Joachim told them. "And the boy's going to be six in not very long, and this is their only chance."

"Actually, it's only the silver mine," Max said. "The littlest children are put to work in the silver mine because the veins are narrowing. The tunnels are small. Little-child sized." He had been imagining it most of the long walk back to the city. "I don't blame her for trying to send them with us," he said.

"Who takes the children?" asked Ari.

Max let Joachim have the pleasure—if it could be called a pleasure—of announcing their discovery.

"There's one soldier, he comes at dusk, bandanna over his face but in an ordinary soldier's uniform. It's always the same one, she told us, but they don't know his name. But I had sketches," he announced proudly.

"Could she identify him?" Colly asked.

"Well done, Joachim," said Grammie.

"Malpenso," Joachim told them.

Mr. Bendiff remarked thoughtfully, "One of the reasons Juan Luc is so interested in producing alpaca wool, I think, is something he said to me that first day. *Mines give out.* He's thinking ahead, like any good businessman."

"Are the mines giving out?" Tomi asked.

"Just the silver mine," Ari answered, speaking as slowly and thoughtfully as Mr. Bendiff had. "But I think—I'm right about this, aren't I, Hamish?—that when Juan Carlos talks, it's never *my mine* but always *the mines,* as if all three of the mines are owned jointly."

"Except we know that each cousin only inherited one," Mr. Bendiff said, "and Juan Carlos took the silver."

"But if it's Juan Carlos who owns the silver mine," Colly said, "and it's giving out, he's got to be running out of money. So what does he have to offer Malpenso for kidnapping the children? To buy him with, I mean."

Into the silence that followed this question, Max began to speak. He had thought he wasn't having ideas when he sat on the hillside, but it had turned out that he was. All during the long walk back to Apapa, he'd been organizing his ideas, and now, with everybody seated at Grammie's kitchen table, he could set them out, just as Joachim had set out his sketches of the soldiers so that the woman could put her finger down on the sketch of the man who rode off with the children held in front of his saddle, facedown and wailing.

Max began, "We don't know what will happen."

"Isn't that the truth?" Mr. Bendiff remarked.

"Let him talk, Hamish," said Grammie, so sharply everyone was surprised. Then Mr. Bendiff also surprised everyone.

"Yes. Sorry." He nodded, and gave Max his full attention.

"We don't know what will happen," Max said again, "so we need a few different plans." Then he listed them.

If his father was found not guilty of murder, they would insist that the King needed to accompany his brother's body to Queensbridge, where William could explain events to his family and where, also, the Queen could give birth in the care of her own doctors. "That will be up to you, Ari," Max said.

Ari nodded.

If his father was found guilty and sent to prison, "I'll have to figure out a way to free him and then escape the country. That'll be up to me. Perhaps the guards can be bribed with gold coins. You take the Queen and return home. Or wait in Caracas if you'd rather, although you shouldn't wait indefinitely," he told his grandmother, who nodded that she understood her assignment. "There shouldn't be any problem taking her with you, if he's in jail for murder."

"What if we stayed on to help you?" asked Tomi, eyes sparkling at the possibility of a heroic adventure.

"Thank you, but no. It'd look suspicious." Max reassured

them, "I'm dead, which makes me either invisible or a ghost. I'll do better alone."

Grammie grunted an unhappy, wordless agreement.

"But how can your father be found guilty of murder when nobody was killed?" demanded Joachim.

Max continued. "If my father is found guilty and sentenced not to prison but to death, then I will come forward. The real problem with that is that I'll be unmasking a false King and also betraying General Balcor's part in all of it. Both in making him King and in the trial, too. I have no idea what Balcor might do then," he admitted. "But we do know what happened to the last royal family. So in case there's too much . . . confusion"—which seemed the safest word to choose—"to make any sense out of what's going on, everybody should follow Joachim up to the farm where the wagon is and I'll bring my parents when I can."

After a long silence, "Was Balcor sincere when he said he wanted law in Andesia?" Ari wondered. "It all depends on that, doesn't it?"

"He did seem surprised to hear about the snake," Max agreed, "and perhaps also about the horse, which we know was Malpenso's doing. So it would be useful to know who Malpenso is working for. It's most likely Balcor, but it *could* be Malpenso acting for himself. Or in the pay of someone other than the General."

"Who is powerful enough to get him to betray General Balcor?" Grammie wondered.

"Or rich enough," suggested Mr. Bendiff.

"Don't forget those countries that sent in the army," Colly said. "Couldn't Malpenso be working for them? As a spy, acting in their interests, stirring up trouble, to destabilize Andesia so they can take over permanently."

"Whoever it is that's responsible," Max said, "if my father is sentenced to death, I'm going to have to come forward and expose the whole sham . . . And what I ask the rest of you to do is return to the guesthouse and follow Joachim up into the hills. Grammie? You'll have to bring the Queen."

"I'll help you," Joachim offered.

"My hope is that as a diplomatic embassy you'll be allowed to leave the country. If I can do it, my father and I will join up with you in Caracas. If not . . ." Max's voice petered out and he needed a deep breath before he concluded, "You'll be safe, and the Queen, too, because once everyone knows she's a false Queen they'll want to get rid of her. That's what I think, Grammie. If everything goes wrong, I'm pretty sure it's the best you can do."

Ari reminded them, "There's no guarantee that our diplomatic credentials will be honored."

"They don't want King Teodor to descend on them with an army," Max argued.

"I wonder if a private interview with General Balcor wouldn't be a better plan," Mr. Bendiff suggested.

"He's already announced the trial," Max pointed out. "I can't imagine he'll go back on that."

"I don't like you putting yourself in such danger," Grammie said, but Max didn't have to remind her that either they were all in danger of their lives or just he and his father were at risk. Which was clearly the lesser of two evils.

"I guess we should do what you recommend," said Pia's father, without enthusiasm. But Hamish Bendiff hadn't gotten where he was by looking on the dark side of things, so he suggested, "Maybe Balcor will pronounce him not guilty."

18

The Rescue

• ACT III •

SCENE 1 ~ THE TRIAL

As the sky turned from silvery gray to a rosy peach to a weak, distant blue, the rising sun spread its light over the plaza and revealed in one corner a tall thing, shrouded in black cloth like a statue waiting to be unveiled. In the corner opposite, water flowed down over the three-tiered fountain, as gentle as the dawn. A solitary figure sat on the rim, *chupalla* low, poncho hanging loosely over colorless trousers and dirty bare feet. He barely glanced at the carved wooden chair set out at stage left or the tall, straight-backed seat at stage right. He couldn't take his eyes off the shrouded thing that waited upstage, between them.

Over the long hours of the morning, the plaza gradually filled. First came soldiers, to line the sides of the space and stand waiting. Then ordinary people arrived, in families for the most part, wives clinging to their husbands' arms while small children swirled around their knees, grown sisters and brothers escorting aging parents, and only one or two women alone, as if an entire family had been stripped from them. They were all talking and talking as if they had months of conversation to catch up on, or as if this might be their final chance to say whatever it was they wished to have said to one another. Nobody, not even the liveliest of the children, approached the tall black shape. A wide space lay in front of it, like an empty stage. Max, who had left the guesthouse when the first band of light edged the mountain peaks, watched everything from under his hat, and he listened, and he waited.

Toward midday, more soldiers arrived. The parade had been canceled because the entire barracks was on duty at the trial. Then, as if a signal had been given—although none had—wandering children were gathered in and the crowd drew back to leave an aisle leading up to the empty stage. Four guards led in the foreign visitors, the Envoy and the man of business first, the rest of their party following at a distance, the two boys and the witch. The Envoy was in his bright uniform and the businessman had on his usual dark suit. The man who drew pictures came last; he wore his paint-stained trousers and blue beret, while the boys wore *chupallas* and ponchos. The witch was hatless, her gray hair and soft, round body disguising her powers.

Max moved forward.

Another set of soldiers now escorted the first families of

Apapa into the plaza. There was Stefano with his two pretty daughters, only their profiles visible under lacy mantillas, followed by his wife and four sons; then the Carrera y Carreras came all together, wives, daughters, sons, and the fathers last in their dark suits, jackets fitted close to the waist, white ruffled shirts, flat-brimmed black felt hats, silver buttons and buckles and spurs glittering in the sun. Captain Malpenso marched half a dozen soldiers in to form a line just to the side of the foreigners, a position from which they could overlook the assemblage as well as the stage.

As the Queen entered, led by soldiers and followed by soldiers, Max moved deep into the crowd. The Queen was swollen with child, it seemed, although Max now knew she was swollen with pillow, and she nodded a greeting to the embassy but gave recognition to no one else. Her bright brown hair gleamed under the shining, three-pointed crown. She sat down heavily in the straight-backed chair, awkward with pretended pregnancy.

The air vibrated with curiosity and anticipation. Occasionally, a booted foot shifted, someone coughed, or a baby gave a cry that was quickly muffled.

This was theater, Max thought. The stage was set, the action poised to begin as soon as the main characters entered to deliver the opening lines of the drama. Unless, he thought, this was the last act, with everything already set in motion and only the inevitable ending to be arrived at.

Max kept the brim of his hat low enough to hide his eyes but not so low that he couldn't look around. He saw his grandmother, Joachim at her shoulder, her eyes and attention fixed on the Queen's expressionless profile. He saw Ari, calmly resting one hand on the hilt of his sword. He noted the way Mr. Bendiff nodded across the aisle to Juan Carlos and Juan Antonio and Juan Luc, nodded to their wives and sons and daughters—probably noticing more than he seemed to, was Max's guess. He was immediately proved right when Mr. Bendiff's glance stumbled briefly on him, and moved on. Tomi and Colly must have melted into the crowd to become just two more heads under *chupallas,* because Max couldn't find them.

The sound of booted feet marching in unison announced the arrival of the prisoner. He arrived within a human cage of eight soldiers, all carrying rifles, as if they thought he might snap the chain that ran between his handcuffed wrists and require them to shoot. The soldiers escorted him to stand at what Max was calling stage right, too far from his Queen to take her hand, and then they stepped back to wait an arm's length behind him.

The King still wore the formal uniform of two days ago, now crumpled and stained, but his crown was gone. He had a two-day growth of beard on his chin. He stood straight and proud, unafraid, although when he looked at his Queen, he did not smile. His manacled hands hung down before him. His feet were a little apart, his high boots unpolished. He did not speak.

The General was the last to enter, alone and unescorted. His uniform was the fathomless black of a midnight sky and its silver buttons shone like distant stars. The General did not remove his plumed shako when he seated himself in the great carved judge's chair at stage left. His gloved hands rested on the sheathed sword that lay across his lap, and for a long moment he stared wordlessly at the King. At last he spoke and the play began.

"You stand accused of murder," the General said. "How do you answer?"

"Not guilty," the King proclaimed, and his voice rang with the truth of that.

They spoke in the King's native tongue, which only the Carrera y Carreras and the visiting foreigners could comprehend. A murmur of discontent spread around the crowd. *"¿Qué dice el General?" "¿Qué dice el Rey?" "¿Esta es tree-ya-la?"*

The General must not have foreseen this difficulty, because he had no translator ready. "Juan Carlos?" he asked, signaling to Juan Carlos to step forward. "Can you act as interpreter to the people?"

Juan Carlos seemed reluctant. "But, General, you have the language better."

"The judge cannot be also the interpreter. You are the most able man here present," Balcor said impatiently. "I ask that you translate my questions and the prisoner's responses, adding nothing, leaving nothing out."

Then Juan Carlos moved to the General's side. The stage now held the three men, two at one side, one standing alone at the other. Between them, impossible to forget, loomed that tall, shrouded shape. Two of the men, the General and the

King, faced one another while the third, the interpreter, faced the crowd.

The General repeated his question and the King answered again, "Not guilty," and the interpreter translated for the crowd. Then, without rising from his chair, the General gave an order. *"Capitán."*

Captain Malpenso walked slowly toward the shrouded shape. His spurs sparkled in the sunlight, his steps sounded like slow drumbeats, his long-legged black figure approached the tall black thing. He halted beside it and turned to face Balcor, ready.

The General gave another order, this time to the crowd: "Remove your hats before the law."

Max's hand had come as high as his shoulder before he remembered that he should not understand the words. Quickly, he lowered it, and did not dare to look around from under the brim of his hat to see if he had been noticed. Juan Carlos translated and Max reached up, again, to uncover his head.

And met the dark eyes—just for one beat—of General Balcor. The General's glance moved on, skimming the crowd, making sure all the men stood with uncovered heads, but Max could not look away from the unsmiling face.

Balcor recognized the boy by his eyes. He thought, as he had when he had first glimpsed him beside the handsome, red-headed Baron, that his eyes were the color of the mountains. Not the lower slopes, where livestock could feed and a hardworking farmer could grow maize and yams enough to feed his family for a winter, but the high, stony reaches of his mountains, worn by winds and water down to their iron-gray hearts, the three peaks that protected his country from outside forces and held in their bellies enough wealth to purchase a decent life for every Andesian. He looked quickly away. He had his own business afoot, and he did not intend to be thwarted by this boy. There needed to be this trial, however much of a mockery it might seem to the visitors. "Now!" he ordered the Captain, and did not trouble himself to see how his poor actor greeted the sight.

Captain Malpenso reached up and pulled on the thick, braided rope. The dark cloth fell to the ground, where nobody paid any attention to it, so fixed were all eyes on the thing now revealed. Max knew it immediately, although he'd never before seen a gallows. The wooden beam reached out over the small platform, and the dismal rope, knotted and ready, hung down.

"Prisoner. I ask again," General Balcor said, from the judge's chair. "How do you answer the accusation?"

Juan Carlos translated.

"Not guilty," the prisoner answered, for the third time.

Juan Carlos translated.

This two-language dialogue gave a stately pace to the proceedings. It was like a man crippled in one leg walking, step-drag, step-drag. Max felt his hands clenching and unclenching and tried to stop them.

"By what reason do you say *Not guilty*?" the General asked.

Juan Carlos translated.

"By reason of self-defense," the prisoner answered. "If a man is attacked, may he not, in this country, defend himself?"

Juan Carlos translated, but when he had finished, he turned to the General. "Sir, I was there, you were present as well, as were many of us, and we all saw. It was the King who first drew his sword."

"Translate that, too," General Balcor ordered.

Max thought now that he could guess Balcor's intention for this trial: to show his people that not even the King was above the law, and thus convince them to entrust their own quarrels to its justice, for which the General would speak. But when you are the only judge, he thought, the law is yours.

The prisoner-King argued his case. "He attacked first, with words. May a man not, in this country, defend his wife's reputation? Which is part of his own honor—and what kind of a man does not defend his honor?"

Juan Carlos translated. To these points, there were a few murmurs of agreement from the crowd, and the prisoner-King stood straighter.

The Queen, Max saw, never took her eyes from her husband's face. He noticed that his grandmother had moved until she was the person in the audience closest to the Queen's chair, and Joachim was still at her side.

General Balcor answered: "A man does not bleed from

words. They are not knives or bullets. Nor are they stones, to merely bruise. A man bleeds his life away from being run through by a sword, which is not the same as a sentence carrying an evil thought, be that thought false or true."

Juan Carlos translated.

The General spoke again: "Words do not kill. It was your sword that killed."

Juan Carlos translated.

"You are guilty," the General announced.

Juan Carlos translated, but Max was watching his father. The King's manacled hand reached out for the Queen, whose own hand lifted slightly, almost invisibly, from her swollen lap, as if the two could clasp hands and raise them in their old coded gesture, *Trouble.*

Tears spilled from her eyes and ran down her cheeks.

So. The play was done. General Balcor, as writer and director and star of the performance, intended to leave the King at the end of the rope and himself in power—perhaps on the throne, perhaps only the land's sole judge—to write and interpret the law. There was the problem, laid out plain and clear in front of Max. The solution, if Max could think of it, would have to put a stop to General Balcor's ambitions, if that was possible; in any case, it would have to somehow save his father's life.

Slowly, the General rose to his feet. He addressed his words to the prisoner, but his eyes were on the assembled people. "William Starling, crowned King of Andesia, the law finds you guilty of the willful murder of another man."

Juan Carlos translated, and murmurs ran through the crowd, in which Max heard repeatedly, as question and as answer, the word *ley,* the law.

"Therefore," the General said, "you are sentenced to hang by the neck until dead."

Juan Carlos translated this and a silence fell. Into the silence came Juan Carlos's ringing voice, "As is right and just!"

There was only one thing for Max to do, and what would happen after that he had no idea. He opened his mouth to announce himself, because if there was no dead man, there could be no murder. After that, the argument marched logically on: If there was no murder, there was no murderer. If there was no murderer, there need be no hanging.

But General Balcor's dark eyes were on him. And the General gave a short, almost imperceptible shake of his head. Shocked, Max hesitated.

Hesitating, Max wondered: Why that shake of the General's head? Why would he want Max to stay hidden? Because Balcor would have a reason—but was it the best reason, as the General claimed, the reason of law, or was it the worst, the reason of greed and ambition, as Max and Grammie had always supposed? More important, could Max best serve his father by insisting on his own plans or by following Balcor's? He could either speak up or stay silent, and both were risky choices. He looked at the General-Judge-Playwright and decided to continue in the role Balcor had assigned him—at least for a little while longer. He was a minor actor, no more than one voice in a crowd, what could he do?

And as if all he had to do was ask the right question, Max saw a chance. Had an idea. A good idea. A possible plan.

He slid backward, deeper into the crowd. When he was so hidden behind two men and a woman with a squirming child in her arms that he would not be noticed from the stage, he remarked to his neighbors, in Spanish that he hoped was convincing, "Andesians are people who kill kings, yes?" He said this as a man might remark on his good luck at cards or his pleasure at the taste of sausage. He must have said it well enough because there were a few murmured responses, both denials and laughing acknowledgments, as Max moved, backward, sideways, to another position.

There, "It takes a brave man to sit on the throne in Andesia," said Max, still low-voiced. "Or a fool," he laughed softly, and moved forward, sideways.

Murmured responses followed him, growing louder. At his next stop, which put him close to the front of the crowd and also to General Balcor, he proclaimed sadly, and more loudly, "We have become a bloodthirsty people."

"Who speaks so?" General Balcor called out, in Spanish, but he directed his accusing gaze to the people gathered close to the Queen's chair, as if the voice had come from there, even though Max stood almost directly in front of him. Max called out his answer, hoping that he might get all of his line spoken before the General found him. "No wonder it was a foreigner, a stranger, they found to wear the crown."

Now a woman's voice answered, in Spanish, "A foolish and jealous foreigner, and see what he has come to."

The General searched over the crowd, and Juan Carlos, standing in front of him, made an effort to quiet the people, many of whom were now repeating Max's words. Some added words of their own. "We should not have welcomed a foreigner!" "Why would any stranger wish to rule here, if not for the wealth of the mines?"

One of the Carrera y Carreras spoke out then, but which one, Max couldn't tell. "Good people, listen to me, please. What will this distinguished embassy think of us, if the blood of another king stains our land? Will they still talk of visitors, coming to walk our fields and climb our mountains and be guests in our homes? Will they wish to take our woven scarves and *chupallas* back to their homeland, as gifts for the women and men of their own country, if we are such a people?"

Several voices answered him. "What's that to me?" "We are beasts to work the fields and the mines, how would visitors help us?" "Will visitors protect my children from the soldier who carries them off?"

The King looked around a little wildly. "What are they saying? What is going on?"

Quietly now, Max asked a woman standing beside him, "Was it not that Captain with the eyes of a hawk? Who took my son away?" His question spread out around him, but in whispers: "Look, isn't that the man?"

Balcor said nothing, not to the King, not to Juan Carlos, but he watched everything, the prisoner-King and the foreign embassy, the first citizens of Apapa clustered together among their dependents, the mass of people that filled the square.

Sometimes his head turned to the gallows, and the dark man standing beside it, as if to reassure himself that it was still there, and he checked the positions of the soldiers who lined the outer edges of the plaza. He did not respond to anything that was being said. He waited for the right moment to speak again.

Max watched Balcor, and moved to a new position in the crowd, but he had no idea what more he might say to stir things up. So, like Balcor, he waited.

Juan Luc stepped forward and then turned to face the people, to ask, "Do you not see? If there are tourists and if there are people in other lands who wish to wear our scarves and hats, then any man who knows the hills and the mountains can be their guide, and earn silver for himself. Any woman who can clean a room and cook a meal can welcome strangers, and earn enough to add a second room onto her house for her aging parents, and ensure her children medicines. Anyone who can spin, dye, and weave, who braids straw, they too can earn for themselves, and the only ones who need go into the mines are those who choose to do so for wages. Those wages will be offered if a man can choose to earn his bread otherwise. Do you see this?"

Louder voices discussed this. The King fulminated and fumed and demanded that Balcor or Juan Carlos translate for him, but both of those men ignored him. The Queen sat tense, her hands tightly gripping one another, her eyes on her husband.

Juan Antonio finished his cousin's argument. "This embassy must not think ours is a violent country. If they do, why would they carry word of Andesia out into the world, except to say that we are a people who slay our kings?"

At that, Juan Carlos called out loudly, "I will not have a murderer for my King! Let there be an Andesian King for Andesia!"

Two things happened simultaneously. The King cried, "What is happening? Balcor, tell me!" and Captain Malpenso gave an order, and the line of soldiers began to move to the front of the stage, rifles held ready. Were they there to protect the General? The embassy? The King and Queen? The process of the law? Max couldn't tell, and they might just as easily have been there to fire into the crowd. People backed away from the soldiers, from the guns. Max pushed sideways to get closer to where his mother sat silent and pale, weeping, and he saw Colly making his way to Ari and Mr. Bendiff, where they waited, alert and unsure. Where was Tomi?

"¡Soldados!" General Balcor called. *"¡Alto!"* The soldiers looked over their shoulders, back to Captain Malpenso, who had ordered them forward, and then to the General, who had ordered them to halt. Everyone watching stiffened and got ready to throw himself on the ground or, in Max's case, toward the Queen.

"Return to your posts!" Balcor ordered, and the soldiers, obedient to their General, withdrew, to stand again at the side of the plaza.

Juan Carlos called out again, "An Andesian King for Andesia!" and the crowd rumbled.

Standing in front of his judge's chair, General Balcor considered this. "Whom do you propose? Yourself?"

Whatever the General might have expected by way of a response, Juan Carlos shrugged, and smiled, and bowed, accepting the honor. A few voices picked up the idea and began to demand it. "Juan Carlos for King," they chanted. "An Andesian King for Andesia." "Juan Carlos for Andesia." Some voices continued, "Juan Carlos for Andesia," while a rumble of angry voices grew in the background. "That Captain, yes, it's him." "I remember those eyes." "He is the man." "Let the law punish the man who took our children away. To slavery, and death, in the mines." "Why should his uniform protect him? We would see *that* law, too, in Andesia!"

"Hang them both!" a man cried. "Hang the Captain beside his King!"

Max looked at his father and saw fear. He saw that Grammie had reached a spot close enough to put a hand on her daughter's shoulder, despite the efforts of a soldier to crowd her away. He looked at Juan Carlos, who seemed to have grown taller, and then he looked at Ari, who was saying something into Mr. Bendiff's ear and looking around him, maybe for an exit route, maybe for Max and the other boys. He looked back at his father and saw fear vanquished by courage, as William Starling transformed himself into a King worthy of the name. Then, finally, Max looked at General Balcor. The man seemed, as always, a small person in a uniform, a small person made taller by his shako and made imposing by his uniform, a man with eyes that watched everything, with a face unaccustomed to smiling.

Small he might have been, but when the General raised a gloved hand, silence spread slowly out before him, spread over the entire plaza, until everyone stopped speaking. Into the waiting quiet, "There has been a murder," the General said in Spanish.

This the General translated himself. At those words, William Starling answered him. Even crownless, even with his hands manacled together, his royal nature was there for all to see. "I will serve the law," he announced.

An impatient and confused murmur answered this.

"Translate!" Balcor ordered.

"With pleasure," said Juan Carlos, who repeated the King's words in Spanish. *"Dice: Yo servirá a la ley."*

Desperately, Max called out in his best Spanish, "That is a true King who speaks."

It was Juan Carlos who answered this, with a shake of the head, denying it. "That is a murderer who speaks. In this land, who takes a life must give one."

"Captain Malpenso," the General ordered, and the Captain came forward, to stand beside the prisoner-King.

Even more desperately, because despite the General's shake of the head Max could do nothing more now than come forward, Max called out, again in Spanish, "Who kills a king is a traitor."

"It is the rope that kills," Juan Carlos answered, and added with a smile, "the traitorous rope."

Max stared at Juan Carlos, who was looking at the Captain while the Captain waited for the General to order the execution to begin. "Easy, Eyes," a voice spoke softly in his ear, while a hand on his arm warned him to silence. But Max understood it now: Juan Carlos intended to have the throne himself, to have the King's shares of the copper mines and the royal treasury, too, for himself, and for that reason he was careless of the failure of the silver mine. Was Juan Carlos, then, in cahoots with General Balcor?

As if to answer that question, Balcor moved to stage center. "Captain," he said, speaking the language of the embassy, "unchain the prisoner." He turned to face the people. "Translate that, Juan Carlos," he said, "and also this: The law will rule Andesia, and that rule will not begin with the traitorous hanging of a crowned King."

Captain Malpenso gripped the prisoner's shoulder.

"Will this foreigner be our King?" Juan Carlos protested, in Spanish.

"Translate," ordered Balcor.

Juan Carlos heard his protest echoing from the crowd behind him and did not obey the General. Instead, he repeated, "Will this foreigner be our King?" and the cries began again, "Juan Carlos for King!"

Soldiers moved around the edges of the crowd. Balcor drew a pistol. With one hand Captain Malpenso turned the King to face him and his free hand moved to his own belt. To unchain the King? Or to drag him to the gallows? Max shoved his way through to his father, with Tomi just behind him, and saw that Ari was doing the same, while Mr. Bendiff stood with the two Carrera y Carrera cousins, consulting with them, it seemed from the quick glimpse Max took. But his father was manacled and weaponless, and judging from the sounds behind him, when they were hidden safe within a mob the people did not fear either Malpenso or the General.

Max didn't know if it was the crowd or his own fear that roared in his ears. Men were pushing forward and women were pulling their children to the rear and he needed to get to his father before the mob did. Two to defend the prisoner was twice one, even if Tomi was armed only with a knife, and if Ari could find his way there it would be three, enough to encircle the King and protect him with their blades.

A shot cracked through the voices. Silence crashed down on the plaza.

For a long three seconds not one person moved, not even Max.

In that frozen time he saw: that Malpenso's left arm was bleeding and in his right he held a long-bladed knife. That his father had his eyes fixed on Balcor's raised pistol and had not seen the real danger.

Max hurled himself forward, knocking his father off balance and onto the ground. At the same time, one of the soldiers who had been guarding the King seized Malpenso and another tore the knife from his hand. Now the voices cried out in surprise and confusion.

The noise subsided, as Max dusted himself off, and in obedience to a small gesture of the General's hand—

The General was writer and director and chief performer, Max reminded himself.

—slipped back into the cover of the crowd. "What is happening?" was the question he heard, although nobody could answer it. "What does this mean?"

Ari had stepped forward to offer the prisoner a hand up, as if it had been he who knocked him down and saved him. Despite manacled wrists, the King rose gracefully to his feet and bowed his head in a brief thank-you. At the same time, General Balcor took two steps forward and the soldiers surrounding the Captain stepped away, so that the hawk-faced soldier stood alone before his commander. "What are you about, Captain Malpenso?" the General demanded, in a voice that filled the entire plaza. "I did not order you to slay the prisoner." He spoke in Spanish but did not bother about translation, as if he knew full well that the Ambassador could understand him.

Captain Malpenso did not answer. His eyes flicked from the General to the Carrera y Carreras, and then to the soldiers lining the plaza, as if looking for an escape. His eyes flicked back to the gallows and his face grew pale.

It was Ari who answered, speaking slow Spanish, his voice calm. "He was about treason, General. For the King is still the King." Ari then spoke to Max's father, translating.

Balcor nodded. He spoke pensively to Malpenso, as if an idea were just occurring to him. "I have often wondered who murdered the last King of Andesia. And his family. All of whom were under my protection. It was a great shame to me when they were slain, and a worry to me when some unknown assailant shot at the new King in Caracas. I knew you had ridden at the head of the escort to the coronation and now I wonder about you, now that I see that you are a man who dares to kill a King."

Malpenso shook his head, to deny the charge, but he had grown even paler and his dark eyes seemed to burn. Ari spoke into the King's ear, Max saw, and Grammie into her daughter's. Every other person in the plaza kept a trembling silence.

General Balcor continued: "With the aid of a chosen few soldiers, I suspect, and they are not so much to blame since soldiers must follow orders. A soldier who is following orders does not share the guilt of he who gave the order."

One of the men standing close to Malpenso was very surprised to hear this, and not displeased, if Max knew anything about reading the expression on a face. This soldier stepped back another pace from the Captain, putting a distance between them.

"And if I, too, was under orders?" Malpenso cried.

"I gave no such command," Balcor declared. "Not then. Not now."

No one doubted his word.

"You are not the only one to give me orders," Malpenso answered.

In the group near Mr. Bendiff, someone stirred, or several someones stirred. Max couldn't be sure.

"Why should I hang alone, when I was told what to do, whom to strike and where and when? As I was. When a bomb was placed into my hands? As it was. And I will tell you by whom. By Juan Carlos Carrera y Carrera! And I was promised his daughter Elizaveta in marriage so that my children might inherit the throne. If I did kill that King, and his family, how do you think I was given entrance to the castle stronghold if not in the company of Juan Carlos Carrera y Carrera?"

"Liar!" cried Juan Carlos. "He lies!"

Malpenso smiled, as a hawk might smile, sinking its talons into a squealing rabbit. "Ask the soldiers what they saw, my General. He has plotted to bring you down!"

Juan Carlos protested again, "He lies!" and turned to Mr. Bendiff. "It was he who had Suela put the snake in the Envoy's rooms." Then he turned to Ari. "Suela will tell you everything."

"Ask the soldiers," Malpenso repeated.

"As if I'd ever waste Elizaveta's beauty on such as you," sneered Juan Carlos.

General Balcor replaced his pistol in its holster and gave the order to the soldiers surrounding the Captain: "Take him to the prison." He turned to point at Juan Carlos. "Take this man, too," he ordered, with a gesture to three more soldiers. "Take him to the prison as well. Both men will be brought to trial," he promised the crowd. "The law will judge them."

This seemed to satisfy the people. Or it may have been

they were too stunned by the events to object to anything. The Carrera y Carreras gathered together, to leave the scene and decide how to understand and respond to everything that had happened. Before they had walked off, however, Juan Luc stepped forward, to announce loudly, first in Spanish for the people and then in English for the foreigners, "What my cousin has done, or not done, the rest of us had no knowledge or suspicion of. I speak for all of us. If Juan Carlos Carrera y Carrera is guilty, he must pay the price. We entrust him to the law."

The family left the plaza with heads bent to conceal faces that were shocked and troubled and, in one lovely case, shocked and angry. People stood back to give them free passage. The people looked to one another, surprised and silent, sensing that there was still something to come. In the silence, General Balcor turned back to the prisoner-King. "There remains this man, who is a murderer," he announced, now translating for himself. "There remains this murderer, who is our crowned King. Under the law, he must die. Under the law, he must not be killed."

To this problem, nobody had any response. All eyes were on the General. He himself looked into the people before him, as if expecting the answer to come from among them, and his eyes did not seek Max out.

But Max was the Solutioneer. He called out the answer, boldly and in Spanish, "This is not *my* King! Send him away! Send him out of our land!" He let silences fall between each

statement, so that each one could hang in the air, as if framed in gold. *"¡Que reine la ley!"* Let the law be my King!

When he heard his cries echoing around him, picked up by voices from all sides of the plaza, Max melted back into the thick of the crowd, to disappear. He left it to Balcor and Ari to work out the details.

19

The Rescue

• ACT III •

SCENE 2 ~ DENOUEMENT

Max returned alone to the empty guesthouse. He noticed, but did not care about, the absence of the usual soldiers at the door. He was not curious to know what people were saying, about the trial, about the unmasking of guilty parties, about the foreigners. Max's job was done.

Once he'd opened all the shutters on the ground floor, put a pot of water on, and set glasses out, Max stood at the back door, looking out at the courtyard, at the stone tower, at the high peaks looming over everything, and it was not so very long before his mother's voice called, "Max?"

They met at the kitchen door. For a long, satisfying, silent time, all he did was stand with her arms wrapped around him and his own arms wrapped around her. He felt the pillow that covered her waist, and grinned to himself at the pillow-shaped deceit they both employed. They were alike, he and his mother.

Eventually, they stepped back, to smile at one another. Grammie took advantage of the situation to move behind Max and pour hot water into the teapot, but she knew better than to say anything. It was one of the many good things about Grammie, Max thought—although he did not look away from the face he was seeing for the first time in months to think it, and he could not take the smile from his own face—the way she knew better than to interrupt strong feelings with words.

When they were seated at the table, however, it was different. "Where's . . . ," Max began, but didn't know what to call his father. My father? The King? But he didn't need to name him, because William Starling was always at the center of his wife's world.

"I think . . . I *hope* General Balcor will put him into the custody of that Baron."

"What else can he do, after pronouncing him guilty?" Max asked.

"We can be sure he has a plan," his mother said. "I only hope that was the last scene we just played."

"What else can happen?" That was Joachim, who entered the kitchen and the conversation at the same time, and fully expected some dismal response to his question.

"Sit down, have some tea," Grammie greeted him.

Joachim didn't take a seat until he had bowed to the Queen. "I don't know if you remember me."

"Of course I do. It hasn't been *that* long."

"It feels long to me," Max said, but not unhappily.

"Certainly not long enough to make me forget Joachim," his mother said.

"Are you really having a baby?" Max asked her then. He knew she was. Grammie had told him she was. But for some reason, he wanted his mother to tell him herself that she was.

She laughed. "When you see me in my morning miseries you'll know for sure."

"Will you be sick all the way until May?"

She laughed again, and told him, "The pregnancy lasts until May, but the morning sickness has already started getting better. How do you feel about becoming a brother, at your age?"

"Pretty good," Max said. "I'm too old to be jealous."

She looked him in the eye, doubting this.

"Not of a baby brother or sister," he specified. "I'm not a child. And yes," he added, "I do know a person of any age can be jealous. But that would be about other things." What he didn't say, because it might hurt her feelings, was that it was sort of a relief to think of them having someone else to take up their attention, because that would leave him more free to live his own life.

"Don't underestimate the boy," Grammie warned. Max signaled her to not say more, with widened eyes that he hoped his mother wouldn't notice.

Luckily, his mother's attention had turned to Joachim. "I

know who you are, but what are you doing here?" she asked. "Here now, I mean. Here with Max and my mother."

"I'm making pictures. Drawing the flora, the people, the landscape, whatever I see that makes a picture. Officially, I'm the party's artist," he told her. "Although I'm not an official member of the embassy since King Teodor doesn't know anything about me." He explained himself, "I was running away, but it turns out I'm not."

This confused Mary Starling, but she had a different question. "So you are a genuine embassy," she said to Grammie. "How did you manage that?"

Max answered quickly. "Ari really is a Baron. The King really did send him, and Mr. Bendiff, too. You remember Bendiff's Jams and Jellies?"

"Beers and Ales?" Grammie added.

"Of course."

"He's the business adviser," Max said.

"You must have wondered why the King would send an embassy to Andesia," Mary Starling remarked, and she looked around at them all, her mother, her son, Joachim, as if she was looking for something she didn't want to find.

Guessing that she hoped her role as a spy had not been revealed, Max suggested, "Maybe he saw the photograph in the newspaper, like we did. He'd recognize you, wouldn't he? Because they came to the theater every summer, didn't they?"

"Several times each summer," she said, pleased at the memory and satisfied with the explanation. "So as soon as you heard about it you asked to be members of the party," she decided.

"We couldn't let it go without us," Grammie said. She understood that Max didn't want to say anything about his own leading role in the events, even if she didn't know why he wanted to keep silent.

Max didn't exactly know why himself, either.

It was Colly and Tomi who brought the first news. As they had hoped, Balcor had announced that the disgraced King would be exiled and remanded him into Ari's custody to be immediately removed from Andesia. The three men would be along shortly. Further news was that the soldiers had all been told that those who wished to could remain in Apapa, to serve under General Balcor in the new Andesian army. The others were free to return to their home barracks.

"Most of them seemed pleased to leave," reported Tomi.

Colly explained: "When you're an occupying army, everybody fears you, and hates you."

"They're soldiers. They want to fight," Tomi added. "If they didn't want to do that, they wouldn't be soldiers, they'd have families and less dangerous jobs."

"What they are is adventurers," Grammie said, and turned sternly to her daughter with an *I warned you* look in her eye.

Max's mother drank her tea and admitted, "This was more adventure than I was looking for."

"And William?" Grammie insisted. "Does he feel the same way?"

"That same William," Max's father announced from the doorway, spreading his arms wide as if it were him welcoming them onto the scene rather than the opposite, "is about to embark on the adventure of another child!"

In his presence, the room filled with life, and energy, and gladness. "Another child!" he repeated. "Think of the possibilities! Look at Max!" he urged them.

Everybody looked at Max. William Starling went to stand behind Max, his hands on his son's shoulders, but not to hold him down in his chair. Max could feel it, the way his father's hands fitted around his shoulder bones, as if he was reassuring himself that Max was real. "I myself am very happy to be looking at Max. Although"—and now he moved around to look at his son's face, with a forgiving smile but also a critical raised eyebrow—"what you were trying to do during that duel I don't understand. Is there no room at this table for a King in exile?" he asked.

Almost unnoticed, Mr. Bendiff and Ari had slipped around William Starling, so the table was now crowded and the teapot already empty. Grammie got up, to reheat the water, and Mr. Bendiff said, "So it was Juan Carlos behind it all, to get the throne. Not to mention the royal wealth."

"Also Malpenso, to get Elizaveta," said Tomi.

"Balcor has rescued her from that, at least," said Colly, and he suspected, because this was something he knew too much about, "It's going to be hard on her, being that man's daughter."

"Did the General suspect him all along?" Ari asked. "I

didn't like the man, but . . . Did anyone here suspect what he was up to? Did you, William?"

Apparently, Max's father and the other two men had had the chance to introduce and identify themselves.

"I never liked him, either. He was *oily.* Does that count as suspicion?" William Starling asked.

"We were kept so isolated. We were told so little," his wife explained.

"Everything we knew came from Balcor, the man of mysteries—who told us nothing," William added.

"I think General Balcor *must* have suspected" was Mr. Bendiff's opinion. "I got the feeling that nothing that happened today surprised him. Will he take the crown?"

"I don't think he wants it," Max said.

"Of course he does," answered the former and false King. "Why wouldn't he?"

"Did you?" Max asked. "*Do* you?"

"It's different for me," his father explained. "As an actor, I never had to have the power of a real king, or the importance, or the responsibilities. Although I think I could have become a good one," William Starling said, and he glanced away from the table to the front door of the guesthouse, and the city beyond. "If you are a king, a king is all you can be; it's what you have to be, all the time." He turned to his wife to ask, "What about you, Mary? Are you sorry that you're no longer Queen of Andesia?"

Max's mother just smiled, and drank her tea.

Max was curious. "How did Balcor manage it?" he asked.

"Captain Francis saw you on the docks, but—" He turned to look at his mother—and lost the train of his thought because—

He was sitting at the same table with his parents and he was looking at his mother's bright eyes and hearing his father's dramatic voice. It made him so . . . so joyous, he almost climbed up onto the table to put a rose between his teeth and dance a fandango. Whatever a fandango was, he thought, and grinned. "But he didn't say anything about seeing *you,*" he said to his mother. Talking to his father again, he said, "He didn't say anything about you looking worried, or troubled, either. What's a fandango, anyway?"

"Ask your grandmother, she knows everything," William Starling answered, but without giving Max time to do that, he told his story: First, the shining, closed carriage that arrived at 5 Thieves Alley, with the three-peaked emblem painted on its doors and the pair of matching horses. This was shortly after Max had ridden off on his bicycle, "To have a class with you, if I remember correctly," William told Joachim. The carriage had taken them to the docks, right up to a gangplank, the railings of which were twined with swags of flowers, "So why would anyone suspect anything?" The couple was greeted ceremoniously by a captain in full white uniform and escorted along a well-lit, carpeted corridor to a door, which was held open for them by a respectful member of the crew, also in dress whites. "And that was the moment when everything turned wrong. Do you agree, my dearling?"

"Absolutely," his wife said. "Although there *was* champagne," she reminded him.

"There *was* General Balcor," he reminded her.

Thus it was, William Starling explained, that he found himself loitering on the docks just in front of the *Simón Bolívar,* asking a gypsy-looking fellow—"untrustworthy ears on him, but beggars can't be choosers"—wandering by, to deliver the note he'd written—"which Balcor read every word of, you can be sure. I had to be quick, *and* clever." He couldn't call for help or attempt an escape. His wife was locked in the cabin of a ship about to sail for who knew what destination, except it was probably not India, and if he gave the game away he had no idea what would happen to her. "As it turns out, probably nothing, but how could I know that I had the essential role? The throne of Andesia could only be inherited by a male of the line," he told them. "Until recently," he added, with a good dollop of self-satisfaction. The note had been the best he could do to leave word of their situation. He'd hoped Max would decipher it. "As you must have," he told his son. "For you've obviously found my fortune to live on, and you will have been staying with Grammie, where we knew you'd be safe, and you did wait—although I presume not patiently—for the next time I could send word."

Max took a quick look at his grandmother and did not contradict his father. Grammie also said nothing, for which he was grateful. He would tell *his* story in his own time. Maybe when he was asked for it? Meanwhile, William Starling looked around the table to say, "I've never seen any of these actors. Where did Max find you?"

"I can't act," Ari said, quite truthfully.

"King Teodor found me," said Mr. Bendiff.

"I'm no actor," Tomi said, and, "Me neither," Colly agreed.

Max could have laughed out loud at the expression on his father's face. "Don't tell me you're a legitimate embassy," the actor protested.

"We have credentials," Ari told him. "We have Teodor's letter of credit."

"So the King really sent you?"

"The royal family always attended our performances," Mary reminded him carefully, as if she was telling him more than her actual words said, as if she was warning him to be careful what he said. "He seems to admire us more than we knew."

Max could have laughed at the two of them. Even being kidnapped and held prisoner, and almost being hanged, too, didn't stop his father. Or his mother, either.

"Max must have persuaded you to let him join you," William told Ari. "And bring his grandmother, too, for which we thank you, whoever you are. Didn't I always say it?" Max's father asked the room in general. "By twelve, a boy is capable of real independence. You do me proud, Max."

Max shrugged and held his tongue. In fact, he *had* done his father proud.

"I'm certainly grateful to all of you," William Starling

went on. "Every one of you, boys included, mothers-in-law included. Did you already know this?" he asked his wife.

"I only heard just before you got here."

"And I was going to ask you two to join the Company," William Starling said, with a rueful smile. "Especially you," he told Ari. "You were the spitting image of that old Baroness, stiff and disapproving in her box, in her black dresses, in her pride."

"I *am* the next Baron," Ari admitted, with a smile for Max.

At that point, Tomi asked the question foremost on all their minds. "Will Balcor really let us leave?"

"We are going with Stefano's wagons in the morning," Ari said, and smiled. "I'm pretty eager to get back."

"It's a good thing we're already packed," Grammie said.

"You haven't said how you feel about becoming a grandmother again," Mary remarked to her mother, teasing.

"You can't *become* a grandmother twice," Grammie snapped, with uncharacteristic uncooperativeness, "the same way you can't *become* a parent twice. The first time does the job, no matter how many others appear and how often."

"There speaks my favorite librarian," said William.

"Not anymore," Grammie said. "And I don't know what kind of grandmothering you two are expecting from me," she went on, with a grumpiness that was just as uncharacteristic.

William Starling looked at his wife and Mary Starling looked at her husband. Alarmed?

Into this quiet came the sound of the door opening,

followed by the sound of booted feet marching. Now everyone was alarmed.

The General came to the kitchen doorway, a soldier at each shoulder. He dismissed his guard and stood, feet slightly apart, his shako held at his side. He looked different, Max thought. Not taller, but for some reason younger. General Balcor was not much older than Ari, Max realized.

Without hesitating, William Starling demanded, "You don't knock?"

Max almost groaned aloud, and he did groan silently. His father seemed to think King William of Andesia was still onstage. Without asking the General to be seated, or to join them for tea, William Starling had his say. "Just for curiosity, Balcor, would you have let me hang?"

This question was answered, and not answered. "The boy would not have allowed it. I came to thank him. I would not have enjoyed watching you kick your life away at the end of a rope."

The image silenced William Starling.

"I have come also because you will have questions to ask," the General announced to the members of the embassy. He might look younger, but he was no less powerful.

"If we are to leave in the morning, what about our trunk of scripts and scenery and costumes?" Mary Starling asked.

"That is being taken right now to the *mercado,* and there is another as well, packed with the clothing made for you during your brief reign." He looked at William to say, "Including those handsome boots you stride about in so well.

You did not disappoint me," he said to his ex-King, with full seriousness.

William's mouth worked, as if trying to force words free, but he didn't speak and Max was glad to see his father for once made speechless—with confusion? outrage? amusement? Certainly not embarrassment. Embarrassment was not in William Starling's repertoire.

Bolder now himself, Max asked, "Back in April, was there really a ticket waiting for me? Or did you plan for me to be left behind?"

"I had no clear plans," the General answered. "Not at that time."

Since questions were allowed, Colly wondered, "Did *you* know all along what Juan Carlos was plotting?"

"The man was too oily not to be up to something," William answered. "The first time I met him, I knew he was up to no good."

"I had suspicions," the General told them, "but I lacked proof. I hoped to put the cat among the pigeons. They are excitable creatures, pigeons, and once excited, once flurrying about?" He shrugged. "I hoped they might make patterns, in which the truth could be glimpsed."

"I was more like a staked goat than a cat," William Starling said.

Balcor nodded, once, in agreement.

"We were bait in a trap," William went on, offended now, but whether at the General's metaphor or the danger he'd been put in, Max couldn't tell. The actor pointed out, "Pigeons aren't killers."

Balcor shrugged again. He looked at Ari. "I understood to whose advantage it was for the throne to be empty, but I had no proof. Today, that proof was given to me, thanks to your embassy."

William Starling disagreed. "I'd say it was thanks to those two or three Andesians who spoke up out of the crowd," he said. "I'm thanking my lucky stars they did—although, I admit it, I am not surprised to have landed on my feet."

"Your lucky stars?" Balcor asked, as if he was confused by the expression. "It was the embassy," he repeated, with a glance at Max.

William Starling maintained a dignified, kingly silence, but Mr. Bendiff wondered, "What will happen now in Andesia?"

"That remains to be seen. Changes have become possible, but real life is a matter of improvisation, not a script. Don't you agree, William?"

"Unfortunately," the actor said, proving that the General wasn't the only person present who could speak ambiguously.

"However, I would like to hope that your interest in my country will continue," the General said to Mr. Bendiff, who answered without hesitation or ambiguity, "It will."

This satisfied Balcor. "I expect that Juan Luc and Juan Antonio will be communicating with you." He turned to Joachim. "I expect also that your pictures—because ours is so wild and beautiful a landscape—will show the world that we are in fact a nation, and *not* a prize to be taken as booty."

"That's not why I will paint them," Joachim told him. He met the General's stern glance with an equally unyielding glance of his own.

"About Elizaveta," Ari began, and hesitated, and decided to continue even if the General might think it irrelevant. "Elizaveta would make good use of an education and, as well, be glad to be away from Apapa for a year or two."

Grammie put her oar in. "There is no school in your country, General, and no library. An educated young woman—even if she marries and has children—might be happy to concern herself with creating a school and a library."

Balcor acknowledged, "The young woman is in my thoughts," but revealed no more, instead saying to Mary Starling, "You understand that the crown and the jewels must remain here in Andesia, to be the wealth of the new country?"

"Of course," she said. "My goodness. I wouldn't know what to do with them, except wear them onstage, and for the stage, crowns need to be bigger and brighter. Lighter, too—more show and less substance. What would we do with those crowns, William? Imagine trying to act under the weight of a real crown."

He smiled, allowing that she was right, but he had a final question of his own. "Why me, General? Out of all the world, why did you choose me for this role?"

This the General answered straightforwardly. "I saw you play Shakespeare's King Henry. When I was traveling with the son of the President of Peru on his grand tour. We visited Queensbridge, and the lake—it was a few years ago, but I remembered. Before your own King, you played a stage King, and he applauded the performance. And you, lady, made a lovely and wise young French Princess, willing to marry him for the good of your country. When I came to Andesia, and had need of a King, I remembered your performances."

This was a satisfying piece of information in answer to the last of the party's questions. The General put his shako back on his head, then, to announce, "Madam, the brooch I sent to you, that is yours to keep, with the country's thanks. If that is all, then—William, Envoy, Mr. Bendiff, Maximilian—the name of a king, is it not?—Mrs. . . . Sevin, did he say? Painter and boys, all of you, I will leave you now. Soldiers will arrive in the morning, early, to take your luggage and escort you to the wagons. I will not be present at your departure, so this is our final farewell." With a quick bow, General Balcor turned on his booted heels, and in six quick steps, he closed the door behind him.

That night, after a makeshift meal taken all together in the dining room, the ex–royal couple took Hamish Bendiff's rooms, while Ari moved into Max's bed to give the older man the better accommodations, and all three boys slept wrapped in alpaca blankets on the kitchen floor. At dawn, with Max again disguised in *chupalla* and poncho, they went to join Stefano, who waited by the wagons. By mid-morning they were rounding the high ridge, leaving Andesia.

20

The Rest of Max's Life

• ACT I •

SCENE 1 ~ THREE INSIGHTS

It didn't take long for Max to figure out that he had a problem. It might be a problem that didn't surprise him, and might even be a problem he'd been looking forward to having, but still . . .

It was his parents, of course.

It was his father, mostly.

With an eye out for snakes and spiders, with a bandanna tied around his head to keep sweat out of his eyes, Max thought about how in Balcor's play, even his flamboyant father had been a minor character, and the rescue party only a plot device. Balcor's play had begun with the murder of a royal family, and it ended when the villain was unmasked and the rule of law begun in Andesia. William Starling's play, which had begun with a kidnapping, had ended in the same scene, but with a rescue. Max's concern now—now that the final curtain had fallen—was *his* play, which also began with that kidnapping. He didn't want *his* play to be over, especially the story of its main character, Mister Max, the Solutioneer. His play had just begun.

That was his first insight into the problem and—since insight is one of the earliest steps toward solution—he thought hard about it.

There was no question that Max was filled with a joy and relief that bubbled steadily inside him, long day of hard traveling after long day of hard traveling. His parents were safe. They were all of them safe, the whole rescue party. He had done it! For the return journey, there was a whole wagon available for those who wished to ride, not walk. Grammie and Joachim had permanent seats, as did William and Mary, but the rest of the party sometimes rode and sometimes chose the exercise of going along on foot, as if by moving under their own power they would arrive sooner at Cúcuta, and Maracaibo, and Caracas—where they would find a boat to take them home.

They were still accompanied by soldiers, and by Stefano, and they were traveling in the opposite of comfort, but they were a cheerful, lively party, slapping at insects or stomping on insects as they jounced along in their wagon, across hillsides and then down into the denser growth of tropical forests, where the insects became more colorful, and larger, and the danger of snakes increased. William Starling was like a gifted schoolteacher, always ready to set off a guessing game or a song or to tell the story of one or another of the many, many plays he knew. Wet and dry, cool and warmer, the days went by quickly enough.

Evenings, however, were a different story, the mood not one of joy and relief but dread. In the evenings, they claimed bowls of whatever stew the camp cook had prepared, carrying them back to eat around their fire, to eat as slowly as possible, as if by eating slowly and talking constantly they could hold back the creeping darkness of this wild country, and hold back memories that—even under a sky so thick with stars that the dense twisting vines couldn't entirely conceal them—slipped in with the darkness. But none of them could, and so every night, eventually, a silence would fall around their fire as each one of them struggled not to remember.

They would look at one another, wide-eyed and pale despite the brightness of flames on their faces. Max couldn't speak for the others, but the memory that grabbed his chest in ice-cold, bony claws was the image of that gallows tree, waiting. It was all too easy to picture how it would have looked with a man kicking his life away at the end of that rope until he was, at last, limp, still, a dead thing. The picture would invade Max's mind and he would look at his father, seated cross-legged by the fire, not limp and dead, and at his mother, close beside her husband, her hand in his as they both looked into the flames, silent and remembering. Max did not like to remember how close they had come to that dangling thing, and he could understand something now about his parents that he hadn't really understood before: They were true adventurers.

His parents had real courage. A spy, even someone spying for a well-intentioned ally, even a woman spy, was in constant risk of being caught, and executed. For whatever reason—and probably for several reasons, many of them contradictory, human beings being what they were—his parents often went out spying for King Teodor. Max had always admired their acting skills and enjoyed their theatrical personalities, but what he especially felt on those dark nights, when he couldn't stop remembering, was pride. They were quite something, William and Mary Starling.

It was because of this second insight that when—as he always did—Max's father broke the grim campfire silence of memory to once again retell the story of his trial, Max held his tongue. Why should he say anything to diminish the brave glamour of his father's heroic moments on that stage? It was William Starling, after all, who had stood in danger of his life, truly mortal danger. They were all certain, although not one of them gave voice to the thought, that General Balcor would have executed his King. Balcor's concern was Andesia, and its people, and the law; if he had not succeeded in unmasking Juan Carlos through the trial, he would have set another trap at another time, maybe even with another King.

Not that Balcor wasn't as pleased as any one of them that things had gone well for the embassy. Max was sure the General would have been genuinely sorry to have to hang William Starling. Just not sorry enough to not do it.

"When they dragged me out of those cells," William Starling would say, and everyone would draw in a little closer to the fire, relieved to have their own fearful memories brought out for an airing, because every airing caused them to grow a little more dim, a little less sharp. William Starling said, "I was blinded by the light—I staggered with the weight of chains, manacles . . ."

He was a good storyteller, Max's father, and so the small changes in the adventure that appeared in each retelling went unchallenged, maybe even unnoticed. Ari grew more stiffly baronial, and Grammie more of a plump, feathery mother hen hovering near her daughter, as the tension mounted. Malpenso's knife blade grew longer, sharper, came closer sometimes to William's throat, sometimes to his heart. Juan Carlos turned into a blustering, ridiculous comic figure, Balcor became more and more powerful and mysterious, like Prospero or some evil alchemist, controlling the scene with an unearthly skill, until . . .

"I thank my lucky stars," William Starling concluded, every night, "and they were surely shining bright. Yes, I thank my lucky stars for whichever of those poor farmers who had been born with good sense finally spoke up. And I thank my lucky stars for whichever of those miserable miners had the native understanding to say the same. And show Balcor a way out." Then he would laugh, adding with a look around at all of them, "But I land on my feet, I always say that, don't I, my dear little mother-in-law?"

All around them, insects hummed and occasionally some

wild creature would shriek, whether in attack on its dinner or defense of its young, they couldn't tell. Only Tomi would look at Max, as if wondering why he didn't tell his father who the men in the crowd had been.

It wasn't until Max stood alone with his father on the deck of the little mail packet carrying them across Lake Maracaibo that Max finally said, "Actually? Actually that was me. That sensible Andesian farmer."

William Starling turned away from the sight of those little houses standing like long-legged herons on their pilings in the quiet water, and he raised doubting eyebrows.

"And the miner, too," Max said.

The wind hummed in the sails, little waves splashed against the side of the boat. After a while, William Starling asked, "You speak Spanish?"

"Some. Enough," Max admitted.

William Starling looked back at the houses, black squares silhouetted against a lowering sun. He turned to look at Max, and bowed, like a gambler honoring his opponent's winning hand. He put his hands on Max's shoulders and squeezed. Then he smiled. "There's no need to tell your mother, is there?" he asked. "Your mother likes to believe in my lucky stars, it keeps her from worrying about things. Especially now, with this baby."

Max could do that, and easily.

Max's third insight came the afternoon of their second, and last, day in Caracas, in the writing room of the Hotel

Magnifica. They had arrived in the soft light of an early-spring evening, and William Starling had instructed the carriage they had hired at the distant dock to take them to the Hotel Magnifica, where "They think we're royalty, wait until you see the welcome we get." After a hot bath, a good dinner, and a long night's sleep on soft mattresses, they met in the morning, refreshed. First thing, they went to the central post office, to send telegrams announcing the success of the embassy to King Teodor (Ari), news of their safety to various people in Queensbridge (Ari and Mr. Bendiff, Colly and Tomi), and notification to various actors that the Starling Theater would soon reopen (William Starling). Waiting for them in the post office was a short stack of letters, most for Ari but one for Mr. Bendiff from his wife and, to his surprise, two for Max from Pia.

That first day, they returned to the hotel's writing room, where tables and chairs awaited those guests who had business to take care of or social lives to keep up with or loving feelings to express. Ari, who wanted nothing more than privacy in which to read his letters from Gabrielle, withdrew to a desk in a corner as distant from the others as the room offered. Nobody wanted to interrupt him, but Max was a different story. Those who had no mail but were accustomed to stage center felt entitled to ask questions.

"What does this girl have to say for herself?" William Starling asked his son.

"What makes you so certain it's a girl?" asked his wife.

"The boy doesn't deny it. What more proof do we need?"

Mr. Bendiff diverted his attention with a question. "Mary?

Aurora? Tell me what you think about this," he said, holding out a page of his letter.

"Doesn't my opinion count?" asked William Starling. "Why doesn't my opinion count, Hamish?"

"It would," Mr. Bendiff answered, "but I don't think you'll have one. You can always prove me wrong. I'm wondering: Would a woman buy pre-prepared apple chutney in a jar? My wife, who seems to have quite taken to running things—"

"Women are like that," William Starling said, adding with a quick glance at his wife and mother-in-law, "and I for one admire and appreciate it."

He allowed the two women time to respond to the inquiry, briefly, before he invited his wife to take a ramble around the city. "Now that we're free to go where we wish, like ordinary people."

"You could never be mistaken for ordinary," his wife answered, accepting his hand and rising from her chair more gracefully now, without a thick pillow at her waist.

All the letterless people decided to go along, and see what was to be seen in Caracas, perhaps visit a museum, have lunch in a sidewalk café, and, most important, find a ship on which the party could travel home, as soon as possible.

"I only travel first-class now," Max's father announced. "Is there enough of my fortune left for that, Max?"

"Actually," Max told him, "King Teodor insisted on paying for everything."

"Well, well," William Starling said, and then, with a little nod, he said it again. "Well, well." He turned to Mr.

Bendiff. "Do you not find your children surprising creatures, Hamish?"

"I find *your* child surprising, if that's what you mean," Mr. Bendiff answered.

"Exactly," said the actor, who then raised one arm dramatically to gather up his group and announce, "Let us begone! The world awaits!"

"Say rather that Caracas awaits," his wife laughed. "You're coming, aren't you, Mum?" She held out a hand to Grammie, who gave an arm to Joachim. Colly mimicked the gesture, holding his arm out to Tomi, and the two boys exited the room laughing.

The next afternoon, back in the writing room, William Starling gave out the responses to the telegrams Ari and Mr. Bendiff had sent, as well as yet another letter for Ari. But one telegram had been returned as undeliverable. This was the one to Colly's grandparents, and Colly was surprised but not unhappy to see from the message stamped on its flimsy yellow envelope that the people who had so reluctantly given him a home for the last eight years, who had hated him so well and treated him so heartlessly, had moved away from Queensbridge, leaving no forwarding address. It didn't worry Colly. "I have a job, I can pay rent, they are as glad to be rid of me as I am to get away from them." It was Grammie who worried, "You aren't eighteen yet, so you're not of the legal age to live alone," and Mr. Bendiff who settled the question, at least temporarily: "We'll think of something."

There had been no telegram for William Starling and he bemoaned the lack. "So soon forgotten! What a fickle place the world is!"

His dramatics were ignored by everyone except Mary, who only smiled and shook her head.

"You are right, as always. I can win back the world," William agreed, then, "How could I have forgotten?" he cried. "I have found a vessel! We sail tomorrow—tomorrow! Isn't that a stroke of luck? *La Freccia.* She's Italian, so the food will be splendid. We will all travel in first-class cabins, together, just as we have all been together in this adventure. You'll see to it?" he asked Max, with the kind of careless gesture common to kings and queens and others who need never carry their own purses.

Luckily for his father, that question gave rise to Max's third insight into his parental problem, by reminding him of who his father was. Max knew how to answer it. "I will secure the reservations," he announced with a slight bow, the Queen's Man acknowledging an order from his King. What William Starling needed, Max understood, what he had been deprived of for months and months, was a stage.

SCENE 2 ~ THE RETURN OF MISTER MAX

If Max hadn't read the Greek myths, he would have thought he was a really bad person, the way he was almost sorry he had masterminded his parents' rescue, the way he kept secret from them his solutioneering and his successes, and especially how much he minded the way his father acted as if he, Max, were only some minor and not very important and pretty inept member of his, William Starling's, theatrical company of a life. However, Max *had* read the Greek myths, so he knew it was normal to feel this way—and that might not have been a solution to his problem, but it certainly was a relief. Besides, Max didn't kid himself, and he didn't want to. You can't be a successful Solutioneer if you refuse to see the whole complicated, contradictory picture, so Max couldn't help but understand that, in a way and without meaning to, William and Mary Starling had given him the new normal life he wanted so badly to keep on living. Of course he was grateful to his parents. How could he not be?

Also, he had to admit how much fun it was to see his father back in action. *La Freccia,* the whole entire long, multilevel ocean liner, became a stage for William Starling, and Mary Starling, too, although not everybody realized this. Her acting was more subtle, quieter and less eye-catching, but no less skillful. Max had always enjoyed watching his parents act, and on *La Freccia* they had many roles to play, changing from one to another with ease. In the evenings, at the Captain's table during dinner, and afterward as the band played and couples moved around the floor, they were royalty in exile. At the breakfast table, when the nine returning citizens of Queensbridge sat together, William and Mary Starling were adventurers returning from a successful excursion. In the hours between breakfast and lunch, they walked the decks, either hand in hand or with her delicate fingers resting on his manly arm, a couple on a romantic ocean voyage, perhaps even honeymooners. And in the afternoons, the Starling Theatrical Company took possession of the ship's library. After all, they had everything they needed for three-person performances. "Why waste our talents?" asked William Starling. "Why waste valuable time? We'll give them Shakespeare!"

Max was expected to take part in these performances, and he enjoyed himself while he was at it. Those afternoons, all three worked together, performing comic scenes and duels, love scenes and heroic declamations, and even the Aesop's fables they had offered in the Queensbridge schools so long ago and so far away. "It *is* good to have our son back with us, isn't it," his father remarked, putting an arm around his wife's shoulder. They both smiled at Max.

"Very," she said.

Max knew they meant it, really meant it, even though the next words he heard come out of his father's mouth were "Every play needs its minor characters."

Which irritated Max.

"And think!" his father went on. "Just think of it! Soon we will have another!"

Which made him really cross.

Only Tomi wondered aloud why Max didn't tell his parents what he'd been up to, during their short reign over Andesia. "I don't get it, Eyes, why the secrecy? It's not as if it wasn't something to boast about, everything you did *and* the way you got the King to send Ari with an embassy, and everything in Apapa, too. Won't they be proud of you? But you usually know what you're doing," Tomi admitted, then pointed out, "Although usually you explain."

But Max didn't want to explain the problem he was working on. He wanted to solve it. If he couldn't think of something, he was going to go back to being plain old Max Starling, son of the famous theatrical couple and still a boy, and also, he suspected, their babysitter and chief bottle washer, and he wouldn't put it past them to ask him to launder diapers, too. Grammie, he knew, had done all those things for them when Max was a baby, then a toddler, and then a little boy. Grammie would still be there, just across the vegetable garden, but this baby was going to be in the same house as Max, probably in the same room. Max would be their most convenient choice. By the time his parents and his brother-or-sister got through with him, there wouldn't be much of anything left of Max, and less than nothing of Mister Max, Solutioneer.

As the first days at sea went slowly by, Max worried away at the solution. He had already taken a first step by announcing that he would share a stateroom with Tomi and Colly rather than his parents. These arrangements had been made before they boarded the ship, leaving the three boys free to spend the mornings exploring the ship, talking to strangers, playing catch and shuffleboard and cards, and eating as much as they could as often as they could, which since the ship served seven meals a day to its first-class passengers was satisfyingly often.

Because William and Mary ate dinners at the Captain's

table, Max was also free all evening, except for the odd moment when he was summoned to verify one of his father's political points—"When I was King in Andesia," William Starling liked to begin—or when his mother wanted him to describe for one of the fashionable women at the table some aspect of life in Queensbridge—"Tell them about R Zilla's hats, Max." Mostly, however, and he did understand this, they summoned him to complete their family. They wanted to have Max standing beside their table, with them—"I don't know if you've met our boy, Max"—to reassure themselves that he was really nearby.

Still, his parents were planning their living arrangements without asking Max if he had any ideas of his own about them, and without asking Grammie if she minded helping raise another child. It was Grammie who put the first spoke in their wheel, and also—although this was not her intention—offered Max a way to maintain the independence he had been forced into, and had learned to live with, and now wanted badly to keep.

The morning after *La Freccia* left the Bermudas, where the ship had refueled and restocked, Joachim had an announcement to make. His chair scraped loudly on the polished wood floor as he pushed it back, to stand up and declare, "I have something to say." He looked around at all of them. "Here's what it is," he said.

At nearby tables, people fell silent, faces turned to watch. Joachim dropped back into his seat. "You'd think a person could make a simple announcement in privacy," he grumbled.

"Just get on with it," Grammie advised, but not impatiently. Not at all impatiently, in fact. In fact, rather as if something was amusing her.

"All right," he agreed. "You're right, I know." He looked up, looked around again at all the waiting faces until his gaze settled on Max, to whom he spoke. "We're getting married. Today. At noon. The Captain's doing it. I'll be returning to Queensbridge a married man," he announced to Max, "and I'm lucky she accepted me. Your grandmother, I mean," he said. "Not—"

Max nodded—he knew not who. But still . . . He turned to stare at his grandmother.

William Starling asked his wife, "Did you know?" and she promised him, "I'd have told you."

"What good news," said Mr. Bendiff. "Congratulations are definitely in order."

Ari echoed this while Tomi and Colly applauded.

Max was too surprised to say anything.

His father declared that his little mother-in-law had quite taken the wind out of his sails.

To her silent daughter, Grammie said, "Don't look so surprised," and to her son-in-law, but laughing, she remarked, "Your sails are never in danger of being without wind." She asked Max, "You aren't *really* surprised, are you?"

"I am," Max admitted. "I never thought. It never crossed my mind. But it's a good idea, a really good idea for both of you. As long as I can still have my lessons," he added, in case she wondered, and then, as if to show her how dumbfounded he was by their announcement, he made what was perhaps the silliest remark of his life so far. "What will Sunny think?"

"Who's Sunny?" William Starling wondered.

"But why now, Mum?" Mary Starling asked. "I mean, why so quickly?"

"We see no point in waiting."

"But a shipboard wedding deprives us of the chance to give you a gala celebration. We could hold it at the theater, you could get married onstage, perhaps at the grand reopening?" William Starling suggested.

"An even better reason to do it now," Joachim said.

Grammie told Max, "We'll live in Joachim's house, with Sunny."

"Why have I never heard of any Sunny?" William Starling asked.

"If we didn't still have Max, I'd feel you were abandoning me," Mary Starling said to her mother, "but he'll make a wonderful big brother and I'm happy for you both, Mum. You and Joachim, I mean. He's a lucky man, isn't he, William?"

"The luckiest in the world except for me," William Starling answered. "But who *is* Sunny?"

Max was so busy taking in this turn of events that he almost missed his own cue. But he didn't miss it. He heard it just in time and spoke the line he'd been rehearsing to himself. "Actually," he said, "Sunny is the dog who was my first job," then added—with a mental apology to his part-time assistant for the self-contradiction—"my first case, I mean. I'll explain later," he promised. Then, knowing what would be a sure and certain distraction, he asked his mother, "What are you going to wear as daughter of the bride?" and, without waiting for her answer, he told his father, "You'll have to give the toast. Are you ready for that?"

After dinner that same day, after the wedding, Max declined Colly's invitation to join in the nightly poker game held in the sick bay. They were not many days out of Queensbridge now, and he was no nearer to solving his parental problem than he had been when they left Andesia. Sometimes he thought it might be insoluble. As he passed close to the Captain's table, on his way out to the quiet darkness of the promenade deck, his father called him over. "You know our boy?" he asked the ten other people at the table, and then, without giving them a chance to answer, he said, "When I was King in Andesia, we gave quite a performance, Max and I. Didn't we, Max?"

Max smiled, but he wished he could tell the whole story, and he wished even more that his father—who, after all, knew better, knew that whole story—would just admit that it had been someone else's play, in which someone else, maybe Max or maybe Balcor, had the leading role. He couldn't say so, but he wished, as he went on his way without saying anything.

Outside—the boat having moved back into the northern hemisphere, where it was fall, not spring—the air had a chilly edge to it. But it wasn't cold enough to drive Max back inside. He stood at the railing and looked out into the night. Stars shone sharp in a black sky. The water gleamed black and depthless, a vast, empty stage.

And anger stepped out onto that stage. This was not a dramatic, operatic anger, dressed out in flames, however. Nor was it an icy anger, carved from slow-moving glaciers. It was just ordinary, everyday anger, wearing trousers and a sweater, hatless, and the actor hadn't even bothered to learn his lines, because—at bottom, at the heart of him—Max loved his parents. He even loved them just the way they were. But he could see no way to be Max Starling, son of William and Mary Starling of the Starling Theatrical Company, and be at the same time Mister Max, the painting Solutioneer. Or was it the solutioneering painter?

Before the boat landed at the Queensbridge docks, he needed a plan. He knew he didn't want to change back into the old Max Starling, and he knew also that he couldn't expect his parents to change. He even understood *why* his parents didn't want to give anything up, not the theater, not the spying, and not their family, either. But what about Max?

That was the problem in a nutshell: *What about Max.*

Dark waves slapped against the high metal sides of the ship and dark thoughts slapped up against Max where he stood at the railing and wondered: Where was the Solutioneer when he really needed him?

Which of course made him laugh.

Before it made him think.

When they were finally alone, just the two of them seated close together at a small table in the brightly lit saloon, William Starling took his wife's hand in both of his. The band had put away its instruments and the only sound was the dull thrumming of the ship's great engines, the occasional clink of a glass being washed and put away. "What has gotten into your mother, getting herself married like that?" he asked.

"Max likes Joachim, and Mum has plenty of good sense, so I think she'll be happy."

"And what *about* Max?" William asked.

"He said he's too old to be jealous."

"I'm not worried about the baby, what I mean is—I think he's up to something, but what can a boy get up to?"

"I agree. Ever since we left Andesia, or maybe it began when we got on the boat? He's had this expression in his eyes . . ."

William Starling put two fingers up against his temples. He was thinking that Max's eyes reminded him of the shadowy areas in the wings, where players waited to make their entrances. He said to his wife, "He doesn't have my eyes. Or yours, either, for that matter."

She told him, "He has *our* eyes, really, as if the colors got all mixed together. Don't you think? His eyes always make me think of the lake, under a darkening sky, all the possibilities of the night. Or maybe when the darkness is just starting to fade, all the possibilities of the day. Our son has hidden depths," she laughed, and for some reason an idea popped into her head. "Have you noticed how all of them, even Hamish, speak to him? You don't think Max organized it all on his own, do you?"

"How would he do that? He's just a boy."

The next morning, Max came to the breakfast table as the hero of *Adorable Arabella,* with Frank Worthy's candid face, plain speech, and subtle understanding of human nature. "I shouldn't tease you like this," he said to his parents.

"No, you shouldn't," his father agreed, so quickly and with the kind of glance at his wife that told Max they had been talking about him. This would work in his favor, he decided. If someone thinks they already know what you're up to, they won't bother to think any more about it. So, "You guessed," he said, and he didn't hide Frank Worthy's admiring disappointment that they had uncovered his secret.

"We *were* wondering," his mother said.

"Although we don't know *why,*" his father said.

"King Teodor sent Ari with an embassy because I asked him to," Max said. He wasn't about to let on that he knew their secret. You didn't have to be Sherlock Holmes, or even Inspector Doddle, to figure out how much their adventuring life as the King's spies meant to his parents. "I told him about the trouble you were in, and asked for help, and he agreed. Because you're citizens of his country, he said."

"You asked?" his mother said. "You simply asked? How did you get to him? Even in Summer, his privacy is guarded."

Max laughed. "It wasn't easy," he admitted, truthfully. "But he'd seen the photograph of your coronation and of course he recognized you, from the theater."

"We'll have to think of a way to thank him, when we get back," William Starling remarked to his wife, and Max heard in his voice confidence that they had not been unmasked. "A private performance, perhaps?"

"I suspect," his wife said, now sure that they knew the whole story, "there's more to this than Max has told us."

"Well, of course there is," Max said with a frank laugh. "Isn't there always more?"

Their table companions spoke, as if on cue. "Always more. Always something else going on. Never as simple as it seems," everyone agreed.

Then Max got to his real point, leaning forward toward his parents, his face a mask of sincerity, Frank Worthy from the top of his head to the tips of his toes. "I've been thinking about you—because you *have* been a real King and Queen, and because, as I happen to know, you don't lack for coins? I'm wondering if it isn't time for you to make improvements in your living arrangements. Maybe hire a cook-housekeeper, to free you for your work in the theater, and especially when you go out on tour. A nurse for the baby, when it arrives. Otherwise," he asked his father, "how can you both continue performing? Grammie won't be next door to help out whenever you need her," he pointed out to his mother. "And I'll be in school," he told them both, "preparing for university. Unless you plan to close the theater?" he concluded, knowing how unlikely this was.

They turned to one another. They hadn't thought of all this, of these particular difficulties.

"What *I* can do to help out," Frank Worthy said, making Max's offer in such a way that, without even noticing it, they would agree to this major change in their son's life, "is give you more room at home. Our house isn't large, as we all know. But if Grammie is going to live with Joachim, I could move over to Grammie's house. That way, I'll be nearby to keep an eye on things, and help with the baby, too, when you are at the theater, or on tour, and I'll still have enough time to do the sets for the theater, even if I'm busy with my jobs or with school."

"So you're still going to school, Eyes? Maybe I will, too, if you're there." Tomi had interrupted at just the right time and said just the right thing, even though Max hadn't told him what he was up to. Tomi Brandt was going to be a good friend.

By the time breakfast was over and only the three Starlings remained at the table, William Starling had settled their future. "Changes are in the wind," he warned his wife and son. "But we are a quick and clever family, and we have the Company to reassemble, the theater to reopen, plays to rehearse, and performances to schedule. We have work to do! How long before we can reopen, my dearling? What are your thoughts?"

At that point, Mister Max, Solutioneer, slipped away from the table and went to find Colly, to offer him a home at 17 Brewery Lane, in Grammie's house.

And after that? After that, he returned to the promenade deck, where he leaned against the rail and considered the wide expanse of clear blue November sky that lay ahead.

EPILOGUE

When *La Freccia* docked in Queensbridge, a small crowd had gathered in the chill November drizzle to welcome her. Among those who awaited the ship was a hat. As well as being stylish, it was a useful hat against the rain, with its wide felt brim, and a useful hat against November, being a bright cranberry red with a cheerful spray of white feathers held in place with a silver *Z*. The hat pushed its way forward, until it stood at the front.

A young woman who had covered her head with only a brown woven scarf stepped aside to make room, with a smile so warm and happy that even the little woman in the red hat had to respond, however much it went against the grain to accept friendliness from strangers. Beside this young woman stood a girl and her mother. R Zilla was pleased to see that the mother wore one of the new winter hats, its two black feathers rising out of a close-fitting crown. This hat lacked a protective brim, so rain had moistened the mother's cheek, but a small hat suited the large blue eyes and strong jaw. As they all watched debarking passengers step off the covered gangplank onto the docks, the mother gripped the girl's hand in excitement, and the girl, in a hat R Zilla recognized by the spray of blue flowers nestled around its flat crown, smiled back at her mother. All three moved closer to the foot of the gangplank.

First onto the docks, as if eager to have his journey done and return to his own life, came a tall older man wearing a blue beret. He seemed unaware of the light rain falling on his head and shoulders. R Zilla squared *her* shoulders, ready to begin her assault, but he stepped aside to allow a younger couple to move ahead of him. The man and the woman were both wrapped around by long cloaks, and at the sight of them, people pushed ahead of her. This couple was known. "Isn't that the actor? And his wife? You've seen them, haven't you? She's Arabella and he's— I had such a pash for him when I was younger. I still do, truth be told. I mean, just look at him! He could be a king!"

Then, "There he is, Mum!" the girl cried as a large man in a dark overcoat, his fedora at a jaunty angle, stepped onto the docks, and beside him—"Gabrielle! There they are!"—a slim, handsome young man, his red hair sprinkled with raindrops.

Now R Zilla could name the woman—it was Mrs. Hamish Bendiff, a good customer. The big man, whom she recognized as Hamish Bendiff, wrapped an arm each around his wife and daughter, but the young redhead only took the kind-faced young woman's hands in his. They leaned toward one another until their foreheads touched and there they stood, as if alone in some mountain meadow, looking into one another's eyes.

Before the tall man in the beret could move, two boys pushed in front of him. Servants? Not likely, these were first-class passengers, although wearing outlandishly large hats of woven straw that did possess, R Zilla admitted, a certain primitive appeal. The boys were unaccompanied and ungoverned—probably someone's wandering sons. Boys were like that, they wandered, and men, too. Men took off at a moment's notice, making it hard work to track down where they might have gotten to, by asking at the railroad station and at the docks, although a persistent woman could eventually learn what she needed to know.

When the tall man, whose gray hair was in need of a trim, in her opinion, finally stepped forward, the hat inched ahead to meet him. But then he offered an arm to the round woman at his shoulder, whose blue eyes sparkled behind the kind of spectacles bookish women wear— Although, actually, she had been beside him all along, hadn't she?

The hat stopped moving. The woman wearing it was no fool. Far from it. She saw how naturally the man's arm was accepted and how the woman smiled up at the tall man and he smiled down at her—

He smiled! Outrageous! How could he smile at this person and never have smiled at her, even when—

R Zilla showed her back to the ship, to the people still waiting by the gangplank, to the docks, to the whole scene.

She did not need to see more. She had seen enough. Her heart was not breaking—she was not the kind of woman to put up with a breakable heart—but it sank, weighed down with disappointment. Her heart was like a feather caught in a rainstorm, she thought, picturing the sodden, sinking, sunken curve rotating gently down . . . Curving down under a chin! Echoing the rounded curve of a cheek! Brushing against a shoulder—or would that be too extreme, a peacock feather brushing against a bare shoulder? Her niece would advise her.

R Zilla rushed toward the carriages for hire that waited beside the Harbormaster's office. She had not a minute to waste. If she really wanted to get herself a husband, she'd take care of that later: The world was full of husbands, but brilliant ideas didn't come along very often, even to her. If she did want a husband, maybe she'd hire that boy to find her one, or—why settle for second best?—she'd wait for the Solutioneer to come back from wherever he'd been. She'd hire the Solutioneer to take care of it, saving her own energies for her art, her craft, her work.

The last of the first-class passengers—or was he the first of the second-class? It wasn't clear from his dark suit, his bowler hat, and the one small valise he carried—stepped onto the docks alone and unnoticed. The fellow seemed to be a stranger to Queensbridge, unknown to, or at least unrecognized by, anyone on the docks—unless the sharp glance from a pair of blue eyes under raised dark eyebrows counted. But he was obviously well-mannered, since when a middle-aged woman in some drab brown housekeeper's coat and hat stumbled in front of him, he immediately offered her his free hand, to steady herself. She smiled her thanks, said something, and walked off.

Max wasn't sure he'd heard the woman correctly. What could she mean: *In three years' time*? Then his fingers recognized the familiar flat, round shape she had put into the hand he'd held out to her and he understood. A button. A summons.

In three years' time he would be sixteen, with three more years of solutioneering experience, and his assistant would be thirteen, which he happened to know was old enough. In three years' time he would have learned whatever history, geography, languages, and psychology school could teach him, and be ready to enter the wider world of the university. He had been given three years to think about it, and decide what answer to give when the next summons came. In the meantime, he expected that there would be plenty of work for the Solutioneer. Max slipped the button into his pocket and moved on through the crowd.

The dignified young man who had moved with such solemn and stately steps off the gangplank and onto the dock stepped into the crowd, but no bowler hat, no dark suit, no stiff back emerged from it. The only person to step away was a boy—visiting the docks on his way home from school for the excitement of an ocean liner's arrival? Reluctant to go home and receive whatever punishment awaited him for whatever boyish crime he'd committed? Hoping to earn a coin or two carrying luggage? The boy strode past the Harbormaster's office, in a hurry, the way boys always are. He was hatless, with his school briefcase in one hand and some round, dark object—probably a soccer ball—under his arm, his jacket over his shoulder, careless of the rain. Turning sharply into Eel Lane, the boy disappeared around the corner.